You're a Dream to Me

SAMANTHA KAY

Also available by Samantha Kay on Amazon

FOUND

GOOD PEOPLE

This Book Is Dedicated To The Redbridge
Early Intervention Team

2011 – 2017

For Without Whom, This Story Would
Never Have Been Possible.

PROLOGUE

It really was the most cowardly thing to do.

I should have been braver, stronger.

I should have thought about the horrible impact it would have on her. But that's the problem when you get in this deep. It feels like there is no other way out; the whole world is closing in on you. The fear of people finding out what you really are, what an utter mess you've got yourself into: that fear is worse than the fear of the act itself.

I couldn't tell her what a mess we were in. I couldn't live with myself having to admit it all. To see the look on her face, for her to think of me as a failure. That feeling scared me more than any other.

We didn't live the most opulent of lifestyles, but she wanted for nothing. Every bill was paid, every mortgage payment in on time, and never once did she have to worry about where the money came from or how much of it was available, and that's not to make her sound spoiled – she was happy, and to be honest, I quite liked it that way too. I was the man, the one with the broad shoulders. It was my job to do the worrying and the fixing, whether it was mending a wobbly table leg or finding the money to pay off the wedding, or the holiday, or the new kitchen.

The guilt I felt was awful. I took vows to love, honour and cherish. She took vows too, to love me for richer, for poorer, for better or for worse, but somewhere along the way a part of me seemed to forget that. Maybe I should've reminded myself of those vows and decided enough. Enough with the lies, enough with the pretending ... but I couldn't.

The note was written, the knot was tied – believe it or not, a fair bit of planning goes into such acts. It was now or never. While the house was empty, and it would be for long enough. It would all be over before her return, by the time she got here it would all be too late. The last thing in the world I wanted was to have to admit to her that the man she married, the man she shared a bed with, the man she laughed at the TV with, was not the man she thought he was.

It was a Saturday afternoon.

As soon as the coast was clear I made my way to the garage and dug out the rope that I had bought a couple of days before.

I made my way upstairs to our bedroom, the only room in the house that had a beam low enough for me to reach, but also high enough to get the job done.

The last thing I decided to do was to write her a note. I didn't want to reveal all – that wasn't the idea. I didn't even want her to understand why I had done it. I just wanted to say goodbye, and tell her that I loved her.

I left the note on her dresser where I knew she would find it. I picked up her small stool and placed it in the middle of the room under the beam. I climbed up onto the stool, tied the rope both ends to where it needed to be, and with one final deep breath kicked the stool away, with it kicking away all my troubles, all my lies; all the worry and hurt I was about to cause, were someone else's problem now.

CHAPTER 1

It was a beautiful summer's day, the 17th of July to be exact. It was early in the morning, around 6.30 a.m., but the sun was already up and so was I. My luck was in, because a July wedding in Britain doesn't necessarily mean sunshine.

My friend Debbie had got married the summer before, and it had rained all day. All her wedding pictures had to be taken inside due to the grounds of the venue flooding, which was just about the saddest thing you could imagine. But that wasn't going to happen to me, not on my day would it rain, no sir! On my day the sun would shine, the birds would sing and all the stars would align, because my day was going to be the very best day of my life. For today was the day Steve and I would finally make it official and become man and wife.

I felt like a princess in my dress. As I looked in the mirror for one last time I had never been so pleased with the reflection staring back at me. My dark-brown hair had never looked this good, loosely curled with a bounce and volume that

I could never achieve myself. My make-up was professionally applied, giving my skin a healthy peachy glow.

My dress was hugging me in all the right places, the white-lace corset pulling me in nicely and giving my bust a very welcome lift, and the long flowing skirt touched the floor, making me feel as if I was gliding along on a cloud.

I was really nervous, but so ready. This was my big day. I was about to become Mrs Lydia Green and no one could've been more excited for me than I was for myself. Before I knew it I was walking down the aisle to meet my future husband, but as I walked, I realised that all the pews were empty. There were no people, no happy smiles, no tears of joy, no flowers; there was no music playing and where the hell were my bridesmaids?

Confused and anxious, I figured the best thing to do was to just keep on walking. But then I saw him, my Steve. My handsome, smart, gorgeous Steve; and I breathed a sigh of relief. There he was, my future husband, waiting for me at the end of the aisle, waiting to make all my dreams come true. As I reached Steve's side, he turned to me, and I collapsed to my knees and screamed out in horror. It was definitely Steve, but not as I knew him, not as he was on our wedding day. Steve's face was white and cold with his jaw just dropped enough so that his mouth wasn't completely closed. I looked upwards and saw that Steve was hanging. Dangling from a beam on the ceiling, a thick blue rope tied around his neck. He was swaying in the air, his feet a few feet off the ground, his blue eyes wide open but dead and lifeless, rolled back in his head. I stared into his eyes while I continued to scream.

It's then that I wake up. I shoot up in the bed, hot and sweaty, my breathing heavy and sharp. I take a quick scan around the darkened room, feeling disorientated, and it takes me a few seconds to remember where I am.

'You're at Ruth's house,' I tell myself in a hushed whisper.

I stay sitting up in bed, lean against the headboard and tilt my head back.

It really did happen. It wasn't just a horrible dream.

After a couple of minutes staring up into the darkness, I lean over to grab my phone lying on the bed next to me and check the time. It's 4.20 in the morning, the date under the clock reading Sunday 19 April. I'm sure I was still awake at around 2 a.m. A small feeling of relief falls over me as I realise at least yesterday is now over. Thank god for small mercies!

Yesterday was not the best of days; but when is it ever a good day to find your husband hanging in your bedroom? And I wonder: Is this it? Will this be it for evermore? Will I never be able to sleep again without dreaming of my husband's corpse hanging from the ceiling? The thought is making me feel panicked, my body burning up again.

I kick off the covers, swing my legs over the end of the bed and perch on the edge. I sit for a few seconds, and soon think I can't sit on this bed any longer and decide to make my way downstairs to the kitchen.

I'm conscious that it's still very early and I sincerely don't want to wake anybody – yesterday was a long enough day for everyone. I decide I won't turn on a light, I'll just feel my way towards the stairs, gripping on to the wall. Moving as carefully and quietly as I can, I can feel that the back half of my foot is on the floor, and the front half is in the air, which must mean I'm at the top of the stairs. Before I know it, all of me is in the air, and I'm flying down at a rapid speed and with a loud thud landing arse first at the foot of the stairs.

My attempt not to wake the house has backfired as I sit slumped on the floor, feeling very sorry for myself with a terrible pain in my left arse cheek. Within seconds I hear stirring and the bedroom door fly open. Ruth switches on the upstairs light, filling the area around us with a bright white light, making my eyes squint while they try to adjust. Ruth comes running down the stairs, followed by her husband Ben who's carrying a hammer that I assume he leaves under the bed for break-ins and DIY emergencies.

'It's okay!' Ruth calls out. 'It's just Lydia, she's been sleepwalking!'

Although strongly focused on my own throbbing arse cheek, I feel embarrassed by the sight of Ben in nothing but a pair of blue boxer shorts. His floppy brown hair sits messily on his head and I note he's without his usual small square glasses, which is a slight concern as I know he's blind without them. Thank god Ruth told him it was me in time, otherwise these guys would have had a double funeral to plan!

'I'm so sorry. I wasn't sleepwalking,' I say, trying to get to my feet with Ruth's help. 'I was awake, I just wanted to get a drink. I'm sorry I woke you both ... go back to bed. Really, I'm fine.'

I look into Ruth's face. She looks utterly exhausted and it's then that I feel a terrible pang of guilt. I shouldn't be putting myself on her like this. I'm twenty-nine years old, I'm a grown-up, I could've stayed in a hotel for the night.

I shouldn't be here, putting her and Ben through this: having to look after a grieving widow who can't even make it to the kitchen without causing a fuss.

Ruth is the person I ran to yesterday. I guess really I should've called the police or an ambulance first, but for some reason my first instinct was to find Ruth.

I met Ruth six years ago, when Steve and I first moved into the street. She and Ben live in the house next door to ours and consequently Ruth and I have become the very best of friends.

I don't honestly think in the years we've known one another that a single day has gone by without our having spoken or messaged or stepped inside each other's homes.

We just seem to get each other in a way others don't, and we love each other dearly for it.

We have an age gap of around eleven years, but you'd never know it to look at Ruth that she'll be turning forty at the end of this year. Ruth has really good skin, quite pale, the sort that would burn easily on a sunny day, but flawless, and she has thick long shiny blonde hair that runs about halfway down her back, the kind of hair many a girl would give their left arm for, myself included!

She's a really good person, which makes me feel bad, because even if she didn't want me staying here she'd never say so.

Ben, confident that all is okay, makes his way back up the stairs to bed with his hammer in tow. Ruth, satisfied I'm stable on my feet, walks ahead of me into the kitchen while tightening the belt of her pink dressing gown around her waist.

I follow Ruth and sit myself down at the table and watch as she fills up the kettle.

'You don't have to stay with me,' I say.

'It's fine, I was awake anyway.'

That guilty feeling washes over me once again. I should be at home, not here. Passing on my problems and grief.

As I sit at the table and Ruth stands by the kettle there's silence between us, neither of us feeling any reason to fill the room with conversation, the only sound being the noise of the kettle coming to the boil. I turn in my chair to face the window that looks out at the garden. The sun's not up quite yet, but the pitch-black darkness of the night before has lifted. I start to watch Ruth in the reflection of the kitchen window. When I said I wanted to get a drink, tea wasn't really what I had in mind. I watch her as she opens up the cupboard door, pulling out two mugs. Then she walks over to the other end of the narrow kitchen, and I assume she's heading to the fridge for the milk, but she walks straight past it and heads for another cupboard next to the oven, opens it, and pulls out a half-used bottle of Bell's whisky as well as a squeezy bottle of honey. That action makes me turn in my chair and face her again. A small smile appears on my face as she looks back at me with a very matter-of-fact expression. I realise this is why she's my best friend: she has the ability to read my mind. Both of us needing something to take the edge off; something to maybe help get half an hour's sleep.

Ruth pours a generous amount of whisky into each of our mugs along with a squeeze of honey and adds hot water from the kettle. She brings over the mugs and places them down on the table and pulls out the chair at the end to sit herself down.

I turn back to face the garden window and Ruth sits facing the kitchen wall, one hand holding her exhausted-looking face, the other wrapped around her cocktail of honey and whisky. We sit in silence for about a minute, this probably being the quietest interaction the two of us have ever had in all our years of friendship.

It's Ruth who's the first to break the silence.

'Did you hurt yourself?'

It takes me a few seconds to realise what she's talking about. I stare out of the window, waiting for my brain to register what I've just been asked.

She's talking about my tumble down the stairs!

'No, I don't think so,' I answer quietly, shifting in my chair slightly, but still staring blankly out of the window.

We both sip our drinks and wait for the whisky to take effect, help ease the suffering in some way. It doesn't taste great in all honesty, but it's a better alternative to staring at the ceiling in a strange bed.

'Is there anyone else you need to call?' Ruth asks gently.

'Just his work, I think. I'll try and call his boss on Monday,' I say, my voice cracking as I try to push down all my raw emotion as a rush of feeling sweeps in. My body is starting to burn up again and I feel tears rapidly filling my eyes.

I try for a moment to compose myself, but then I remember where I am. I'm sitting at the kitchen table of my best friend, drinking whisky from a tea mug, I don't need to pretend to hold it together here, and so I don't. I let the tears stream down my face and I start crying out loud as if I'm in some kind of physical pain. One hand is holding my sobbing head, the other resting on the table. Ruth reaches over and gently holds my hand. She doesn't move or react, she just sits there, letting me cry out all the pain.

CHAPTER 2

The bing-bong of the doorbell startles me out of my sleep.

I've no idea what the time is exactly or how long I've been lying here, but I feel some relief in the knowledge that I've managed to get some shut-eye, albeit on the sofa in a pair of Ben's joggers and one of Ruth's old pink T-shirts.

I slowly pull myself up as I hear Ben trotting down the stairs en route to the front door. When he opens it and I hear the unmistakable sound of my mother my relief instantly melts away.

'Is she here?' she demands to know, her voice gruff as she storms her way past Ben into the living room.

I suddenly feel conscious of my lazy attire in a way I'm not sure is normal in front of your own mother. I peel myself from the sofa and stretch out my arms, unable to raise anything that resembles a welcoming smile.

'Lydia,' she says, her eyes large and sympathetic, her head tilted slightly. 'You look awful.'

Having expected nothing less from my ever-loving mother, I flop back down on the sofa rubbing my eyes, wishing her not to be there when I open them again, but unfortunately no such luck.

She looks her usual self: run ragged. Never having enough time to pay a great deal of attention to anyone or anything in particular. Her mousy greying hair is thrown up on her head in a messy half-ponytail, half-bun manner and she's dressed in her usual leggings and the same denim jacket she's been sporting for the past sixteen years.

She does look more tired than usual. The lines around her small eyes deep set against the new dark circles under them, and I wonder if they're a result of her being awake half the night worrying about me.

She wastes no time in making herself comfortable, plonking herself down next to me on the sofa.

'What are you doing here?' I ask, grimacing as she bangs her feet up on the coffee table whilst riffling around her handbag.

'Oh, charming, that is! I come all this way on the bus, on a *Sunday,* I might add, and that's the welcome I get,' she says, the frustration in her voice tangible.

Mum works a couple of jobs. She does night shifts at a petrol station as well as cleaning; offices as well as anywhere else that requires her services, and if there's one thing my mother hates more than anything, it's being disturbed on her day off.

'I told you last night, there was no need to come, I'm fine,' I say, rubbing my forehead in frustration and exhaustion.

'I asked her to come,' Ruth says sheepishly as she enters the living room.

'Why?' I ask Ruth, unable to mask my annoyance.

'She said she was worried about you.'

'I am here, you know,' snaps Mum, digging out a box of cigs from her bag.

'And don't I know it,' I mumble.

'Ruth, you couldn't make me a tea, could you, sweetheart, milk, two sugars, oh and bring us an ashtray as well. There's a good girl,' instructs Mum, taking out a cigarette. She shoves it between her lips and shielding the end of it flicks her lighter to it.

'Actually, Sue, I'd rather you didn't smoke in the house if that's ...' Ruth doesn't bother to finish her sentence, watching in silent horror as Mum lights up, quickly taking one long pull and releasing the smoke into the fresh clean air of the living room.

I watch Ruth scurry from the room, my guilt multiplying. Not only are Ruth and Ben having to shoulder the burden of me this weekend, but now my mother as well.

Knowing I haven't smoked in years, Mum points her box of cigs towards me, her way of a grand gesture.

I shake my head before rubbing my forehead once again. Mum places a hand on my shoulder and I fight the urge to recoil.

'Come on, sweetheart. Tell me what happened,' she says in her most sympathetic voice.

'You know what happened,' I utter, my voice tight, my eyes quickly filling with tears.

'Ruth said you found him hanging in the bedroom,' Mum says softly, as if needing confirmation.

I nod silently as my tears run down my cheeks of their own free will.

'I was only gone an hour, maybe not even as long as that ...' I say, the pain of re-living that very moment almost too much to bear, but I push on, knowing well enough that Mum won't let up until she hears my full account.

'I'd gone to the supermarket to get some bits for the week, and I knew something was weird when I got home because usually he helps me bring in the shopping from the car, but I thought, maybe he was in the toilet or something ... so I brought in the shopping, left it all in the kitchen and I went upstairs just to check if he was all right. I got to the top of the stairs, and I saw him ... in the bedroom,' I tell Mum through sobs and short sharp breaths, unable at this precise moment to go into any further details about my discovery.

'Here you go, Sue, it's not an ashtray, but you

can use this,' says Ruth, reappearing with an old tea mug and placing it down on the coffee table next to Mum's feet, looking concerned at the growing, unsteady stick of ash at the end of her cig.

'Do you know why he did it?' Mum asks, finally taking her hand off my shoulder and tapping her ash into the mug.

'No, I don't know why he did it! What sort of question is that!' I shout through a loud wet sob, feeling angry that I let myself believe for two seconds that my mother could show an adequate level of sympathy.

'What? People don't just hang themselves for no reason!' says Mum, looking at Ruth for some kind of back-up, believing her question to be a completely reasonable one.

Ruth looks sympathetically towards me.

'No, I don't know why he did it, and quite frankly, I don't know why you're here!' I rant, standing from the sofa and wiping my nose with the back of my hand. I notice Ben pop his head round the kitchen door at the sound of all the commotion, before slinking back in, keen to stay out of the way.

'Because I'm your mother, Lydia. And believe it or not, I was worried about you, because I've been where you are now and I remember it weren't no picnic,' Mum rants back at me.

I watch as she takes a hard pull on her cigarette and I notice her cheeks redden slightly and her eyes well with tears, but like a true pro, she swiftly wipes her eyes, pushing away any sign of emotion.

'It's not the same. What happened to Dad. That was an accident,' I say, wiping my dripping nose with the back of my hand again before reluctantly returning to my seat next to her on the sofa.

'Same outcome,' says Mum with a sigh, looking down at the floor, and I find it hard to gauge her thoughts. Is she feeling sorry for me, or silently chewing over her own sorry situation?

'What have the police said? Did they say when you can return home?' she asks, pulling herself out of her trance.

'Yeah, they said the house was ready, I can go back today. I just wanted to try and get some sleep here first.'

'I'll come with you, Lyd, back to the house, you shouldn't do it alone,' says Ruth, sitting herself down on the matching sofa opposite me and Mum, a look of grave concern etched across her face.

'That's good of you, Ruth, but I'm her mother, I'll go back with her,' insists Mum.

'No one's coming back with me,' I interject bluntly.

'But you're still in shock, Lyd, you shouldn't be on your own.'

'Ruth is right, sweetheart. I'll come back with you, and maybe I'll stay a couple of nights, just until you're settled.'

'Okay, that is absolutely not happening,' I blurt out, almost laughing at Mum's suggestion, unable to think of anything worse than having her stay in my house against my will.

'I'm going home, not to a strange foreign land. I'll be fine,' I say, aware of trying to convince myself as well as everyone else.

A silence falls, no one knowing what to say next.

'How's that tea coming along, Ruth? I'm gasping over here,' says Mum.

I roll my eyes, feeling embarrassed, but grateful she isn't putting up a fight about coming home with me.

Ruth dutifully stands from the sofa and goes off to the kitchen, and I wonder if she's beginning to regret so willingly inviting my mother into her home.

'Who knew we'd ever have so much in common, eh?' says Mum with a heavy sigh, stamping out the end of her cigarette in the mug.

I look at her blankly.

'Me and you. Both widowed before we're thirty,' says Mum, her words triggering my tears once again.

I feel my bottom lip tremble and my insides begin to crumble once more. Unable to hold it all in, I begin to sob loudly and in a dynamic that's most unusual for us, Mum affectionately wraps her arms around me, letting me cry it all out safely in her hold.

CHAPTER 3

Ruth stands at her street door with a smile on her face, issuing me a small wave. Whenever I return home after visiting her, she waits at the street door with a wave and a smile, making sure I'm safely inside. But today's wave and smile are tinged with something different, an air of worry and deep sadness.

With Mum packed off to her own home and with a strong cup of coffee inside me, I finally feel ready to tackle the biggest challenge of the day – going back to mine.

Ruth was quite insistent on coming in with me, but I was just as insistent that she didn't. My home had always been my happy place, I told her. A place I couldn't wait to return to, a place filled with love and countless happy memories, and although today's return home would not be on quite the usual level of joy, it wouldn't scare me to enter alone.

However, as I stand here now, my street door before me and Ruth's spare key in my hand, an unbearable level of nerves takes over my body. My hand begins to shake with such vigour I have trouble pointing the key towards the lock, all my focus aimed at opening the door in a timely enough manner so Ruth can't see quite how much of a state I'm in.

I look over at Ruth; she's no longer waving, her smile weary. I fake an animated smile and dig deep inside myself, forcing my shaking hand to open the door.

To my own surprise I manage to navigate my hand quickly enough so as not to panic Ruth into taking any action.

I push open the door, flash Ruth one last smile and step inside, swiftly shutting the door behind me.

I stand with my back to the door looking up at the hallway ceiling, and I can feel my heart beating at the kind of speed one would experience after a 10 km run. I take a minute, allowing myself a chance to calm down whilst also taking a moment to congratulate myself on making it this far.

I imagined returning home to feel rather emotional, but if anything, I just feel ... lost. As if I'm a guest in somebody else's home, the house sitting in an eerie silence.

With no idea what to do, or where to begin, I eventually make the decision to move away from the door, cautiously taking one step at a time until I reach the kitchen, where I'm met by the sight of several shopping bags taking up the counter space. Having almost forgotten about my discarded shopping, I feel a rush of surprise that the kitchen should look exactly how I left it. I imagined maybe the police might have turned the house upside down looking for clues or something, but maybe the man hanging in my bedroom was clue enough, and he was a pretty easy one to find!

I walk over to the counter and see my handbag lazily resting on the work surface, and I have a quick rifle through to check that my keys and purse are all present and correct, unsure as to why I think they shouldn't be.

I decide my first job should be to make a start on putting the shopping away.

I dive into the nearest bag and instantly pull my hand back out with a fright, the inside of the bag wet and cold. I take a look and groan loudly when I realise the bag with all my frozen food has been left out in a warm kitchen for the past twenty-four hours.

I pull out a sodden frozen-pizza box which falls apart in my hands. The tub of ice cream has melted all over everything else, turning it all to a sticky sodden mess.

I take what's left of the pizza box over to the sink and dump the remains in there, the ice-cream residue dripping all over the floor and counter.

I skulk back to the offending bag, pull out a soggy packet of (no longer) frozen peas and put it on the counter. I riffle further through the bag and pull out a plastic packet of minced beef. Even with the contents saved from the ice-cream massacre, I realise they can't possibly be salvageable after sitting out in a warm kitchen all day and all night.

With my emotions high and my nerves fraught, it seems a bag of ruined frozen food is just one issue too many. In pure frustration and anger, I shove the packet of minced beef back into the bag and with one loud scream I throw it down with force onto the kitchen floor, along with myself.

Collapsed in a heap, I reach out to the upturned bag on the floor beside me and grab the packet of minced beef. I pull it onto my lap and cry my heart out on the kitchen floor, wishing with all my might that Steve was here to help put the shopping away.

I wake in the living room, uncomfortably scrunched up on the sofa. I check my watch and see the time is a quarter to six in the morning. Significantly earlier than I would usually rise, even on a Monday morning. I must have eventually fallen asleep in front of the TV, but in truth I had no intention of venturing upstairs to the bedroom, the very idea of doing so creeping me out.

It's the start of a brand-new week, and there's a lot to do. Unfortunately, none of it involves the humdrum of readying myself for work or racing down to the train station, but making the necessary arrangements in the aftermath of my husband's suicide.

Like the absolute gem she is, Ruth said she would contact work on my behalf to let them know why I won't be in for a while. I work in town on the reception desk for an advertising agency, which doesn't involve much beyond drinking coffee and answering the phone. I don't love it, neither do I hate it. I've worked there for about three years. It's not overly challenging and doesn't pay all that well, but I've never been much of a career girl.

Earning enough money to pay for all the necessities was always Steve's job; one he took very seriously and did very well. Steve worked for an American investment bank. He was no Charles Rothschild, but he earned a decent sum which was topped up with very generous bonuses. If I'm honest, the only reason I went to work at all was to bide my time until I got myself pregnant. But seeing as my period arrived two days ago and my husband is now dead, I might have a wait on my hands until I can take advantage of that particular work break.

The people at the agency are nice enough, but I just can't face making the call to explain things, so I was keen to take Ruth up on her offer when she said she'd call for me. Although I may have wriggled out of having to call my own boss, there's still another dreaded phone call waiting in the mix. Steve's family were contacted straight away with the help of Ruth and Ben, meaning the only phone call I have left to make is to Steve's work.

The police asked me if there was anyone I would like them to contact on my behalf, and as tempting as the offer was, I declined. Steve was my husband, and even if I don't feel completely up to explaining my own absence to my colleagues, the very least I can do for Steve is explain his; hopefully in the most dignified and eloquent way I can muster.

I stretch my arms above my head, and I'm met by the unpleasant waft of body odour. Still dressed in Ruth's old T-shirt and Ben's joggers, I realise it's been two days since I last had a shower, which is horribly unlike me. I decide before I do anything else the first order of business should be to jump in the shower. With some reluctance, I peel myself from the sofa and drag myself up to the bathroom.

I emerge from the bathroom feeling fresher, but not a great deal better. With my body and hair wrapped in fluffy towels, I lie on my bed staring up at the bedroom ceiling.

I took a fair amount of time to goad myself into the bedroom. If I had it my way, I'm not sure I would have ventured in here ever again, but I wasn't totally prepared to abandon my clothes and walk around naked for the rest of my days, and so here I am. Lying back on what was once 'our' bed, now simply mine, finding it so strange how everything around me is exactly the same, yet everything in my life is now so very different.

Left to my own devices, I'd happily lie here staring into space for the rest of the day, but I'm aware there are a number of things I need to deal with today, item number one being to call Steve's work. I take hold of my phone lying next to me. Swiping the screen, I see the time is now almost half past seven, still rather early, but I know Steve's boss is always in early and I'm sure he'd rather hear the news of Steve's death now, rather than in the middle of the day, when he'd be wondering why Steve hadn't turned up for work.

I sit myself up, find Steve's work number on my phone, inhale a deep breath and hit the call button.

The line rings for a while, and just as I'm about to hang up, assuming it's too early for anybody to be in, a young, well-spoken female voice answers the phone.

'Good morning, Jackson Goldberg, how can I help?'

'Oh hello, I er, I need to be put through to Richard, please.'

'Do you have a surname for Richard, madam?'

Shit! Richard ... ? Richard ...? What was his last name?

'Um, no, I don't, I'm afraid. I know he's a manager in Foreign Exchange,' I say.

The line falls silent for a moment, and I wonder if I've just been cut off.

'Richard Williams? He's the head of Foreign Exchange,' says the voice at the other end.

'Yes, yes, that'll be him.'

'Can I take your name and the nature of the call, please?'

'Yes, please tell him it's Lydia Green calling, wife of Steven Green.'

'Thank you, transferring you now.'

The phone at the other end begins to ring once again, and I can feel my heart beating out of my chest. Part of me hopes that he won't pick up, which is ridiculous as I'll only have to call back later. All too soon the ringing stops and a very middle-class male voice answers the phone.

'Hello.'

'Oh, hello, is this Richard?' My voice is high-pitched and shaky.

'Richard speaking.'

'Hi, Richard, my name is Lydia Green, I'm Steve's wife.'

'Lydia, Lydia, oh yes, we met at a Christmas party a couple of years ago.'

'Yes, um, yes, anyway, Richard, I'm afraid I'm calling with some bad news. Um, you see, well what it is ...' My voice begins to break, I'm struggling to find the words for the bombshell.

'You see, at the weekend, Steve, well, he, he passed away.'

Richard is silent for a little too long and I start to wonder if he's still there. Suddenly I hear him clear his throat, as if trying to contain his own emotions on hearing such devastating news.

'I see. I really am truly very sorry to hear that, Lydia. Do you mind me asking what happened?'

'It was, um, an, an, an accident ...'

'Oh my goodness, what kind of accident?'

'A ... car ac-ci-dent ...'

Oh god. What did you just say?

'Christ, Lydia, I'm ... I'm so sorry—'

'Yes, well, it's been a really difficult couple of days. I thought I should call you as soon as I could ... I didn't want you to think Steve just hadn't turned up for work.'

Richard's end of the phone has gone silent again which I assume is because he's feeling quite emotional himself. It can't be every day you're notified of a colleague's death.

'Lydia, Steve hasn't worked here for a while now. He was let go, around six, maybe seven months ago.'

Now it's my end that has fallen silent.

'Lydia, are you there?'

'Yes, yes, I'm here, sorry, I don't understand. What do you mean, Steve doesn't work there anymore? Of course he does,' I say, utterly confused by what Richard is saying.

'Well maybe he just didn't want to worry you —'

'No, Richard, I don't understand. Steve works there, for you, he travels to work every day.' I can feel myself becoming irate, baffled as to why Richard should be speaking such nonsense.

'Listen, Lydia, I can understand that this must be a very, *very* difficult time for you, and I'm—'

'No, but, Richard, you're not making sense. Steve works at the bank. Are you sure he hasn't just moved departments or something?' I ask, desperately looking for some kind of explanation.

'Not as far as I'm aware, Lydia. Would you like me to see if I can put you in touch with HR, maybe they can—'

Before Richard has a chance to finish his sentence, I end the call, my mind frantic as I try to register the information I've just been given. Richard must've got his wires crossed. There's no way Steve could've lost his job and not told me, it's not possible.

With my phone still in my hand, I sit completely dumbfounded, staring blankly at the wall, when suddenly the doorbell rings, startling me from my trance. Assuming it's Ruth calling by to check in on me, I clamber from the bed, wearing nothing but my towels, and make my way downstairs to the front door.

When I open it I feel my jaw drop in embarrassment. Ruth is nowhere to be seen and before me stand two burly middle-aged men dressed in matching white shirts, black trousers and what look like stab-proof vests.

'Hello, madam, is Steven Green at home?' one of the men asks, a serious expression etched onto his face, a black clipboard held between his hands.

'Er, no, he's not. Sorry, who are you?' I ask, keeping tight hold of my towel, trying to protect my modesty.

'I'm a High Court enforcement officer, madam, and we're here to collect Steven Green's outstanding debts,' he explains.

'Outstanding debts? What outstanding debts?' I ask.

'According to my paperwork, debts of fifteen thousand pounds,' says the officer, looking down at his clipboard.

'What?' I mumble, totally bemused by what I'm hearing.

I rub my forehead with the heel of my hand as the officer hands me a sheet of paper. I release my other hand from the towel to accept the paper, forgetting about my loose state of dress. Totally dazed, I take a second or two to realise that the officer in front of me has looked away, while the other is giggling to himself, his gaze firmly on my chest. A slight draught passes over my left boob, the sensation and the utter humiliation of exposing myself to two complete strangers on my doorstep springing me back to life.

'Oh god!' I yelp, making a grab for my towel. 'I need to get dressed.' I turn away to escape up the stairs.

'Good idea, madam. We'll wait down here for you,' says the officer, both of them stepping inside my house without being asked and closing the front door behind them.

CHAPTER 4

It was two years ago on a Friday afternoon as I approached the end of another uneventful day at work when Steve phoned me in a terrible state of panic to let me know that he'd arrived home early and decided to put a wash on, but somehow the washing machine had flooded the entire kitchen. The new floor was ruined, and he'd kept calling the plumber to no avail.

I grabbed my things and rushed home as fast as I could, so worried about the damage to our new kitchen it never occurring to me that the scenario was rather odd. Steve never left work early for no reason, and even if he had, putting on a load of washing would never be top of his agenda.

When I arrived, the house was in complete silence. There were no lights on, there was no sound coming from the TV. It didn't even seem as if he could be home.

I walked through our small hallway, peeped into the kitchen and everything looked completely fine; I could see no evidence of a flood or any other type of carnage.

'Steve!' I called, utterly confused as to where he could be or what was going on. From the panic he'd been in, there was just no way he could possibly have got everything back in order so quickly.

I noticed the living-room door was closed, which although that might sound daft was odd, because we always left that door open.

I went in and there he was, on bended knee, surrounded by the glow of candles (honestly, it was so hazardous, they were everywhere, on every available surface), small tea lights twinkling along the entire parameter of the floor along with hundreds of red rose petals scattered all around.

I remember seeing the small box he was holding and I dropped my handbag in complete shock. It landed with a thud by my feet as I placed my hands over my mouth.

'What's going on?' I whispered as I slowly approached him, feeling very nervous but extremely excited.

'Lydia,' he said, his eyes meeting mine. 'Will you marry me?' he asked, opening the box to reveal the most stunning diamond ring I'd ever seen.

I remember so clearly the sparkle in his eyes and the huge smile plastered across his face, no hint of nerves, just joy. Pure unadulterated joy.

Of course I said yes, as the acoustic version of the Ella Eyre and Sigala song 'Came Here for Love' played softly in the background – that going on to be our wedding song a year later.

It was quite simply the most romantic moment of my life, even more so than our wedding day because it was so unexpected.

I used to love telling people that story. I used to love rubbing it in people's faces how wonderful and romantic my husband was. Never in a million years could I ever have imagined that two years on from that most wonderful moment of my life I'd be standing here now in the very same room, saying goodbye not just to our shared memories, but to our home.

It's been just over two months since Steve's death and just over two months since my whole life was turned completely on its head; with today almost the culmination of the whole sorry calamity that is my life. For today has been one of the very hardest so far, the day I have to leave our home.

Who knew the day I discovered Steve's body in our bedroom would be the simplest so far.

Once I'd hung up the phone on the person who did indeed turn out to be Steve's former boss and flashed my boob to two complete strangers, it seemed the lies that Steve kept had finally caught up with him; with everything violently erupting to the surface for the whole world to see.

Steve hadn't worked for months, at the bank or anywhere else; that much I was just about able to get my head round, but it seemed that was merely the tip of an enormous iceberg.

Debts had been piling up even before Steve lost his job, eye-watering amounts. He was overdrawn on every account, owing on numerous credit cards and that was just the start. It didn't even include what was owing on our general living expenses, or the mortgage and the car instalments that had remained unpaid for months.

I had no idea where to begin, the clean-up operation far greater than my capabilities could manage. It was never my intention to burden Steve's parents with the financial turmoil I found myself in, but they were looking for answers and I couldn't lie to the face of two parents who were about to bury their son.

They were actually very helpful in navigating me through the financial fuck-up I found myself in and I'm grateful for their help, but it seemed no matter what way round we looked at things, the quickest and easiest way to clear the shedload of debt was to sell the house.

There's simply no way I can afford to stay here on my own, not with debts being cleared against the house; that's why it was suggested it went to auction, that being the quickest way to raise a sale.

So, after lots of tears, today finally marks the very last day of my old life.

As I anxiously twist the engagement ring and

the wedding ring on my finger, I can feel myself about to break.

An arm wraps itself around me.

'You okay?' asks Ruth.

I stare at her blankly for a second before shaking my head.

'I ... I'm not sure,' I answer. The last couple of months have taken such a toll on my emotions that I'm unsure at this precise moment how I actually feel.

Ruth pulls me in, engulfing me in a well-needed hug.

'I'm really going to miss you being next door,' says Ruth, her voice strained, this day a tough one for both of us.

'Me too,' I say, trying my hardest not to cry.

'But we'll still see each other. We'll always be friends,' Ruth reassures me, holding me a little tighter.

'Gawd, if you spent as much time helping as you did moping maybe we wouldn't still be here. Honestly, *Tipping Point* starts in half an hour!' says the unwelcome voice of my mother.

'I'm so sorry my emotional trauma is getting in the way of your TV viewing!' I bark, unhooking myself from Ruth's embrace as I make my own contempt clear.

I don't even know why she showed up today. With Ruth and Ben's help, I've been more than capable of getting everything done here. All she's done is moan and get on my nerves.

'I need a fag,' huffs Mum, reaching into the pocket of her denim jacket.

'Not in the house,' I groan, it being the ten thousandth time I've asked her not to smoke in my house over the years.

'What do you care, it's not even yours anymore!' says Mum, ready to light up against my will.

'It is while I'm still in it! Go outside!' I snap, finally reaching the end of my tether, and not needing another reminder that in a few short moments I'll no longer have any authority over what goes on in this house.

Wisely choosing to avoid any further conflict, Mum skulks her way out of the living room.

'She's driving me mad,' I say to Ruth, unable to hide the exasperation in my voice.

'Don't worry. In a couple of hours from now we'll have you all settled in your new pad,' says Ruth chirpily. Doing her best to cheer me up, but her words are nothing more than a sad reminder of how far I've fallen.

After everything, there was just enough money left over for me to put a deposit down to rent a tiny studio flat.

'Don't remind me,' I groan, dreading the idea of moving from my lovely spacious home to a tiny studio flat above a bookmaker's in Seven Kings.

'It could always be worse,' says Ruth, her eyes full of sympathy.

'Could it?' I ask, not quite convinced.

'I know it's not the Palace of Versailles, but it won't be for ever, and it'll be yours. You'll have your own front door and your own space. And at least you don't have to move back with your mum. That really would be awful,' says Ruth with a small chuckle.

I nod, knowing Ruth is right, but I still can't shake this crushing feeling of utter, utter sadness. I bite down on my bottom lip, worried I'm about to break once more, when a voice interrupts my train of thought.

'Right, I think that's everything, Lyd,' says Ben coming into the living room, looking sweaty and tired from lugging my belongings around all day.

'So that's it then,' I say sadly, wishing we had just one more item to move, one last box or cushion, something that could drag out my time here a second longer.

'You ready?' asks Ruth.

'Yeah, I'll meet you outside,' I say.

Ruth nods with an understanding smile and meanders out of the room, followed by Ben.

I take one last lap around the empty living room. Tears surface in my eyes as I stare at the very spot on the floor where Steve proposed. I think back to that moment once again, remembering how completely he took me by surprise. A lot of planning and organising must have gone into it. I suppose I should have realised then just how very good Steve was at keeping secrets.

I take a deep breath and walk from the room, closing the living-room door behind me.

I can officially confirm that today has been a long one.

I had no idea moving into this tiny flat would take so much time, and if I'm honest, I was starting to worry I'd never get sorted at all, but at almost midnight, it seems the painful procedure of moving is finally complete.

To my own amazement, most of the boxes are unpacked. As I stand here looking around me, maybe for the first time I start to feel a slight sense of belonging.

Although most of my worldly goods are now residing in Ruth and Ben's spare room (much to their delight), I did bring as much with me as I could to try and make this place feel like home.

The flat did come with all the basic furnishings. A tiny grey sofa and a bed that at last is clear of boxes and neatly made. My kitchen area finally resembles a kitchen with my kettle and toaster decorating the work surface, and most of my clothes are put away, although I do still have some five or so boxes of clothes stacked against the wardrobe that I need to sort through.

The flat certainly feels a little more personal than it did a few hours ago and I feel really quite pleased with myself. I take myself to my sofa and sit myself down. I've been on my feet all day and I can feel the bottom of my back starting to ache a little.

I lie down on the sofa and turn my head towards the wall where my TV is now hanging, when I notice up on the pine shelf next to it a silver picture frame, displaying a photo of Steve and me on our wedding day, but oddly I don't remember putting that picture out or coming across it in any of the boxes.

I sit up and drag myself off the sofa and reach over to the picture frame on the shelf and just as I make a grab for it, the frame vanishes. I turn away in surprise and look out towards the large window at the back of the flat and it's then, as I peer through the window out at a dark night sky, I see Steve, alive and well, smiling at me in his smart wedding suit. I run towards the window, but with every step I take Steve moves further away, to the point that I'm now straining to see him as I press my forehead up against the glass, until finally the image of Steve in his wedding attire disappears from view completely.

I turn and in a panic look frantically around me, and it's then I see him again, right in front of me. Steve's back in his wedding suit levitating in front of me with the noose of a blue rope tied around his neck and his blue eyes wide open staring lifelessly at me and just as I begin to scream, I wake up.

My breathing is short and sharp and I can feel that my bedclothes are wet through with sweat. It's dark in the flat, and I reach over to my bedside table for my phone to check the time. It's 1.32 a.m. I close my eyes in despair, frustrated to have had another night of broken sleep. I feel annoyed at myself, and I feel angry at Steve for haunting my sleep yet again.

I kick off the covers in an effort to try and cool my body down and roll over to lie on my side so I'm facing the flat's large window. There are no blinds or curtains to draw across the window, and so I stare out at the dark night sky of nothingness, unable to view any stars due to the heavy cloud coverage.

I lie in the lonely darkness of my flat, the only sound the low hum of the passing traffic outside on the street below, and I think of nothing but Steve, and how much I miss him.

I feel my eyes fill up with tears and quickly they start rolling down my face and onto my pillow. I wrap one leg over my duvet and hug into it. My breathing is under control now but my tears are continuing to flow. I start to slowly feel my eyes getting heavy, and finally they close, with me still cuddled into my duvet pretending that it's Steve.

CHAPTER 5

Never before in all my life have I been quite so happy to be sitting aboard a cramped and stuffy train carriage. Usually, the smell of other people's bodily functions and secretions is enough to make me turn my nose up in disgust, but today it's the welcome aroma of a familiar environment and routine, for today is the day I am finally returning to work.

Today is a day of mixed emotions.

On one hand I feel pure dread at the idea of returning to work a wholly different person to the one that left two and a half months ago, but on the other I feel an enormous sense of relief.

I've never felt any great passion towards my job, but I feel ready to get back to some sense of normality and I feel grateful that I simply have somewhere to go for the day. Living in my shoebox-sized flat was supposed to be a more desirable option than moving back in with Mum; but knowing I haven't been at work, she might as well have moved in with me, for she won't leave me the hell alone.

She got herself a key cut, without my

knowledge, I might add, and just 'pops by'. Her visits unannounced and most unwelcome. I wouldn't mind so much if she was like other mums. Stopping by to make me soup and do my washing, but instead, I get lectures on my life choices. Yesterday she told me if I'd paid more attention at school, maybe I wouldn't be in such a mess right now.

Ruth assures me it's just her way of showing she cares, but it's driving me insane.

Mum's continual presence coupled with the fact that I haven't slept properly since the day Steve died has left me in a constant state of exhaustion. Whenever I do get to sleep, I'm woken by a disturbing dream that keeps me awake for hours afterwards. It's then, as I lie in the darkness all by myself, I feel so incredibly lonely.

Now the busyness of sorting Steve's funeral and moving house is over, I feel as if my life completely lacks purpose, as if this great huge chunk of me has just been cut off and thrown away. My husband is gone, my home is gone, our future children, holidays, anniversaries, birthdays, our entire for ever after ... all just gone. Every night, I lie awake in my tiny flat, unable to comprehend where it all disappeared to.

As tired as I feel, I'm hoping a familiar routine might just be the tonic I need to feel a little more like myself again.

The man sitting next to me starts to cough

rather violently and doesn't seem to feel any great need to place his hand over his mouth. I see tiny splatters of saliva shoot from his mouth and land on my lap, and I think it sad that in this moment where I could well be contracting a deadly virus, it's still a far better option than spending another day at home crying alone.

The train gradually begins to slow down as we approach Liverpool Street Station. As the train chugs along on the final stretch of our journey I stand from my seat with a renewed sense of purpose. Today I will go to work, and for the first time in such a long time, I will take my role seriously, be open to learning opportunities in order to better myself.

The train stops and the doors beep open. I step out onto the platform with a great deal of anxiety, but feeling ready as ever to start my day.

Feeling more nervous than I'd like to admit, I step over the threshold into the office.

Things are quiet. It seems I'm the only person here and so I take my time meandering to my desk, allowing myself a moment to have a quick scan around.

Everything seems pretty much as I left it. The same coffee stain marks the carpet tile by my chair. I notice some new stationery in the form of brightly coloured Post-its that must belong to whoever's been covering for me. The plastic ficus plants by the window are still thriving, the same unopened magazines are fanned out neatly on the low table in the middle of the room and I note the same light aroma of coffee is seeping its way through from the kitchen area next door.

Satisfied that all seems as it should, I pull out my wheelie chair, plonk myself down and proceed to turn on my computer. I've no idea who's been covering for me or how much work I might be returning to. My contact with work has been extremely limited during my time off.

Ruth dutifully made the initial phone call to tell them I wouldn't be in for a while.
Of course, the obligatory bunch of flowers was sent to the house, but other than that no other contact was made. I've had far too much to get my head round to worry about work, and it was only when I received a text from my manager Bev, telling me they wouldn't pay me for a third month off, that I decided on making my big return.

My computer quickly fires up and as I click through the screen to load my emails I hear the door to the main office swing open. I look up, and from my right in walks Phil Collins – not the international superstar, but the ever so slightly creepy finance manager from the second floor. Phil is somewhere in his late forties. He wears glasses and is clinging on to his thinning mousy brown hair with bloody fingernails. He's recently divorced and it unsettles me greatly that I can always see his nipples through his shirt.

'Oh, hello, stranger ...' he says with a big smile on his face as he approaches, two mismatched coffee cups in his hands.

'Hiya,' I say with a small smile.

Uninvited, Phil bounds over to my side of the reception desk. Leaning over my chair he tightly wraps his arms around me, forcing my face to squash awkwardly into his shoulder.

'It's so good to see you back,' he says over my shoulder, hugging me far too tightly for my liking. Not a moment too soon, he lets go and looks at me with wide eyes full of pity, before not so subtly dropping his gaze to take a fleeting look at my chest.

'Thanks ... how've you been?' I ask with fake interest, before glancing back at my computer.

'Oh, you don't know,' says Phil, a look of anguish flashing across his face.

I stare at him blankly. Indeed, I don't know about a single thing that has gone on here in the last two months.

'I've been off sick for the past two weeks, today is my first day back,' says Phil, placing his mugs and his behind down on the desk, making himself comfortable.

'Nothing too serious, I hope,' I say, turning to my computer, subtly hinting it is now time for Phil to leave.

'I had a UTI,' says Phil in a hushed voice.

'Oh ...' I say, struggling to muster genuine concern as my inbox alerts me to 485 unread emails.

'I've had two rounds of antibiotics, and if truth be told, I'm still not one hundred per cent. It was like peeing barbed wire. You ladies think giving birth is bad—'

'Well, I'm yet to experience either,' I say, trying to steer my focus away from Phil's infected urinary tract and back to my emails.

I'm pretty sure most of these can be deleted but I guess it's still important to check what's here. I decide to sort them into date order first and start opening the earliest ones.

'Listen to me, harping on about myself. How are you, Lydia? I hear you've had a tough time of late,' says Phil, showing no sign of fucking off.

Taken a little by surprise by Phil's question, I suddenly pause on clicking through my emails.

I guess such a question was to be expected and I feel disappointed in myself for not being better prepared. Maybe I should have had an answer rehearsed, but instead I just stare blankly at Phil for a second, trying to think of something to say.

'Er ...' I muster, before clearing my throat. 'I'm okay ... I've been better, but I'm okay,' I say, believing myself to have given a perfectly appropriate and polite answer.

Phil nods sympathetically.

'Well, I'm here if you ever need to talk to anyone.'

I nod my thanks. It's a sweet offer, I'd rather eat my own foot – but it's a sweet offer all the same.

'It can't have been easy for you ... I had an uncle that killed himself. Threw himself off an overpass,' Phil says thoughtfully, and I feel my stomach hit the floor.

'Sorry,' I mutter, Phil's words taking me completely off guard.

'My uncle, threw himself off an overpass, onto the A127,' says Phil.

'Yeah, I heard you. Why are you telling me that?' I ask, taking my eyes off my emails and looking desperately at Phil who's still sitting casually on my desk.

'Your husband, that was it, wasn't it, hung himself?' Phil says in a quiet voice, as if filling me in on the facts of my own life.

'How do you know that?' I ask, absolutely horrified that this person before me who, quite frankly, I don't even like that much, should hold such intimate knowledge about my life.

'It was in the email,' says Phil and I can sense his bemusement at my horrified reaction.

'What email?'

'The email Bev sent out.'

'What? When?' I ask, my voice high with urgency.

'I don't know ... a couple of months ago ...'

I turn away from Phil and start rapidly clicking through my emails when I soon come across one from Bev. I see the sent date and realise it was only two days after Steve's death and I click into the email.

The first thing I notice is the amount of recipients at the top, it being clear that this email was sent not just to a few 'need to know' contacts, but the entire company. I frantically begin to read through the words on my screen.

Hello, All
Today I received some sad news regarding Lydia Green.
A good friend of hers called to notify me that over the weekend Lydia's husband was found hanged at their home, having committed suicide. Lydia found his body – to the best of my knowledge the death is not being treated as suspicious.
During Lydia's compassionate leave the front reception desk will be manned by a temporary member of staff. The exact date of her return to work is to be decided.
I'm sure Lydia will take great comfort in your keeping her in your thoughts and prayers at this most difficult of times.

Should you find this email triggering, please see the link below where you can make contact with the Samaritans as well as other helpful organisations.

'What the ... how is that appropriate?' I ask, unable to hide my outrage and utter shock. I feel my hands begin to shake out of anger and absolute horror that the whole company should be privy to such details of my private life.

'You know Bev, she likes to have complete transparency with everyone,' says Phil, his calm response in no way matching my building hysteria.

'*Transparency*? Fuck transparency! What happened to confidentiality?' I rant, my words leaving my mouth at a much louder volume than I intended as I stand from my chair and tears begin to flood my eyes.

Finally sensing my distress, Phil lifts his buttocks from my desk and stands beside me, attempting to comfort me by placing a hand on my shoulder.

'Don't take it personally, she just wanted to make everyone aware,' he says sympathetically.

'But I don't want everyone aware, there must be over fifty people included on that email!' I rant, pushing Phil's hand off my shoulder.

'Come on, look, I'll make you a coffee and we can sit and have a chat,' suggests Phil, his best attempt at damage control.

'I don't want a coffee and I certainly don't want to sit and chat ... oh god!' I say, tears finally falling from my eyes.

'Come on, Lydia, there's no need to overreact,' Phil says calmly.

'Overreact! She emailed the entire company telling them how the girl at the front desk found her husband hanged in their bedroom!'

'I'm not sure she mentioned it was in the bedroom,' says Phil, casually peering at my computer screen to scan over the offending email.

I can feel my body burning up in a mixture of rage and sheer humiliation. As if the last couple of months haven't been hard enough, I've arrived at work today totally unprepared for the full exposé on my husband's suicide.

With a whole day here ahead of me and no idea how to face it, I make a bold decision and quickly make a grab for my handbag.

'I need to leave,' I say with as much composure as I can muster, swiftly wiping my teary eyes with the back of my hand and marching towards the exit.

'Lydia—' I hear Phil call, but before he has a chance to say anything more I'm out of the door and on the pavement. Without looking back, I walk away as fast as my feet can take me, with no idea where to go, or how to spend the rest of my day.

Terrified by the idea of bumping into somebody from the office, I make the decision not to seek refuge in the nearby Starbucks. Feeling drained, I find myself shuffling back inside Liverpool Street Station.

The station is still busy with people rushing about in all manner of directions like thousands of ants crawling into every available crevice. I walk towards the huge digital departures board in the centre of the station, bobbing out of the way of the never-ending stream of people heading towards me.

I look up at the board and notice the time, 9.29 a.m. With no other plans for how to spend the next few hours, I decide to head home. I scan the departures board for my train and see that it's here, platform 17, and ready for departure in two minutes.

I'm standing outside platform 5: my platform is a whole twelve away.

Not wanting to stay here a single second longer than I have to, I quickly assert myself and awkwardly run the length of the station towards platform 17. Feeling out of breath from my sprint, I reach the ticket barriers and dive into my bag, frantically looking for my purse containing my ticket. Unable to locate it, I dump my bag onto the floor and drop to my knees to riffle through it, desperate not to miss my train.

Finally, in the depths of my handbag, underneath a whole heap of crap I really don't need to carry around with me, I find my purse! I get up off the dirty floor and slam my purse down on the ticket reader.

The barrier doors flap open, and I run towards the train just as the doors begin to beep. I leap onto the train at the first carriage I reach, just in time before the doors slide shut behind me.

As the train rolls back out of the station I feel a great sense of relief, as if I've just orchestrated my escape from prison. I'm safe now, and all I can think about is going home. Not to my shitty flat, but home … the home I used to return to every day where I'd snuggle down and watch TV in bed. The home that had vibrant bright flowers decorating the garden in the summer and a very ornately decorated tree in the living room at Christmas.

The place I lived happily with the man I loved, a man who would make me a cup of tea and a banana sandwich if I'd had a rough day. But that place doesn't exist anymore. Now home is a tiny, rented, lonely room above a bookmaker's … and I've just walked out of my job.

How am I ever going to pay my rent? How am I going to afford food? What if I have to move back in with my mum?

Oh god, what have I done? How could I be so stupid?

Maybe I should go back to the office … but I can't show my face there, not with everyone knowing. I can just imagine it. The sad sympathetic smiles, the wide eyes of pity, the gossip in the kitchen: *Lydia's back … Who's Lydia? You know, Lydia, the girl whose husband killed himself.*

No, I can't go back there.

As my panicked mind races, my body starts to burn up. This part of the train really is quite crowded, more so than I would expect it to be for this time of the morning.

Wedged into a corner by the doors, I feel beads

of sweat starting to form on my forehead and my upper lip. I could really do with a sit-down but there are no seats available even if I was near one. I attempt to roll up the sleeves of my blouse, but it has little effect on cooling me down.

My body is becoming even hotter, as if a small campfire is burning in my stomach, making its way up through my chest and neck; even my underarms are starting to feel moist. I'm beginning to feel a little woozy, so I try to take some control over my breathing, taking deep breaths in and out through my nose.

A ringing begins to sound in my ears, the ringing quickly getting louder and louder until it becomes a high-pitched buzzing. My eyes feel heavy, wanting to close themselves. More than happy to escape, I don't fight the feeling ...

On opening my eyes I realise that I'm still on a packed train but in a horizontal position, staring up from the floor at a sea of concerned faces.

What. The. Fuck?

My arms are either side of me, reaching out slightly, like when a baby is telling you it wants to be picked up and cuddled, expect I'm not a cute baby. I'm a pathetic mess of a grown-up, lying on the floor of a dirty train somewhat concerned that my skirt has shifted since my transit to the floor and I'm displaying my knickers to a group of people that no less than two minutes ago were all strangers, now united in concern for their fellow passenger's welfare.

'Don't worry, don't worry. You're okay,' says a man's voice.

It's not said in panic, but gently and reassuringly. It takes me a minute to place who or where it's coming from, but before I can figure that out, I feel the support of someone behind me. Helping me to my feet, one hand gently holding my upper arm and the other firmly on my back, slowly easing me up from the floor.

I notice as I stand that the train doors have opened again, not in my honour, but because we've just reached the next stop, Forest Gate. Before I have a chance to take in what's just happened, I'm being escorted off the train onto the platform, the same man beside me, guiding me to safety. We go along the platform for a short while until we reach an empty bench.

'Sit yourself down there for a minute,' says the man, and I slump myself down on the bench. As I try to make myself comfortable, my head fuzzy and feeling slightly nauseous, I take a look at the person that's just walked me here.

He sits himself down beside me, perching on the edge of the bench, concern in his very handsome hazel eyes. He looks genuinely worried and a little uneasy, shifting slightly in his seat, looking behind me to see if there are any station staff around that might be able to help.

He's dressed for work, real man's work, in a tight black T-shirt, showing off muscular arms, teamed with a pair of orange high-vis work trousers and tan-coloured work boots, the kind with steel-capped toes. I reckon he must be in his early thirties, maybe mid-thirties at a push? He has fair spiky stubble around his face that matches his fair cropped hair and eyebrows. His face is very chiselled, with a perfectly shaped nose and lips. He really is very handsome, which is further aiding my embarrassment.

'Aren't you supposed to put your head between your legs after you pass out? I think that's a thing,' he says, sounding a little doubtful of his first aid knowledge while still doing a scan of the platform for some help.

I'm not willing to drop my head between my legs, but I lower my head into my hands and stare downwards, and it's then I notice his hands. They're not smooth like Steve's were, but hands that know hard graft, with dry skin and half-eaten grubby fingernails that are holding on to the handles of a black rucksack which sits on the ground by his feet.

'I'm so sorry,' is the first thing I manage from my mouth. 'Have I made you miss your train to work?' I say, finally lifting my head up and looking back up at his handsome face.

'No, not at all, I'm actually on my way home. I'm finished for the day. Anyway it's you we need to worry about. Would you like a bottle of water or something?' he says, looking at me and leaning himself back into the bench, becoming gradually less anxious.

'No, really I'm okay, but thank you.'

'How about you? Are you going to be late for work now?' he asks.

'Ha, no. Let's just say that passing out on the train wasn't the worst part of my day so far,' I answer, hoping that he can't sense the shame I feel around the whole sorry affair that was my morning.

'Oh dear, sorry to hear that,' he laughs. 'Well, you were only out for a few seconds. I managed to catch you in time, just to stop you hitting your head, but then I thought to lie you down, just until you came round.'

'Thank you,' I say coyly, feeling a slight rush of excitement on hearing how the handsome man caught me in his arms.

I gently absorb the sight of him. He really is very easy on the eye. Out of all the people who could have rescued me, I got lucky with him.

'I'm Lydia by the way,' I say and reach out my hand to him. He pulls a hand away from his rucksack and shakes my hand firmly, my small hand engulfed in his.

'Scott. Nice to meet you, Lydia.'

I turn my head away from Scott and notice a train in the distance making its way down the track.

'Are you jumping back on?' I ask.

'No, this is me, I'm going to walk home from here. Are you okay to jump back on though?'

I rise to my feet and Scott mirrors my action.

I feel a little disappointed that my time with the handsome stranger is over, but I'm eager to get back home. My tears of shame won't cry themselves into my pillow sitting here.

'I'll be fine. My head's a little fuzzy still, but a sit-down was all I needed.'

The train is pulling into the station now, slowing right down.

'Thank you, Scott.'

'No problem. Get home safely,' says Scott just as the train stops. As the beeping sound of the doors opening plays out I climb on board and straight away turn round to face Scott on the platform. He beams a huge grin and lifts his hand, giving me a small salute. I beam a smile back and salute back to him.

As the doors close, I stay standing in my chosen spot in a much less packed carriage than the one before. Scott doesn't move from the platform and we both smile a little awkwardly at each other until the train begins to roll along the platform and we finally disappear from each other's sight.

CHAPTER 6

'Oh my god, Ruth, and that's not even the half of it. Then on the way home on the train I got myself in this whole massive panic and I passed out!'

I'm back home now, pacing up and down the flat while talking Ruth through the whole disaster that was my day over the phone.

'Yeah, someone did stop to help me, a very nice man.'

A very handsome man, in fact. As the thought of his handsome face enters my head, I feel ashamed of myself. My husband isn't even cold and I'm cooing over some handsome stranger. I really am a terrible human being.

I continue pacing around while talking on the phone when there's a knock on the door.

'Oh, hang on one sec, Ruth, someone's at the door.'

I pull my phone down from my ear and trot over to the front door to open it.

To my horror, standing in front of me on the other side of the door is Steve, wearing a smart white shirt, scruffily untucked from his smart black work trousers. I stare into his face, and I can see that his eyes are red and his cheeks are wet. I notice tears slowly rolling down his face. As I look on, he begins to sob. I stand perfectly still looking on while Steve begins to break down uncontrollably in front of me, the tears now streaming down his face. His body suddenly starts to shudder and unable to maintain his composure any longer he begins wailing aloud, just like I did the day I found him in the bedroom. He drops his head into his hands and collapses to his knees.

I'm at a complete loss as to what to do. I'm shocked and frozen to the spot. I've never seen Steve cry and certainly not like this. I feel a vibration and look down at my hand to see that I'm still holding on to my phone. It starts to ring as I continue to stare at it, my grip on it loosening, and I watch as it smashes onto the hard wooden floor with a loud bang, the noise making my eyes open.

Suddenly wide awake, I bolt up on my bed drenched in a cold sweat from yet another nightmare. I can still hear the ringing of my phone along with a loud buzzing sound coming from down below, a result of the phone's vibration on the hard floor. I lean over the bed, still fully dressed in my work clothes from earlier, and pick up my ringing phone from the floor. I take a look at the screen to see that it's Nick calling – my brother.

Nick is four years younger than me. Once an absolute horror, he was advised to join the army as a more productive option than the alternative – prison. He was never on trial for murder or anything, but if Nick had continued down the path he was on, he would have been heading in exactly that direction.

Nick joined the army and has never looked back. It seems he finally found his calling and has morphed into the very best version of himself. He's currently stationed out in Poland, and as a result I don't get to see him a lot; he wasn't even able to make it home for Steve's funeral, but that aside, he has been making more of an effort at keeping in touch, which I appreciate.

I swipe the screen to answer.

'Hello,' I say, my voice a little hoarse from having just woken up.

'Hiya, sis, you all right?' asks Nick and I can hear the slight concern in his voice.

I clear my throat quickly in an effort to sound more alert.

'Yeah, I'm fine. Sorry, I was asleep.'

'Sleeping on the job, is that allowed?' questions Nick with a small uncertain laugh.

'I'm not at work,' I groan, rubbing my tired forehead and standing from the bed.

'Why?'

'Who are you? The police?' I ask, making my way to the front door. I open it just a little, taking a peek outside; double checking Steve isn't there as he was in my dream. With the coast clear I close the front door and meander over to where I was.

'No, I just thought today was your first day back.'

'Yeah, it was, and consequently my last,' I groan.

'Oh shit, what happened? Did they sack you?' asks Nick, outraged before aware of the facts.

'No, I just decided that I don't want to work there anymore,' I say, not wanting to get into the details right now.

'Right ... okay, so what's the plan?' Nick asks cautiously.

'I'll find another job,' I say assertively.

What else am I going to do?

'Okay, well make sure you do. You don't want to move back in with Mum,' laughs Nick, both of us unable to think of anything worse.

'Trust me, that's not going to happen,' I say, just as my front door starts to unlock itself. Momentarily terrified, I panic that my dream is about to become a reality and Steve really is here.

'Oh god,' I gasp.

'You okay?'

After a second, I come to, and realise it's not Steve, but something much worse – Mum.

'She's here,' I say to Nick, the annoyance in my voice clear.

'Right, gotta go,' says Nick, eager as ever to avoid unnecessary conversation with Mum.

'Git.'

'Bye,' he says, hanging up the phone just as the front door opens.

'What you doing here?' asks Mum as she walks through the door, clearly not expecting me to be here.

Suddenly I'm catapulted back to being a wayward fourteen-year-old and it takes all my will power not to blurt out 'free period'.

'Shouldn't I be asking you that?' I say, quickly asserting myself, wondering why she should think it's okay to enter my home when I'm not here.

'I need a phone charger. Sucked mine up with the hoover today and broke it.'

'Then go and buy a new one,' I snap, wishing her to leave.

'I will, but I haven't got time today, and you're on the way to my next job.'

'Fine,' I huff, pointing towards my bedside table where my charger lives.

'What are you doing home?' she asks, walking over to my bed. She dumps herself down and plugs in her phone.

I stay silent, scared to approach the subject, not caring for the lecture that's about to ensue.

'Lydia!' snaps Mum, becoming impatient, a stern look etched onto her face.

'I left my job,' I tell her.

'What do you mean you left?' questions Mum, screwing up her face.

'I left my job,' I repeat, unsure how what I've said can be misconstrued.

'Did they sack you?' she asks, unable to fathom such a decision.

'No,' I answer, offended that this seems to be the common assumption.

I take a seat on my sofa, trying to keep a notable distance between us. I watch as she dives her hand into her handbag, pulling out her box of cigs and a lighter.

'Mum, don't smoke in here,' I bark, at which Mum rolls her eyes, reluctantly shoving her cigs and lighter back into her bag.

'Then why did you leave?' she asks.

'Because I didn't want to work there anymore,' I explain, omitting all vital information.

'What? That's not a reason.'

'Of course it is,' I say, trying to remain breezy, sure this really is none of her business.

'No, Lydia, a reason to leave your job is because they've sacked you, *or* because you've found another job. Have you found another job, Lydia?' Mum asks in her most patronising tone.

'Not yet.'

'Then I recommend you go back to your job until you do.'

'I can't do that,' I utter, unable to look Mum in the eye.

'Lydia. How do you expect to pay your rent?' asks Mum, and I can tell she's beginning to lose her patience.

'I'll find another job. People do leave their jobs and get new ones, you know. It's a thing,' I reply, sounding a lot more confident than I feel.

'Well, you better. God knows I can't subsidise you like Steve did. I'm not a charity worker!' says Mum, her voice becoming irate.

'No, you're not, you're my mother, and a bit of fucking sympathy wouldn't go amiss!' I snap, my words spoken loudly, my irritation quickly exceeding hers.

'Sympathy!' barks Mum, not taking too kindly to my comments.

I roll my eyes, aware I've woken the dragon, and dreading the row that's certain to follow.

'*Honestly*, I thought a daughter of mine would be made of stronger stuff than this! Tell me, where do you think we'd all be if I'd just lain around all day watching telly after your father died? Where do you think we'd be if I'd just gone around pleading with everyone to *sympathise* with me!' rants Mum, her lecture laced with her usual mix of detestation and anger towards me for the cards that life has dealt her.

Internally seething, but not willing to get into a full-blown row after an already difficult day, I decide to take the high road and remove myself from the situation by marching towards the front door.

'You know if you'd spent as much time studying at school as you did bonking Darren White ...' she continues, lifting herself from the bed and following me.

I cringe at the idea of her having such intimate knowledge of me. I always denied I was 'bonking' Darren White, and she always knew I was lying.

'What on earth has that got to do with anything!' I shout back, unable to understand why she should feel the need to slur me with a random scenario from the past as I determinedly put on my shoes.

'Maybe then you'd have some prospects! Options!'

'Maybe if you'd been around a little bit more I wouldn't have been bonking Darren in the first place!' I yell back, that being my first open admission to 'bonking' Darren, and I see a look of smugness creep across her face in the knowledge she was right all along.

'And Nick wouldn't have been out shoplifting and god knows what else!' I continue, making a grab for my bag on the floor.

'Oh well, sorry I was too busy trying to keep a roof over our heads!' she shouts, clearly offended by how ungrateful I am for all her hard work and sacrifice.

'What do you want, a medal!' I yell, ever so slightly concerned I may have stepped over the line.

I forcefully open the front door, storming out of my own home, keen as ever to get away before things get even more heated.

'Where are you going?' she demands to know.

'Out!' I shout, sure I don't need to explain myself. Fuming that her mere presence makes me revert back to being a stroppy teenager. I slam the front door shut with no idea where to go.

CHAPTER 7

Sitting in a draughty church hall somewhere in London's Forest Gate and nursing the final drops of a rather grim cup of instant coffee, I relax in an uncomfortable plastic chair as Ruth belts out her own rendition of Shania Twain's 'That Don't Impress Me Much'.

Ruth is a professional singer – by which I mean people pay her to sing at weddings, parties, pubs and clubs, as opposed to the O2; but that's not to say her career hasn't been without its high points, it being a colourful and somewhat successful one. Ruth has sung aboard cruise liners, at foreign-holiday resorts and in the very early noughties she was one fifth of a girl band that made it to number 35 in the German pop charts.

Recently she performed at the opening of a retirement home. Dressed in a 1940s Army Girl costume, Ruth sang her heart out to all the Vera Lynn classics as the elderly and their families milled around drinking tea and eating biscuits.

Recently she joined a band that were looking for a new singer – The Dancing Shoes. This evening they're rehearsing in a draughty church hall ahead of their first big gig this weekend, a wedding in Bromley.

After storming out on Mum I called Ruth. She very kindly suggested I sit in on rehearsals and promised we could go for a drink afterwards. I miss not living next door to Ruth. In another time I'd hop next door, slump myself down on her sofa and we'd put the world to rights for as long as we pleased, the change in our routine just another adjustment I'm struggling to deal with.

As the song comes to an end, I give a solo round of applause which the group seem to appreciate, none more so than Ruth who beams a smile at me and takes a bow.

'Brilliant, Ruth!' gushes the keyboard player. 'I think that's a good note to end on, what do we think?'

The drummer and guitarist nod in agreement and Ruth gives a thumbs-up.

Whilst the band discuss their final notes for the evening I take that as my cue to gather myself together, eager to start analysing my horrible day with my best mate.

With rehearsals over for another day, I gladly follow Ruth out to the busy main road where Forest Gate train station sits large and proud on the other side. Ruth guides us slightly left down the road and, true to her word, we quickly stumble across a pub directly opposite the station and a small off-licence.

Ruth and I walk through a gap in the pub's low black iron railings that leads us to the concrete beer garden and past a tall black iron pole that's missing the pub's sign at the top. The empty frame leaving a vacant square-shaped hole, framing nothing other than a small section of the evening's light blue sky. The pub's large black sign sits high on the whitewashed walls, the gold writing reading 'The Prince of Wales'. Large round hanging baskets bursting with colour hang at the entrance, adding some much needed vibrancy to the otherwise run-down and cold-looking façade. We walk past some black weather-beaten picnic tables that sit empty, doing their best to make the concrete beer garden look as inviting as possible.

Inside we're met with the faint smell of stale beer. The pub is fairly busy with mostly middle-aged men and a few women in attendance. Ruth and I stand at the door and scan the area for a vacant table. The pub's mahogany wood panelling gives the place a warm homely feel, but also makes the wide space seem enclosed, almost a little claustrophobic. The long bar stretches the length of the pub, with a handful of uncomfortable-looking wooden stools scattered sporadically along it.

Ruth is the first to catch a glimpse of an empty table, just in front of us in a cosy corner next to another small round table with two used pint glasses on it. I follow Ruth and pull out a chair. Not wanting to place my bag down on the sticky table, I decide to keep it securely on my lap and try to make myself comfortable as Ruth heads straight to the bar.

It's been almost an hour since Ruth and I arrived at the pub, in which time I've managed to give her the full rundown on my disastrous day.

'She has got a point, though ...' says Ruth, referring to Mum's earlier outburst, taking a sip of her G&T.

'Oh, don't side with her!' I protest, crossing my arms on the table like a moody teenager, feeling rather defensive.

'I'm not, I swear, I'm just saying, I'm not sure quitting your job was the right way to go about things.'

I know Ruth is right, but it's done now. There's no way I can show my face in the office again. The only thing to do now is to sit and dwell, whilst I panic about what to do next.

'It was a shit job anyway!' I declare, trying to stand strong in my decision, even if I am having doubts.

I notice the pot man has appeared at the table next to us. He scoffs a small laugh at my comment as he starts wiping down the table with a damp cloth.

'Was it so bad?' asks Ruth, not quite convinced.

'Well, it wasn't what I want to do.'

'Right ... and what is it you want to do exactly?'

'I don't know, maybe something creative, or something with kids ... or animals,' I say, rattling off ideas, none of them actually sounding all that appealing.

'Well ... it's good to see you've really thought this through,' quips Ruth, taking another sip of her drink.

Sensing Ruth is losing some patience with me, I slump my head down on the table in despair, releasing a loud groan.

'I don't know,' I moan into the table. I lift my head again. 'I think, after everything that's happened, I need a change. I need to do something different. I can't just carry on with parts of my old life, pretending things are still the same,' I say, a little worried I might start crying, so I stop, not wanting to create a scene.

Ruth nods and gives a sympathetic smile, knowing all too well just how difficult the past couple of months have been.

'When you were little, what did you want to be when you grew up?' asks Ruth.

I guess this is her way of trying devise a plan, but I suddenly feel myself go shy, as a long-buried memory emerges.

'I wanted to be a bunny,' I say coyly.

'What, like a bunny girl?' questions Ruth, somewhat confused as to why a small child would want to grow up to be a sexy pin-up. However, that assumption is less embarrassing than the truth.

'No, just a bunny. Like a rabbit. I used to have this book when I was really little, and there was this really pretty bunny in it, she had this pink bow and big eyes, and I used to think, one day, when I grow up, I want to be just like that bunny,' I say, speaking with building enthusiasm.

'Jesus Christ,' mutters Ruth with an eye roll and a shake of her head. Realising I am beyond help she takes a large gulp from her drink.

'When I was a little lad, I wanted to be a cowboy,' says a voice in a strong cockney accent to my right.

To my horror, the pot man who was wiping the table next to us has pulled out the seat next to me and sat himself down at our table.

Everything about this man is round.

He has a round bald head surrounded by blond whitish hair, small round glasses that rest on his round snub nose and a large round belly.

I'm not really feeling up for small talk with strangers right now, but I sit up anyway, pretending to engage.

'But it wasn't meant to be. What with the severe shortage of ranges in the East End, coinciding of course with my inability to ride an' 'orse or even come within ten miles of one, my dreams of becoming the next John Wayne remain just that. So, tell me, what was this job you just packed in?' he asks, and I note the volume of his voice and the confidence in it, as if he could well be addressing a large audience.

'I was a receptionist, in town.'

He nods approvingly before folding his arms over his large belly.

'And tell me this, have you ever considered bar work?'

'Er, no, I can't say I have,' I say with a shake of my head.

'Well, I'm afraid to say I haven't got any bunny rabbit vacancies going, but I might just have something,' he says with a small chuckle, and I feel my cheeks flush with embarrassment.

'What's your name, girl?'

'Lydia, Lydia Green.'

'Nice to meet you, Lydia Green. Jonathan Briggs, but please, call me Jon. Landlord and general dog's body of this fine establishment.'

Jon reaches out his hand for me to shake. I pull my arms from the table and shake Jon's hand. He gives a tight firm handshake which leaves my small hand hurting a little after he lets go.

'You see the problem with the pub game, girl, is that most people just see it as a means to an end. Your students, backpackers, mums who want a bit of pin money and the like, which is fine an' all, but not many people realise that there is a career to be had in the pub industry; should they want one of course.'

I nod as Jon speaks, feeling a little unsure as to where his speech is going.

'You see, for a while now, I've been looking for a

new manager to take over the general running of this place.'

I feel a mixture of excitement and confusion rush through me. Could it be this simple? Could a job as a bar manager be falling this easily into my lap? I wonder.

'You want me to manage your pub?' I ask aloud, unable to keep my excited speculation to myself.

'Ha ha ha ha!' he laughs, at an embarrassingly loud volume. A huge bellowing laugh that very much matches his loud speaking voice.

He lifts his glasses slightly and wipes his small blue eyes with the tips of his stubby fingers.

'No, girl, do I look like an idiot? You said it yourself, you have no experience!'

'But she's very keen to learn,' Ruth chimes in.

'Yes, okay, thank you, Ruth,' I say, embarrassed at how I'm clearly reading this whole situation wrongly.

'Look, my dear, don't let this 'andsome face and boyish charm fool you, I'm quite a bit older than I might look. I would like to one day to do a little less around 'ere and be able to leave it in the hands of someone I can trust. Now I'm not going to appoint you as my bar manger today, or even tomorrow or next week in fact, but I'm willing to give you a chance. We'll start from the bottom and work our way up. Sound fair?'

I nod my head eagerly.

'I take it you don't have any pressing engagements tomorrow?' asks Jon.

'No no, nothing at all.'

'Wonderful! I shall see you here tomorrow morning, ten o'clock sharp. Wear something smart and comfortable shoes.' Jon pushes back on his chair to stand up, and picks up the empty pint glasses and cloth from the table next to us.

'Great, lovely, thank you so much,' I say with extreme gratitude, enthusiastically standing up from my seat for no reason.

Jon nods his head and smiles at me, then does the same to Ruth before slowly walking away towards the bar.

CHAPTER 8

It's 10 a.m. and I'm standing outside the pub ready to commence my first day's work.

Already having knocked on the front door to no answer, I now have my forehead nervously pressed up against the door's frosted-glass window. I can just about make out the bar, where I can see a load of empty glasses, proof that life has been in existence, but there's not a person in sight, the bar in complete darkness.

'Morning, girl!' bellows a voice.

I yelp in shock, spinning round to see Jon standing behind me holding a small white mug of black coffee in one hand and a lit cigarette in the other.

'Ha ha ha ha, sorry, my dear, I didn't mean to startle you. I thought you might turn up while I had me morning fag,' he says, reaching into the pocket of his short-sleeved shirt where I can see a carton of Benson & Hedges. He opens the lid with the box still in his pocket and pulls out a fag to offer to me.

'Oh no thanks, I don't smoke,' I say, at which Jon shrugs and places the fag back in its box.

In actual fact, I would love nothing more than a fag right now. I used to love smoking, but Steve hated it and would never let me smoke in the house. I only finally gave up after a particularly nasty chest infection set in one winter and I didn't smoke a single fag for three weeks. Once I was better I never really fancied it again, and I haven't smoked since. Although, with the stress and trauma I've been through recently, I think I deserve a medal for not turning back to my old friends for a little comfort, although, saying that, I'm not even sure it's a habit I could afford right now. I enviously watch Jon take one long pull on what's left of his cigarette before he throws it in his half-full mug of coffee. I have been guilty of some bad fag etiquette myself over the years, but that is disgusting!

'Come on then, girl,' says Jon.

I follow him at a slight jog, trying to keep up with his wide strides which are quite fast considering he has such short legs. We walk past the front of the pub and I'm led through a narrow alley that runs along the side of the building. Keeping my head down, I notice a small skeletonised bird lying on the ground amongst the weeds that are growing up the side of the building, the sight of the bird leaving me feeling a little squeamish. We reach the end of the alley and are met by a small wooden door with its black paint peeling off.

Jon reaches into the pocket of his trousers and

pulls out a large bundle of keys. He stands for a second, sifting through them, then once he finds the key he's looking for he unlocks the door and walks on through.

'I'll give you the grand tour in a short while, I'm just taking you via the scenic route,' says Jon without even looking behind him to check I'm still following him as he leads us through to an area situated behind the bar, out of sight of the general public.

A set of empty brass coat hooks hangs on the wall in front of me, next to a large oval-shaped mirror.

'Bag, jacket,' says Jon, pointing to the set of hooks on the wall.

I nod my head at Jon's instruction, remove my jacket and hang it up along with my bag.

Jon then continues to walk ahead, until we're both now standing behind the bar, which is, as suspected, completely littered with last night's dirty glasses.

All the chairs are placed upside down on the tables. The jukebox is playing softly in the background, filling the silence nicely with an old swing song, the original version of 'Mack The Knife'.

'Right, so your first job. Glasses. They're dirty, they need to be loaded into the dishwasher. The clean ones in the washer need to be put away. Once and only once you've done that we'll stop for a cuppa and a fag, or just a cuppa in your case.'

'Okay, I can do that.'

'I should hope so.'

I turn round to ask Jon the location of his dishwasher, but as I do, he's already walking away, whistling along in tune to 'Mack The Knife' and making his way up the stairs behind the bar area.

Wondering if this is some kind of idiot test, I suddenly feel overwhelmed by a scene that is completely alien to me. I decide to start the process of looking for the dishwasher by taking a slow walk along the bar. Under the bar top sit rows of clean glasses. Walking along the sticky floor I spot a white square sink sitting underneath a set of brass beer taps. I notice the ends of the taps are all wrapped in cling film, a concept I don't understand. Behind me along the wall hangs a long row of upside-down spirit bottles and lower down along the floor there are several small waist-height fridges containing bottles of soda water and other soft mixers. After walking a full lap of the bar, I'm still none the wiser as to where the dishwasher is.

Just when I'm about to give up all hope and burst into tears of frustration, I'm startled by a female voice in a strong cockney accent just like Jon's.

''Ello, love, you must be Lydia.'

I turn to see a very brassy blonde lady, much the same age as Jon. She's quite short and rather overweight. She's done up to the nines with a full face of make-up on heavily tanned wrinkled skin, the orange hue to her skin highlighting the brightness of her shoulder-length platinum-blonde hair. She's wearing a knee-length denim skirt and a bright purple V-neck blouse showing off an eyeful of cleavage as well as a tattoo of a rose at the top of her right boob.

'Hiya,' I respond nervously.

'I'm Norma, lovely to meet you,' she says with a welcoming smile.

Norma reaches towards me and I shake her limp hand, she quickly letting go to rescue the handbag that's slipping from her shoulder while she holds on to a set of keys.

'I work the lunchtime shift. Jon told me you'd be starting with us today. Where is the miserable sod? Don't tell me he's left you here all on your tod,' says Norma.

'He asked me to put the glasses in the dishwasher, but, er, well, I can't find it,' I say, the confidence in my voice faltering.

'Right there, sweetheart, in front of where you're standing,' says Norma with a gentle chuckle, pointing to a large chrome unit directly in front of where I am in fact standing.

I feel my cheeks burn with embarrassment at not having been able to find it.

'Don't worry, sweetheart, many hands make light work! We'll get this lot sorted in no time,' says Norma, the presence of a friendly face finally putting me at ease.

What I originally dreaded would be a mammoth task is now all done and dusted with the help of my new best friend Norma.

Shortly after Norma's arrival, Jon came downstairs armed with three bacon sandwiches. To some it may just be bacon and bread, but I was really touched by the gesture. Once the three of us had eaten, Jon then, as promised, gave me the grand tour of the building, including the kitchen area and the toilets as well as the upstairs flat, which is where Jon lives.

Now I'm back behind the bar there isn't long to go until 'showtime' and while Jon has disappeared to take care of a few things, I'm alone with Norma. After being given a quick master class on the ideal way to chop lemons, I'm left in sole charge of lemon cutting while Norma stands a little further along from me, unwrapping the cling film from the beer taps and placing the nozzles back on.

'So where were you working before here?' asks Norma, showing a keen interest in her newest colleague.

'I was working in town, on a reception desk,' I answer, keeping my attention firmly on my lemons.

'Aw, let go, were you?' asks Norma with an air of sympathy as I try not to grimace wondering what it is about my general demeanour that makes everyone assume I was fired.

'Something like that,' I say, it being an easier response than the truth.

'Those are some very nice rings on your finger,' says Norma, and I wonder if this woman is always so goddamn nosy.

I look down at the rings in question. One a simple platinum band, the other also a platinum band but with three stunning clear diamonds, a large square-cut stone in the centre with smaller square shoulder stones either side. They really are beautiful rings, the only things I now own of any real value, sentimental or otherwise.

'You been married long?' asks Norma, the question not at all uncalled for or too personal, but one I'm suddenly struggling to answer.

'Er, no. I wasn't married for all that long,' I say, almost mumbling as I struggle to hide the sadness in my voice.

'Oh. Divorced?' asks Norma outright, seemingly unfazed by the awkward ground she's just stumbled upon.

I feel quite taken aback by the directness of her question, but I also hold some admiration for it. There's been many a time in my life when I've wished I could just cut out all the bullshit and be that direct with people, and so I choose to be just as direct with my response.

'Widowed actually,' I say, lifting my head to look at Norma, trying to sound confident.

I can tell Norma's a little shocked, pausing at the beer taps with her eyes widened. She tilts her head to the side and gazes at me with a look of sympathy, a look that I'm becoming increasingly used to, if a little bored of.

'Oh Lydia darling, I am sorry to hear that.'

'Yeah, well. It's just one of those things,' I say, lowering my head to focus back on my lemons.

'How long has it been?' asks Norma, who's now turned away from the beer taps to give me her full undivided attention.

'Not long,' I answer, feeling proud of myself that I've managed to get this far into the conversation without breaking down in tears.

'He must have been so young,' says Norma, full of curiosity.

I feel a tightness in my stomach. I'm starting to feel uncomfortable at Norma's digging into the finer details of my husband's death.

'You know, I really don't like talking about it,' I say sheepishly, sincerely hoping that I've not caused any offence.

Norma quickly shifts her weight and turns her attention back to the brass beer taps.

'Christ, sweetheart. I'm sorry. I shouldn't be prying like this anyway. It's me own fault. Too nosy for me own good!'

'So how long have you worked here for?' I ask, keen to change the subject.

'Oh I don't know. Twenty years now? Maybe less, maybe more?'

'Wow, a long time,' I reply.

'Forty years I've known Jon, longer than you've

been alive, I 'spect?'

I nod and smile at what I think may have been Norma subtly asking how old I am, another piece of information I'd rather keep to myself.

'I was friends with Jon's wife Val. She was my best mate, I'd known her all my life. Our families lived only four doors apart,' says Norma, staring knowingly into the distance.

'Yeah, knew Val all me life. I was her bridesmaid at her and Jon's wedding. He's had a rough time of it, has Jon. Him and Val had a girl. She would've been about your age now, late twenties, early thirties?'

'Did his daughter pass away?' I ask, wanting to be sure of understanding the past tense in which Norma spoke of Jon's daughter.

Norma nods her head gently.

'Sarah, her name was. Gorgeous little thing, she was all Val. Blonde hair, blue eyes. She passed away a week before her tenth birthday. Yeah, must be coming up twenty years ago now, I'd say.'

Norma holds on to the end of the beer tap as she speaks, looking straight ahead of her as she lovingly remembers a little girl who clearly meant so much to her as well as her parents.

'That's really sad,' I respond, conscious that I'm stating the obvious, but at a loss as to what else to say.

'She never really got over it, did Val, I mean, you never get over the loss of a child, but she *really* never got over it. She passed away a couple of years later.'

Norma tells her story of loss as if it's a story she's told many times. Almost as if it's no longer even a story, but just a few pieces of factual information. But that aside; I can still sense the sadness in it.

Feeling fragile as a result of my own recent loss I feel a tear free itself from my right eye and speed its way down my cheek.

'That's sad,' I croak, hastily wiping my face with the back of my hand, trying to hold back my sudden rush of emotion.

Norma, having finished screwing the nozzles back onto the beer taps, makes a grab for the damp J-cloth in the sink under the bar and starts wiping down the bar top.

'That's when I started working here. I never did bar work before then, but Jon weren't coping at all, and he needed someone to take the reins while he sorted himself out. I just do part-time these days, but I've been here ever since. He's a sound bloke, Jon. A bit rough around the edges, but he's got a heart of gold. I can see why he hired you.'

'Why?' I ask, intrigued.

'Aside from the fact that he's a sucker for a pretty face, he knows loss and hardship all too well, sweetheart. He'll do whatever he can to help a distressed damsel,' says Norma, laying out the green beer mats on the bar top.

It's been four hours. Four hours of standing on my feet, clearing glasses, fucking up the till and total utter confusion. Pulling a pint was a lot more difficult than I first thought, but fortunately for me most of the lunchtime crowd are lonely old men. Although not all that easy on the eye, they are very patient, and they seem to be enjoying the novelty of someone new and inexperienced behind the bar.

It's nearing the end of the lunchtime rush, and I'm glad. I'm not sure what time I finish, but I'm happy enough to keep going. I have nothing to get home for after all. Every hour here is another step away from eviction!

Jon has asked me to go outside to clear some of the empty glasses so I do just that.

It's been a bright day and plenty of people have been drinking in the concrete beer garden. I move between the picnic tables, picking up empty glass after empty glass, different shapes and sizes, and struggling to cling to them all at once, even after stacking some of them inside each other. Deciding I've hit my limit, I turn to head back inside the pub. As I do so, something or someone barges into me with enough speed and force for me to lose my footing and stumble, causing me to drop all the glasses onto the hard concrete ground.

'Oh shit, shit, shit,' I whisper loudly to myself.

'Shit. I'm so sorry,' says a man's voice behind me.

I bend down and hurriedly pick up the shards of glass with my bare hands, mortified by the mess I've just made. Suddenly I feel a sharp scratch along my left palm. I choose to ignore the pain, my mind too distracted by the urgent clean-up I'm keen to get underway, until I notice large blobs of blood dripping down onto the concrete and over the broken glass.

'Oh no, stop, you're bleeding,' says the man, gently taking hold of my wrist and moving my bleeding hand away from the shattered glass, and it's his hand I notice before anything else.

A working man's hand with rough skin and bitten grubby fingernails; and just as I thought, when I stand up straight and look at the face of the person I've just barged into, I see it's him, my handsome saviour from yesterday's train journey, Scott. He's back in his work clothes, an ensemble of orange high-vis trousers and a snug black T-shirt. He's standing so close that I can literally smell him, a smell of a hard day's work, of dust and a hint of deodorant. It's no Hugo Boss, but the scent of real man and it's very sexy.

'Leave those, let's get your hand sorted.'

Quickly taking control of the situation he keeps a gentle hold of my wrist, raising it high above my shoulder, and places a hand on my back, escorting me carefully away from the shattered glass and back into the pub.

'Oh Scott mate, what've you done to 'er?' laughs Jon from behind the bar as we walk inside, his good humour making me feel relieved that he's not angry about all the glasses I've just broken.

Jon lifts up the bar top and Scott lets go of my wrist, allowing me to walk through to the area behind the bar. I see Jon make a grab for a small green first aid box that sits on one of the shelves under the bar.

'Come on, girl, get yourself in the karzy,' bellows Jon, pointing towards the toilet door in the corner of the pub.

I let Jon lead the way, following him like a lost puppy.

Jon pops his head round the door before walking in and I follow him inside towards the sink. Jon turns on the tap and points, silently ordering me to place my hand under the running water.

'Get that clean and we'll take a look at the damage,' he says, placing the first aid kit down next to the sink, then rummaging through to find a suitable bandage.

'I'm so sorry, Jon,' I say with far more emotion than necessary.

'Ha, you're not the first person to drop a load of glass on the floor, girl, and you certainly won't be the last.'

Jon pulls my hand away from the running water and takes hold of my hand to inspect the damage.

'I think you'll live. But next time come in and get the broom. I can't keep disappearing into the karzy with me barmaids, people'll talk!'

Jon chuckles as he performs a plaster application like a pro with his short stumpy fingers.

With my hand patched up with two large plasters, I go back behind the bar to continue work.

Scott's sitting at the end of the bar on one of the wooden bar stools with a pint of something in front of him next to a half-folded copy of the *Sun* newspaper while he looks down at the phone screen in his hand.

Feeling unsure whether to approach him or not, I hover awkwardly behind the bar, when suddenly Scott lifts his gaze from his phone and looks directly at me, flashing me a very sexy smile.

'You've not had the best week!'

'How'd you mean?' I reply, accepting the invite of conversation but choosing to remain a little vague as I walk over to his end of the bar.

'Passing out yesterday. Cutting your hand open today. God knows what'll happen to you tomorrow.'

I feel a rush of excitement at the knowledge that he's recognised me.

'So now you know, I'm just a walking disaster!' I joke, trying my best to keep the conversation alive for a few more seconds.

'Nah, I'm sure you're just having an off week. Anyway, I'm sorry, that was my fault walking into you like that. Is your hand okay?'

I lift up my bandaged hand.

'I'll live to fight another day!' I say with a smile.

'Pleased to hear it,' Scott says, smiling back with a flirty wink, which makes my tummy flutter.

Unsure the conversation has anywhere else to go, I slowly start to pull away, deciding to leave Scott alone to enjoy his drink in peace.

'Have you worked here long?' asks Scott after I've already turned my back to him.

'No, today's my first day,' I answer, turning round to face him.

'I thought it might be, I've not seen you here before.'

'Where do you work?' I ask, expertly directing the conversation away from myself.

'I'm a rail engineer. I work weird shift patterns, usually somewhere along the Central Line. I come here sometimes after work. It can take me a couple of hours to wind down. If I didn't go somewhere after work I wouldn't see civilisation for days at a time.'

I nod in agreement. 'Ha, yeah, I know what you mean. If I don't leave my flat for a couple of days I feel like that too. As if the whole world's out enjoying themselves while I'm just sitting in bed alone watching telly and stuffing my face.'

'Your husband not the best company then?' Scott asks, taking a sip from his pint.

I stare at Scott in utter confusion, wondering what part of what I just said gave him the impression that I presently have a husband.

Looking a little bewildered by my reaction, Scott points towards my left hand.

'Sorry, I thought you were married,' he says, confused as to why I should be so shocked by his observation of my wedding and engagement rings.

I look down at my hand and feel a deep stab of sadness.

'Um, no, not quite,' I say looking down at my rings. 'It's a little more complicated than that,' I add, looking back up at Scott.

'Separated?' he asks with sympathy and curiosity in equal measure.

'I guess maybe you could say that. It's complicated.'

Scott arches an eyebrow, having not received the straightforward answer he was maybe expecting.

'Oi, Scotty boy, stop chatting up my new barmaid,' bellows Jon, as he comes up behind me to open one of the small fridges.

Scott smiles, shifting a little uncomfortably on his stool at Jon's interference.

I take that as my cue to move on and do some work and leave my handsome saviour to finish his drink in peace.

'Enjoy your drink,' I say to Scott, then I turn my attention to the elderly man with thinning white hair and white stubble waiting to be served. 'Yes, sir, what you having?'

CHAPTER 9

It's been a month or so since I started my job at the pub, and so far, so good. The work is certainly more labour-intensive than I'm used to, and it really doesn't pay that well, but it's serving me well in keeping my rent paid and just enough food in my belly. The role is so far removed from my usual type of work I have to concentrate, and it's a relief to focus my mind on something other than crushing loneliness and general failure.

It's a bright and sunny Sunday evening and I'm sitting outside The Prince of Wales at one of the weather-beaten picnic tables, enjoying after-work drinks with Ruth and her very oldest friend Gavin.

Gavin is tall and broad and could easily be mistaken for some kind of hooligan if he wasn't so unbelievably camp. His strawberry-blond hair is starting to show signs of grey but his clean-shaven complexion is as flawless and fabulous as ever.

Like Ruth, Gavin is an entertainer. The two of them first meeting years ago when they would frequent the same dodgy pubs and night clubs to sing for their supper. These days Gavin concentrates primarily on his drag act, the one and only Orgasma Sanchez, one of the most glamorous and outrageous drag acts around. I've seen Gavin perform at many an event in the years I've known Ruth. Whether we're watching him on stage in a sparkly gown or sharing a bottle of wine with him, it's always an absolute delight to be in his company.

'It certainly has a … charm about it,' says Gavin, absorbing my new surroundings for the first time and taking a sip from his glass of red wine.

'That's one way of putting it,' I say, looking around at a less than glamorous environment.

'I've worked in worse places, darling. Once when I was working in a pub, I slipped in someone's piss,' says Gavin, his words followed by his signature cackle.

'You did not!' says Ruth, refusing to believe something quite so disgusting.

'I swear to god. I tell no lies, darling.'

'Are you sure it wasn't just beer?' I question.

'It was certainly a very pissy-smelling beer if it was. It was a gay pub in Dalston, absolute cesspit. God, I loved it!' muses Gavin with a filthy laugh. 'It is a shame no one here is that easy on the eye for you, darling,' continues Gavin, just as Jon appears to collect some empties.

'Speak for yourself! I'll have you know it's taken me a lifetime to perfect this physique,' says

Jon, rubbing his round belly with pride as he continues to walk on by.

I like Jon. In the month or so that I've worked here he's been super patient and really kind, greeting me every morning armed with a cup of tea and a bacon sandwich, but that aside, he still remains something of a closed book, revealing very little about the person outside of this place.

'What can I say. You can't have it all!' I say, taking a sip from my drink.

'I loved bar work. Really, I did. Do you love it?' asks Gavin with an air of excitement I'm struggling to match.

I smile thinly and take a second before answering.

'It's okay … right now I think it's good for me, just while I get my head together,' I say with a small shrug.

'I agree,' says Ruth with a small smile and sympathetic eyes.

'Oh, I take back what I said about the lack of eye candy,' says Gavin.

I turn my head to follow Gavin's gaze, and soon realise he's spotted Scott meandering out into the beer garden with a drink in his hand.

Through chatting to Scott over the past month, I've learnt that he's thirty-two years old and lives right here in Forest Gate. He doesn't like prawn cocktail crisps, he broke his wrist last year playing football, he never learnt to swim due to a scary incident as a five-year-old where he fell in a pool on holiday, and one day when he wins the lottery, he hopes to go on an African safari.

As we chat I usually stare at him and have inappropriate sexual fantasies about all the things I want him to do to me, which of course is something that I've kept completely to myself. I'm in no way looking to enter a new relationship, but a girl can dream about the handsome rugged man who sits at the end of the bar most days, can't she?

'That's Scott,' I casually inform the group.

'Friend of yours?' enquiries Gavin with a mischievous grin.

'Suppose so,' I say, unsure if Scott really qualifies as a friend.

'SCOTT!' shouts Gavin, waving his hand to gain Scott's attention.

'What are you doing?' I hiss at Gavin, mortified.

'What? You said he was your friend,' says Gavin.

'He's really not, he's just a customer,' I say, urgently correcting myself.

'Too late now, he's coming over,' says Ruth and I can see excitement dancing in her eyes.

'Hi,' says Scott.

I turn round to look at him. He's dressed in his usual work attire of orange hi-vis trousers and a tight black T-shirt, looking as gorgeous as ever.

'Hi,' I say back a little bashfully.

'You not working today?' asks Scott.

'I was. For a few hours, but now I'm done for the day,' I say, feeling just tipsy enough not to feel as embarrassed as I should.

'Cool, me too.'

'Lydia darling, move up, let Scott sit down,' insists Gavin.

'Oh, I don't want to interrupt,' says Scott.

'Nonsense, darling, please join us. Any friend of Lydia's is a friend of ours,' says Gavin, at which point I shuffle up and make room. Scott willingly takes a seat next to me, flashing me a smile.

'So, Scott, tell us all about yourself,' says Gavin, tilting his head to one side, eager to learn all about the gorgeous man at our table.

Although I was never in any rush to head home tonight, I wasn't planning on staying out quite this late. Ruth and Gavin left some time ago, leaving Scott and me behind in our own little bubble of flirty conversation.

It's almost half ten and I've no idea where the last few hours disappeared to. We're still sitting on the same weather-beaten picnic table and I have to say, it's been lovely, really lovely in fact, to chat without the constant interruption of work and customers.

I can see Scott only has a small drop of beer left in his glass, and I wonder if it might soon be time to call it a night, but while the conversation is flowing I feel no need to hurry things along.

'Honestly, I felt so bad. It's so typical of me not to look where I'm going. I walked into a lamp-post a while ago while I was looking down at my phone,' says Scott, referring to the day he barged into me in the beer garden.

'Ouch, I bet that hurt,' I chuckle.

'It really did. I was just embarrassed I didn't have a better story to explain the huge bump on my forehead. How is your hand now?' asks Scott.

'It was a bit gunky for a few days, but it's fine now,' I say, lifting my left hand and baring my palm to reveal a faint scar, scarcely visible under the evening sky.

Scott looks down at my hand, tracing his fingers across the small scar, his rough fingertips moving gently with ease across my palm.

'Looks like it's healed really nicely,' he says.

I don't move, or pull away, if anything I relish the moment, enjoying the feel of his skin against mine, utterly transfixed.

'I'm gonna charge you two rent if you stay there any longer,' says Jon, seemingly appearing from nowhere, a tower of used glasses balanced in his hands.

I pull my hand away from Scott, a little resentful of the interruption.

'I think that might be our cue to go?' I say.

Scott downs the last drop of his drink as I swing my legs out from under the table.

'How you getting home?' asks Scott as we slowly walk our way out of the beer garden to the main road.

'Oh, my chauffeur will be here in a minute. He picks me up in this giant red car with an upstairs. I wait for him down the road just there,' I say, pointing towards the bus stop just a few yards from where we're standing.

'Okay, I'll wait with you,' Scott suggests and I scoff a small laugh.

'What? What's funny?' he asks.

'Nothing. It's just I don't think a boy has waited with me at the bus stop since I was about fifteen.'

'Oh, well, I promise, no funny business,' says Scott and I find myself releasing a little giggle.

We walk the few short yards to the bus stop together and I take a look down the road to see no bus is on the way just yet.

'So, do you work anywhere else?' asks Scott while we wait, using our last few moments together to find out a little bit more about me.

'No. Right now I'm just working here while I figure some stuff out,' I say, aware my answer may sound a little vague.

'What kind of stuff?' asks Scott looking down at my wedding and engagement rings, no doubt curious as to why a married woman would spend her evening drinking and casually flirting with another man.

'Just stuff.'

'Good stuff or bad stuff?' Scott asks curiously, his eyes meeting mine and holding contact for long enough that it becomes a little disarming.

'Really … crappy stuff,' I say, my defences dropping, but only slightly.

'Sorry to hear that,' Scott replies sympathetically and I see his eyes narrow slightly as if he's wondering why I'm incapable of giving a straight answer.

'It's okay. Everyone has their stuff, right?' I say.

Scott nods knowingly, good-natured enough not to push me any further.

'Is this you?' asks Scott, looking into the distance behind me.

I look round and see my bus coming down the road.

'Yes, it is. Thanks,' I say, reaching out my arm to alert the driver.

'Okay, well get home safely,' says Scott as the bus pulls up beside us, and before the doors have opened he places his face next to mine. His stubble gently brushes against my cheek as he quickly plants a small kiss there.

As soon as he's made contact he pulls away again, leaving me feeling a little giddy.

'You too,' I say as I climb aboard the bus, a huge grin tugging at my mouth.

I plonk myself down on a seat near the front of the bus, and smile at Scott through the window. He lifts his hand, issuing me a small salute, which I match with a smile before the bus finally pulls away and the image of Scott is left behind me.

I smile to myself and open my hand, taking

a look at the faint scar on my palm once again. I follow the line of it that Scott ran his fingers over, all the way along to where it finishes at the base of the finger where I wear my wedding and engagement rings.

I urgently look away and anxiously begin to twist my rings with my other hand as a strong wave of shame crashes into me, instantly wiping the smile from my face. Any remote feeling of happiness replaced by a feeling of gut-wrenching guilt.

CHAPTER 10

When I was employed as a receptionist, it would have been wholly inappropriate for my mother to be perched at the end of my desk while I worked. Unfortunately, in my new pub environment, her hovering nearby while I work seems to be perfectly acceptable practice.

The pub is pretty sparsely attended this evening. Mum could take herself to any available table of her choosing, but she has decided to sit herself at the end of the bar within talking distance of me. As Mum drones on and on about a topic I take no interest in, Jon calls for my attention.

'Lydia love, will you serve this gentleman for me, please. I've got me hands full 'ere.'

On Jon's request I spring into action. Happy to be relieved from the torture of having to listen to my mother.

I look to see who's waiting to be served and to my surprise and delight I see Scott standing on the other side of the bar. He smiles at me and I smile back and without waiting for him to say anything, I pour him a pint. I place it on the bar top when I feel the force of something gripping my wrist. Startled by the brutish conduct I look up. Scott is nowhere to be seen and the tight grip crushing my wrist is Steve's, his hand refusing to let go.

The action shocks me. This isn't my Steve, my lovely gentle caring Steve.

I try to pull my wrist away. I look up at Steve and I notice his pleading eyes, his tear-stained face. His cheeks are red and he looks desperate, scared even.

I shake my head, unable to fathom why Steve should be here in the first place. I try to move my wrist and break free from his grip, but he won't let go. Just as I begin to panic, Steve pulls me in closer to him. The bar isn't there anymore, Steve gets nearer and holds me against him, his arms wrapped tightly around me, he's crushing my body with his. Unable to understand what's going on, I look around me for Mum or for Jon, for anyone to help, but there's nobody, not a soul, the few people that were here disappeared into nowhere.

I scream at Steve, begging him to let me go, and it's then I wake up.

I bolt up in my bed, my heart beating furiously inside my chest. My skin feels moist and even in my panicked state I can feel my bedclothes are drenched in my sweat.

I sit for a moment, trying to get my breathing under control. I take a quick scan around my dark and lonely flat, confirming I am alone, no immediate threats present.

Eventually, I feel myself begin to calm down and I see that during my disturbing dream my pillow has fallen to the floor. Exhausted, I slide myself off the bed and wearing nothing more than my underwear I retrieve my pillow, pulling it into my body as I slump to the floor. Wrapping my arms tightly around my pillow, I bury my face in it and begin to wail, never having felt so alone.

I didn't sleep well last night. Actually, I haven't slept well for the past three months. More specifically, I haven't slept very well since I found Steve hanging from a rope in our bedroom. My problem doesn't seem to be getting to sleep as such but staying asleep. It seems not a night goes by when I'm not interrupted by a disturbing dream featuring my dead husband and if I'm honest I'm feeling royally fed up with being in a constant state of exhaustion. So I've finally booked a doctor's appointment and I'm hoping it will be worth my while and they'll be able to offer me something to take the edge off.

After what feels like an age in the busy waiting room, the electronic board in front of me buzzes and displays my name in lights, directing me to Room 1. I leap from my seat, pull down the silver handle of the shabby white door and open it to see a stunningly beautiful young Asian woman sitting behind a large desk.

She has the most perfect features with big brown eyes and beautiful long thick black hair. Her natural beauty makes me feel tatty in my jeans and T-shirt, but I think the thing I'm most in awe of is her age. I stand at the door and stare at her for a few seconds and feel like a complete failure in her presence. She's my age, maybe a couple of years older, but still of my generation.

Just as the feeling of inadequacy overcomes me, Dr Patel turns on her wheelie chair and flashes me a welcoming smile.

'Come in, Lydia, take a seat,' she says, her voice calm and soft.

I step inside the room, making sure to close the door behind me, and make my way to the plastic seat that's perched at the end of her huge cluttered desk.

'I believe this is the first time we've met?' says Dr Patel as I sit down.

'Yeah, it's been a while since I came here last,' I reply awkwardly.

'So what brings you in today?'

I look into her flawless face. She's clearly achieved so much, academically and otherwise, to have become a GP at such a young age, and here's me … one dead husband, living in a poky rented flat and barely earning above the minimum wage.

I so desperately don't want to tell the beautiful young woman in front of me what a mess my own life is in.

I look down at the floor and I can feel myself crumbling from the inside. I take a deep breath and try my level best to keep my composure.

'It's um, I uh, my ... my feet,' I answer.

'Your feet?' repeats a chirpy Dr Patel.

'Yeah, they hurt.'

'Okay. What kind of pain are you experiencing?'

'Like a stabbing kind of pain, in my heels, and in the balls at the front. I'm on them all day now, for work, and they hurt, and sometimes the pain, it stops me from sleeping. So I would like something to help me sleep, so I can sleep through the pain as it were. I don't think I've had a proper night's sleep in about three months or so, because of the pain ...'

The more I speak, the more I impress myself as I become rather confident in my bullshit tale. However, Dr Patel on the other hand looks a little confused. I'm guessing this may well be the first time she has had a patient link foot pain to insomnia.

'So the pain in your feet is stopping you from sleeping?' confirms Dr Patel.

'Yes,' I answer assertively.

Silence falls between us as the pretty doctor looks at me, then raises a small smile, quite possibly out of embarrassment.

'You see the thing is, Lydia, rather than give you sleeping pills, what I'd really like to do is sort out the pain in your feet.'

'Well you see the thing is, Doctor, all I really

want is a good night's sleep.'

Dr Patel doesn't respond, but slowly moves back on her wheelie chair and turns away from me to face her computer screen. She places a hand on the mouse and spends a few moments looking at the screen while the room falls silent.

Dr Patel turns back to face me and slowly moves closer towards me in her chair.

'It's been a while since we've seen you here, Lydia. Would you mind if I took your blood pressure and your weight?'

I nod in agreement, happy to comply.

Once my blood pressure and weight are taken, I sit myself back down in my seat and put my shoes back on. Dr Patel is facing back towards her computer, updating my records.

'Is everything okay?' I ask, keen to hurry the process along.

'Your blood pressure is a little higher than I'd like it to be,' she says, gently tapping on her keyboard. Dr Patel quickly makes the last few taps on her keyboard and turns round to face me once again. 'Also, you're a little underweight. Lydia, do you think maybe the reason for your lack of sleep could be linked to something else?'

'No, no, I think it's just my feet,' I answer casually.

'Hmm, okay. Lydia, I'm not going to push you or make you feel uncomfortable, but while your feet may well be causing you pain, I do feel that your lack of sleep could be linked to stress, maybe?'

I think I've been rumbled. Although utterly embarrassed, I feel myself relax slightly, knowing I no longer need to keep up this pathetic façade. I look towards the large bay window to my left, feeling too embarrassed to look at Dr Patel. The blinds are down, but open, letting in the warm rays of sunlight from the car park outside.

'I just want to get some sleep, that's all I want. It's every night. I can get to sleep, that's not the problem. It's just the dreams I keep having.'

Tears begin to stream down my face, but I can't pull my eyes away from the window.

'My husband, he killed himself ... and I keep seeing him, and it's like when I found him. I found him. In our bedroom, hanging from the ceiling.' The more I speak, the more I sob, finally feeling broken enough to turn and face Dr Patel who's looking with wide eyes at the crying mess in front of her.

'And that's it, once I'm awake, I can't get back to sleep, so I'm only getting maybe three hours a night, and I'm just so tired all the time. And now I'm working in this pub, and it's okay, but it's not much money, and I'm worried about my rent, and I really am on my feet all day, and my feet, they really do hurt.'

I could go on, but the more I speak, the more incoherent I seem to become.

To her credit Dr Patel doesn't flinch or seem at

all embarrassed by my breakdown.

She doesn't speak straight away, giving me a moment to compose myself, and maybe also giving herself a moment to plan her next move. She leans forward and pulls a couple of tissues from the box that's resting in the middle of her desk and hands them to me.

'I definitely think that all your worries and stress are manifesting themselves physically. I'm happy to give you something to help you sleep, but really, Lydia, I think the one thing you may benefit from the most is some kind of support group.'

I roll my eyes at the suggestion, honestly unable to think of anything worse.

'Can I not just be referred to a counsellor, I think I'd rather something more private.'

If I must to be subjected to this.

'I can refer you to counselling, but the waiting list for a counsellor with the NHS can be a lengthy one.' Dr Patel pushes back on her wheelie chair and reaches down, opening one of the drawers in her desk. She pulls out a wad of leaflets, placing them down on her desk and sifting through them.

'I know the idea of attending a group sounds daunting, but honestly, you'll be amongst people who have been through very similar experiences, and that's something that people tend to find very comforting. You'll be surprised how much it can help.'

She hands me over three different leaflets. I take them from her and glance down at them.

Support After Suicide Loss reads the top one in large bold white lettering with a deep purple background.

'Thank you,' I say, placing the leaflets into my handbag.

'Now before you go, let's see if I can sort you out with something to help you sleep.' Dr Patel turns back to her screen once more to issue me a prescription.

I head straight to work from the doctor's, starting a couple of hours later than my normal time. Norma is in her usual spot behind the bar as I walk on through and I have to say, I feel a little relieved to see things don't seem particularly busy.

'All right, Lydia love? You okay?' asks Norma on my approach, looking a little concerned.

'Yeah, why?' I ask.

'You look rough. Don't she look rough, Jon?'

As used as I'm getting to Norma's bluntness, I'm a little put out by such a harsh observation.

I shake my head. Unable to fathom a polite reply. I skulk my way past her into the back to hang up my bag and ready myself for work.

'Been awake all night thinking about ol' Scotty Boy, I'll bet!' bellows Jon, laughing at his own joke as clutching a red and white tea towel he follows me into the back.

I roll my eyes, annoyed with myself at not doing a better job of hiding my very obvious attraction to Scott.

I look into the oval mirror, checking my reflection one final time before starting work. Norma's right, I do look rough. My eye make-up damaged from my tears at the doctor's, causing the dark rings under my eyes to look all the more prominent. In an effort to salvage something of my looks, I decide to top up my lip gloss.

'You know I'm only joking with you, girl, about Scotty,' says Jon, his tone a little softer.

'Yeah, I know. It's fine,' I say, wishing my dreaming about Scott really was the extent of my sleep deprivation as I dig my hand into the depths of my handbag.

'Everything okay? You get on all right at the quack's?' asks Jon.

'Yeah, all good,' I say, not wishing to elaborate.

After a few short seconds of rummaging, I locate my lip gloss in my handbag. As I pull my hand free, it seems some other contents have got caught up in my search and without any warning, a half-used packet of chewing gum falls onto the floor by my feet along with the leaflet given to me earlier by the GP.

My eyes widen as I watch in horror Jon chivalrously kneel to the floor to pick up my things. He looks at the leaflet, the writing so big and bold it's impossible to miss. He stands and saying nothing at all nonchalantly hands me back the leaflet.

I stay frozen to the spot, my mind a whirl of worry and sheer embarrassment, and watch as Jon leaves to head back behind the bar.

CHAPTER 11

I feel exhausted. It's been a long day, even with starting a little later than usual.
Today, I'm working until closing time. I still have a few more hours to go and although I feel like utter shit, I'm hoping the way I feel means that when I hit the hay tonight I might actually slip into a coma without having to pop a sleeping pill.

This evening Ruth has swung by after band rehearsal and is propping up the end of the bar with a G&T. The pub isn't that busy tonight. With just the same old boys monopolising the corners, I'm able to spend plenty of time chatting with Ruth in between serving, which would be nice if I could muster enough energy to actually listen to her.

'Lydia. Lydia!' barks Ruth.

'What, what?' I reply, barely able to keep my eyes open.

'You're not listening. I said, did you see the message I sent you about the gig this week.'

I think for a second, unable to recall seeing anything, but in my defence, Ruth sends me so many messages about upcoming gigs that it's hard to keep up with them all. As I desperately try to rack my brain, I'm distracted by a familiar figure, the very sight of him transforming me from an exhausted mess to bright and alert.

I stand a little straighter and run my fingers through my hair in a lame effort to tidy it just as Scott spots me behind the bar. He's not in his usual work clothes, but in a white T-shirt and blue jeans and even though he's dressed casually he looks so god- damn handsome.

He flashes me a smile which I match and I feel my excitement building as he approaches.

Ruth turns round, curious to see what or who could possibly have had such an effect on my tired stance. She turns back round, and I pretend not to notice the dirty big smile spread across her face.

'You fancy him,' she says in a quiet voice, her finger seductively circling the rim of her glass.

'I do not,' I hiss back, hoping Scott didn't hear her.

'Oh, you so do! Hi, Scott,' beams Ruth as Scott takes his place at the bar next to her.

'Hey, I don't usually see you here at this time,' I say, trying to sound breezy as I casually fetch Scott a drink.

'I know, I have a few nights off. I thought I'd swing by and say hello.'

'Aw, that's nice. Isn't that nice?' gushes Ruth and as much as I love her, I really wish she would shut the fuck up.

'Very nice,' I mumble, conscious I might just be blushing.

'I was just telling Lydia about a gig I have coming up this week.'

'Yeah, right, which one is this?' I ask, feeling slightly guilty at not being able to remember.

'I told you, it's the opening of a new gallery, somewhere along Brick Lane. Apparently the artist is the next big thing. They want contemporary but sultry.'

'What kind of artist are they?' I ask, struggling to mind.

'I don't know. I don't really care as long as they pay me. So, are you coming?' asks Ruth.

'I dunno, Ruth. I'm not sure it's how I want to spend my night off,' I say as I place Scott's pint down in front of him.

'Right, because you have so much else going on. You've hardly been anywhere other than work and home for months,' says Ruth, slight annoyance in her voice.

Scott looks curiously between me and Ruth, no doubt trying to piece together why I'm so tragic.

'Just sounds a bit naff,' I say, trying to wriggle my way out of having to go, fully aware I may well have a battle on my hands as I put Scott's money into the till and hand him back his change.

'Sorry it's not the O2, but it's a night out. I'll get you a free drink! Scott, will you tell her,' says Ruth, not backing down.

'A free drink. Nothing naff about that,' says Scott, taking a sip from his pint.

'See. It's not that bad. I'll tell you what, Scott, if you can drag this one along, I'll get you both free drinks and maybe even a tray of canapés,' says Ruth and I'm not completely sure if she's joking or not.

'Don't listen to her, Scott, she doesn't have that kind of power,' I say jovially, but inside I'm starting to panic a little, worried I might well be climbing into something I'm not ready for.

'Well in that case, we can always skip the canapés and get something proper to eat. I know some nice restaurants round there,' suggests Scott, cool and collected.

I notice a huge smile spread across Ruth's face, but I don't react. I stand by completely dumbstruck, as if someone's just hit my mute button, the atmosphere turning from light and jovial into something a bit weird and awkward.

'Okay, sounds great,' says Ruth on my behalf, just as the sound of a ringing phone cuts through the awkwardness.

Scott reaches into his jeans pocket, pulls from it his phone and takes a quick glance at the screen.

'Oh, sorry, I should take this,' says Scott, moving away from me and Ruth towards a quiet corner.

'What the hell was that?' I snap at Ruth, confident Scott is out of earshot, finding my volume button at last.

'What?' says Ruth, in no way matching my building hysteria.

'I'm not ready to date,' I plead.

'Why not? He's hot.'

'Because my husband died,' I remind her, almost on the verge of tears. Unable to fathom why Ruth would think railroading me into a date a good idea.

'Steve died. Not you. And this whole hermit thing you've got going on at the moment, it's not healthy and frankly it doesn't suit you,' says Ruth, looking at me with a serious expression.

I know Ruth is right, but I feel so incredibly panicked about the very prospect of dating again.

I see Scott standing in the corner of the pub. He's still speaking on the phone when he looks over at me, flashing me a warm smile.

I raise a smile back, trying to mask my fragility.

'You two clearly fancy each other,' says Ruth, throwing back the final drop of her G&T. 'Why not see where it goes?' she says with a small shrug.

'Lydia girl, if you do insist on gluing yourself to that spot all night, could you at least empty the dishwasher!' orders Jon, his not so subtle way of telling me to do some work, but I'm happy for the interruption, the last few moments a little too overwhelming for my liking.

'Right, I'm going to love you and leave you. Be good, and if I don't see you before, I shall see you and that handsome man in a couple of days!' says Ruth, readying herself to leave.

'Oh Ruth, you shouldn't talk about me like that, we'll get tongues wagging!' says Jon, gently laughing to himself.

Ruth cackles in return at the friendly banter, waving and smiling on her way out, leaving me behind in a thick fog of apprehension.

Today's double shift is finally over and to say I'm tired is an understatement.

My head is heavy, my feet are sore and my whole body aches, it wanting nothing more than to run home and jump straight into bed.

I'm standing out the back getting myself ready to leave for the night. I pull my handbag off the brass hook on the wall and throw it over my shoulder, then walk back out to the bar, ready to commence my journey home.

'What'll it be, girl?' I hear Jon say with his back to me, as he reaches up to bolt the top lock on the front door.

I move out from behind the bar, not taking too much notice of what Jon has just said. I look around the empty, dimly lit pub, the only light coming from the small spotlights above the bar, and I quickly realise it's only Jon and I here.

Jon turns round to face me and raises his eyebrows over his small round glasses, awaiting my answer as he goes behind the bar.

'Um, a vodka and Coke, please,' I answer, feeling unsure as to what's going on, wanting nothing more than to head home after such a long day.

'Lovely, take a seat then, I'll bring 'em over.'

I hesitantly walk towards the small table nearest to me and sit myself down.

I feel my stomach come alive with the heavy flutter of butterflies, concerned that I could be in some kind of trouble, that maybe this is Jon's very tactful way of firing me.

'So Scotty boy, he seems like a nice bloke,' says Jon, his voice accompanied by the slushing sound of Coke being sprayed into a glass.

'Are you gonna tell me there's a policy against dating customers?' I say coyly, feeling my cheeks flush in anticipation of a telling-off.

'Ha, no, my dear. I'm not that petty about such things,' says Jon, walking towards me holding a tall glass of vodka and Coke in each hand.

Jon places the two glasses down on the table and pulls himself out a chair, sitting himself down opposite me. He slides his glass closer.

'I've worked in pubs for … oh I don't know, forty years? Stopped keeping count a while back. Something that you'll soon discover, my dear, the longer you do this job, is that you are so much more than just a barman, or barmaid. You're the keeper of the secrets, an unqualified therapist, basically, a professional listener and not to mention amateur spy. My point is, you develop a skill for people. You learn how to read them, and the longer you do this job, the less people surprise you. Now, I'm not saying I'm some kind of mind reader, but not much gets past me, and might I be right in thinking that it's not been long, has it?'

I assume I'm right in thinking this intervention is to do with the leaflet Jon saw fall from my bag this morning. I'm relieved that I'm not in trouble, but I'm horrified that Jon has taken it upon himself to approach me on the subject.

A silence falls between us as Jon waits for my answer, leaning comfortably back in his chair, moving his drink even closer.

'I take it you've spoken with Norma. What did she tell you?' I ask defensively, casting my mind back to my first day and my conversation with Norma at the bar. I lift my glass to my lips and take a large gulp from my drink.

'Nothing I didn't already suspect, my dear. But what I will say is that Norma weren't wrong when she said you were looking a little run-down and what I wanted to say was, you should give it a go, the group thing.' Jon pauses and takes a small sip from his drink. 'It'll help, trust me.'

I take another large gulp from my drink, the only sound that of my glass being placed back down on the wooden table. My silence makes me feel I'm the one that's winning, but at what exactly, I'm not sure.

'If you want a night off to go, or if you want someone to go with—'

'I don't want to go,' I snap, cutting Jon off before he has a chance to finish.

Jon doesn't respond, but waits to see if I have anything more I want to add to my short sentence.

'I just … I don't see the point. It's not going to change anything. It's not going to bring him back,' I say, so quietly I wonder if Jon has even heard me.

'No it won't. But it might make you feel a little better. No good will come from bottling it all up, trust me on that,' says Jon, his words full of wisdom and worldly experience.

'Is that what you did?' I ask, finally feeling confident enough to look up at Jon. 'Did you go to counselling after your wife died?'

Jon drops his gaze down to the glass in his hand and lifting the glass to his lips takes a huge gulp from it, his silence worrying me. I may have stepped over the line by asking such a personal question.

'By the way, don't try and talk yourself out of going out with that Scott fella.'

I roll my eyes and let out a small chuckle.

So he heard that!

'I'm just worried it's too soon,' I say, feeling a little glum as we approach this particular subject.

'Maybe. But you said it yourself, girl, he ain't coming back. Don't stop yourself from being 'appy. I don't know much about him, ol' Scott, but he seems like a sound bloke, and I'll tell you this for nothing, he's keen on you, girl.'

I smile at Jon's observation. I feel flattered by the attention I've been paid by our most dreamy customer, soon followed by all-consuming guilt because it I feels like I'm betraying my dead husband. I take another large gulp from my glass. I can feel the alcohol helping me to relax and feel safe in the non-judgemental environment.

'Three months. That's how long it's been,' I say, finally giving Jon the information he's been fishing for.

'Not long,' confirms Jon.

'Nope,' I say, staring into my glass and letting out a deep breath, at which Jon and I both lift our glasses at the same time and drink in unison.

'Don't be afraid to be 'appy, girl. You're allowed to be. And do me a favour and 'ave a think about those groups?'

I nod. I will think about it. I have no plans to go, but I'll certainly think about it.

'I'll call you a cab,' says Jon, reaching into his shirt pocket and pulling out his phone.

'No, that's fine,' I say. I finish the last drop of my drink and stand up, knowing that a cab ride home is a small luxury I simply can't afford, not something I'm willing to admit out loud.

'It's okay, it's on me,' says Jon as if he's just

heard the thoughts in my head, and signals with his hand for me to sit back down and wait as he holds his phone to his ear. 'Yes, hello, can I have a pick-up from The Prince of Wales to, sorry, one sec, what's your address, girl?'

CHAPTER 12

I feel sick with nerves; so sick I'm afraid I might actually vomit.

After my chat with Jon and some not so gentle persuasion from Ruth, I've decided to be bold and accept her gig invitation, with Scott as my willing companion. I'm totally unsure if the night ahead qualifies as a date, the lack of clarification quite possibly aiding my nervousness.

It's almost seven o'clock and Scott has very chivalrously offered to pick me up from my flat and is due here any minute now.

Over the last few days Scott and I have exchanged some flirty messages and there's certainly a part of me that's really looking forward to spending some time with him away from the smell of stale beer and work interruptions. I just wish I could convince the gut-wrenching guilt festering in my stomach that tonight is a good idea.

Dressed and ready to go, I get up from my bed and decide to carry out one last check on my appearance in the bathroom mirror. I look good, dressy, but relatively casual in a white skater dress I did well not to drop any make-up on. I bare my teeth in the bathroom mirror, checking for lipstick, when I hear my mobile ring from the other room.

I trot out of the bathroom and retrieve my phone from my bed to see it's Mum calling. Far too preoccupied to deal with her I drop the call and toss the phone back down on the bed. As I make to ready myself for Scott's impending arrival, my phone rings again. I let out a huff of frustration and without looking I answer the phone, worried Mum won't give in until I've let her know I'm alive.

'What do you want?' I groan down the phone.

'Oh, er, sorry, it's me, Scott, I'm outside.'

'Shit,' I mouth to myself, pulling the phone from my ear, checking the screen a second too late, the name indeed displaying 'Scott', not 'Mum'.

'I buzzed your number, but I don't think your buzzer's working,' he says hesitantly, taken aback by my brashness.

'Sorry, Scott, I thought you were someone else. That buzzer's rubbish, I can buzz you up, come in for a sec,' I say, walking towards the intercom at my front door. I press down on the release button and pull open the door.

I watch as Scott climbs the short flight of stairs to my flat and I'm a little taken aback by how very sexy he looks. He's dressed in a snug dark shirt, the sleeves rolled up showing off his strong, toned arms, teamed with a trendy pair of light blue jeans.

'Hi. You look lovely,' he says, stepping inside.

'Thanks. You look lovely too,' I say, catching a waft of his aftershave, the smell and sight of him almost erotic.

'So, this is your place,' says Scott, gently closing the front door behind him as he takes a subtle look at my half a square foot of home.

'Yeah, it's not much,' I say, wishing I could show more enthusiasm towards my home.

'It's nice,' Scott says.

I'm pretty sure he's just being polite, but it's still kind of him to say.

I make my way over to my tiny sofa where my handbag is lying on its side. I plonk myself down and shove my phone inside, getting myself ready to go.

'Would you like a drink?' I ask, almost forgetting my manners.

'No, I'm okay, thanks,' says Scott.

I look at him and I notice he's looking around him a little anxiously. He seems a little nervous, but I can't imagine why.

'So ...' he says.

I wait, intrigued as to whether there's an end to his sentence.

'Look, I don't want to step over the line or anything, but what's the deal here? Are you married, separated? I just don't want some bloke calling himself your husband to jump out of a cupboard and give me a black eye,' says Scott.

I get the sense this subject might have been playing on his mind; and for that I feel bad. I'm not entirely sure if tonight is a date or something more platonic, but I do know if the person before me is going to be any kind of fixture in my life, then the very least I owe him is an honest answer to his question.

'I'm no longer married … but I never separated from or divorced my husband.'

Scott narrows his eyes, waiting for me to give him a straight answer.

'I'm widowed,' I blurt out.

I notice Scott's eyes widen and his lips part slightly, and I think it's safe to say he's displaying a reaction somewhere in between surprise and relief.

I'm too surprised, but in my case at how easy that actually was, and I feel a massive sense of relief at having finally laid bare my uncomfortable truth.

'Would you like to sit down,' I say, sensing some kind of conversation is waiting in the wings, for which all parties involved should be sitting comfortably.

Scott takes a seat next to me on the sofa.

'Lyd, I'm so sorry. It didn't occur to me.'

'It's okay, why would it? Widows are supposed to be eighty-year-olds with bad hearing, right?' I say, trying to keep things as light as I can between us.

'Has it been long?'

'No, not really. Only a few months,' I say, and I can feel myself becoming nervous again, worried as to how much information I might have to divulge right here from my tiny sofa.

'I'm so sorry ... how, I mean what happened?' asks Scott, the words leaving his mouth clumsily as he tries to gather all the facts.

It's a simple question and a perfectly reasonable one. But for some reason I feel my heart as good as stop inside my chest. The sick nervous feeling that had so nicely petered away is suddenly back with a vengeance as I contemplate how on earth to answer Scott's question, when suddenly my mobile starts to ring, the ringtone sharply cutting through any tension.

I roll my eyes, sure it's Mum calling me again.

'Sorry,' I mumble, quickly rooting through my handbag.

I pull out my phone and on looking at the screen I'm surprised to see it's not Mum calling, but my brother Nick. I tried calling him earlier and I got no answer.

'Did you want to take that?' says Scott, ready to stand and politely offer me some privacy.

'No, it's fine, it's just my brother,' I say.

I know it's nothing urgent so I drop the call, vowing to try Nick again later.

'Sorry, where were we?' I say, feeling a little

flustered.

'Your husband, how he ...'

Right, we're still on that!

I look blanky at Scott, completely unable to string any kind of explanation together.

Just the very word 'suicide'. It sits in my mouth like a piece of filth that I'm desperate to spit out, but I can't, through fear of people knowing, seeing the kind of dirt I've done so well to keep hidden.

The screen on my phone flashes, alerting me to the missed call from Nick, and I don't know how or why, but without even thinking the words just come tumbling out of my mouth.

'He was in the army,' I say, my voice small and unsure.

Scott raises his eyebrows, waiting for me to tell him more.

'My husband. He was in the army. That was how he died,' I say, my words spoken a little more confidently as I shove my phone back into my handbag as if hiding the evidence.

'Oh, that's horrible. How, I mean, where ...' splutters Scott and I get the distinct feeling he's unsure as to what it is he's trying to ask exactly.

I inhale a deep breath before answering, quickly scraping together all the knowledge I have on British Army deployments, trying to decide which country to base my late husband's fictional army career.

Think, think. Somewhere dangerous, hostile.

'Iraq, mainly,' I say.

Scott's eyes dart from side to side.

'Are the army still in Iraq?' he questions.

I feel my stomach flip, wondering if he can see through my lie.

'Yeah. Some are still there,' I say, answering quickly and confidently, knowing that to be the case. 'But actually, he was in the Special Forces, so I'm not really allowed to talk about it. I may have said too much already,' I say, quite impressed by how quickly I managed to piece that bullshit together. I'm deliberately creating a certain air of mystery around the circumstances, hoping it will deter Scott from asking any further questions.

'God, I'm so sorry, Lyd. I had no idea you'd been through so much,' says Scott, shaking his head in disbelief.

I look down at the floor, too ashamed to look him in the eye, embarrassed at how easily the lies were able to pour out of me as I contemplate if I really am ready to move on with my life. If I can't be honest about my past, how on earth can I consider the future?

'If I'm honest,' I say, fully aware of the irony, 'I really like you, but I'm not sure if I'm entirely ready for anything too heavy ... yet,' I say a little hesitantly.

Scott smiles thinly, absorbing my words for a second.

'I really like you too. And you know, this ... us

… it doesn't have to be anything you're not ready for,' he says, and I sense he feels a little defeated in the knowledge this evening isn't quite headed in the direction he might have hoped.

An awkward silence hangs between us for a second that I feel compelled to fill.

'I'm sorry,' I say.

'What for?' asks Scott, looking a little baffled.

'I don't know …' I say with a shrug.

For being a lying emotional wreck of a human being.

'It's not a race. We can move at whatever speed we like,' says Scott, his words reassuring me that not all hope is lost between us. 'Do you still want to go tonight?' Scott asks hopefully.

'Of course,' I reply, worried he should have thought otherwise.

'Come on then, let's get going,' Scott says with a happy gorgeous smile, lifting himself from the sofa, readying himself to go.

'Okay,' I say with a small nod and a smile, feeling like we've landed in a place of agreement.

I follow Scott's lead and begin to make my way out of the flat feeling a great sense of relief. I've managed to lay my cards on the table and to my surprise and delight he hasn't bolted for the door. If anything, I think I like him even more; he's kind and understanding. I just hope he's still so understanding when he realises I've told him such a whopper of a lie.

As we head down the stairs to the street door I

start to fret, wondering how the hell I'm going to safely manoeuvre myself around the minefield of lies I've laid before myself.

Scott and I arrive at the corner of a quiet street just a stone's throw away from London's Brick Lane.

'I think this is it,' muses Scott, peering up at a very ordinary-looking red-brick building, not overly confident in our find, the exterior giving very little away.

We walk along the outside of the building until we find an open door, where only a hazy light seeps through the narrow entrance. We step cautiously into a small, dimly lit foyer when I step back and gasp in horror at the sight of a woman lying bound and gagged on the floor in front of us.

I grab hold of Scott's arm and I feel him tense as he too instantly takes a step back in shock. Just as I feel I'm about to suffer a stroke we find ourselves in the calming presence of a woman with engine-red hair.

'Welcome,' she says, handing us both a leaflet, her smile showing off a silver piercing in her gum above her two front teeth. 'Don't mind Wanita. She doesn't bite.'

After taking a second to compose myself, on closer inspection I see the woman bound and gagged on the floor is in fact a mannequin, which judging by her position should have been obvious. 'Wanita' is lying on her stomach, her bound arms reached backwards with her legs bent upwards and bound at the ankles. A red ball gag sits in her open mouth, her blonde bob perching a little haphazardly on her head.

'Is this the Ghalib Golshan Exhibition?' I ask, sure we must have stumbled into the wrong place.

'It most certainly is,' says the woman in a soothing voice.

I look at Scott, his eyes scanning frantically over the leaflet in his hand.

I take a look for myself: *Ghalib Golshan presents a tantalising exploration of human sexuality through paint and sculpture.*

'Okay, thanks,' I say with a grateful smile, truly flabbergasted.

With no more to add, Scott and I slowly meander our way through the foyer, when I hear the unmistakable sound of Ruth singing, confirming that we are indeed in the correct place.

The light in the main gallery is brighter and straight away I see Ruth at the back of the room standing behind a microphone and in front of a giant painting of a man with not one, but three giant penises.

I feel my cheeks flush with embarrassment as I stare at Ruth.

She spots me, looking at me with pleading eyes as she mouths the word 'Sorry' in between her sultry rendition of Take That's 'Could It Be Magic'.

In the centre of the gallery another 'Wanita' style mannequin hangs motionlessly from some kind of makeshift sex swing suspended from the ceiling. Like her partner in crime in the foyer, she's dressed in black PVC underwear with her legs bent behind her head, a small group of onlookers admiring her pretzel-like position whilst sipping flutes of champagne.

I look at Scott who's scanning over the room, when I notice his gaze fix on the wall behind me.

'There's a whole wall of people masturbating behind you,' utters Scott.

I turn round and I can indeed confirm it: on the large wall hang ten or so paintings of people masturbating. Thin people, fat people, men and women all brazenly pleasuring themselves for all the world to see.

'I don't know what to say,' I say, feeling beyond embarrassed, the amount of explicit sexual content rather overwhelming.

'It's certainly ... original,' says Scott with a small awkward laugh, us both a little lost for words.

'There's a painting of a giant vagina in the next room,' says an excitable voice I recognise.

I turn to see Ruth's husband Ben, her most loyal fan/roadie/lackey. He's dressed smartly, a half-drunk flute of champagne held in his hand as he glances around him in complete awe.

'You all right, Lyd,' he says, greeting me with a peck on the cheek. He turns to Scott. 'You must be Scott. I'm Ben, Ruth's husband.' He shakes Scott's hand. Although Ben's tone is friendly, I notice him not so subtly looking Scott up and down, giving him a mental once-over.

A smartly dressed waitress glides past us holding a tray of full champagne flutes and we don't hesitate in taking a glass each, before turning our attention back to the exhibition.

'I think Ruth might have mis-sold this to me,' I say.

'Ha, maybe, but surely it's better than another night stuck indoors,' says Ben.

I roll my eyes and take another look around the room, momentarily mesmerised by a painting of an elderly naked woman with large saggy breasts and nipples the size of satellite dishes.

'Lyd's been a bit of a hermit lately. I don't know if she's mentioned much to you,' Ben says casually to Scott.

'Ben—' I interrupt, keen to shut down this particular area of conversation.

'I'm just making sure you're okay,' says Ben, defending his right to look out for me, at which point I take a much-needed sip of champagne.

'Yeah, Lydia did mention her husband being in the army,' Scott says cautiously, at which point I spit my champagne back into the glass.

'In the army?' questions Ben, narrowing his eyes, confusion plastered all over his face.

'I'm fine, Ben, really. We don't need to talk about it here,' I say, trying to remain cool and casual, desperately not wanting the conversation to develop any further.

Before Ben has a chance to ask any follow-up questions, we're interrupted by the piercing sound of Ruth's microphone feedback echoing through the gallery.

'Excuse me, I'd better check on the speakers,' says Ben, hurrying away not a moment too soon.

Suddenly keen to make an exit, I put a suggestion to Scott.

'Are you hungry? Shall we find somewhere to eat?' I say, eager to avoid any further unwanted conversation with Ben.

'I don't think we should leave before seeing the giant vagina next door,' says Scott, taking a sip from his glass of champagne.

'Giant vagina, then dinner?' I suggest.

'Sounds like a plan,' nods Scott with a small laugh as we make our way past the sex swing into the next room.

Not all that far from the gallery, on another corner of another quiet back street, Scott and I find ourselves sitting by the window in a small Chinese restaurant. We may have over-ordered, our small table loaded with plates of spring rolls, rice and other ooey-gooey-looking dishes, which have left their mark on the clean white tablecloth.

For the past few minutes Scott has been trying his best to teach me how to use chopsticks, but it's no use. With each try my food either ends up on the table or on the floor.

'How did you learn to use these?' I ask, impressed by Scott's dexterity; finally giving up and opting for my humble knife and fork.

'My dad, he's an electrical engineer, and when I was seven, he took a job in Japan. So, our family relocated for the year, and that's where I learned valuable life skills such as ...' Scott taps his chopsticks together and like a pro he shows off his skills once more, picking up a piece of chicken with ease.

'Wow. So do you speak Japanese?' I ask, intrigued.

Scott shakes his head.

'No, we went to an English-speaking school with all these American ex-pat kids. I might have known a few words, but if I'm honest, I don't remember a huge amount about it now.'

'Even so, what a cool part of the world to live for a year,' I say, shovelling more rice into my mouth.

'I suppose. What about you? You must have travelled a little, what with your husband being in the army,' says Scott, his voice quietening on the mention of Steve's pretend time in the services.

I smile before looking down at my plate and awkwardly pushing my food around.

'Not as much as you might think. He was only ever deployed to really dangerous places, so I never went with him,' I say, confident I've provided a satisfactory response on the matter.

'So, are you close to your family?' I ask, quickly changing the subject.

'Yeah, I guess. I'm the youngest. I have two older sisters. They used to terrorise me growing up, but now the three of us are pretty close. What about you? Do you have any brothers or sisters?'

'Yep, I have one brother, four years younger,' I say, proud to have given my first honest answer of the evening.

'You guys close?'

'Geographically no, he's in the army. Right now he's stationed in Poland, so I don't get to see him a lot. What about your parents? Are you close to them?' I ask, anxious not to stay on army-related subject areas for any longer than necessary.

'Yeah, Mum and Dad are pretty easy-going. They're happy as long as we're happy. What about you? You close to your parents?'

'My mum ... it's not the easiest of relationships. And my dad actually passed away when I was little,' I say.

'Was your dad in the army too?' Scott asks with interest, wrongly assuming the British armed forces to be responsible for killing off all the good men in my life.

I shake my head.

'No, he wasn't. He was a roofer. And one day

when he was at work ... he fell off a roof,' I say, giving my shoulders a small shrug, not choosing to add any further detail, allowing Scott to fill in the blanks for himself.

'That's horrible. How old were you?'

'I was eight. My brother was four.'

'I can't imagine what it must be like to lose a parent that young,' says Scott, placing his chopsticks down on the table, granting me his undivided attention.

'It was pretty shit,' I say, unable to articulate a better answer.

'You must really miss him,' says Scott, his gorgeous hazel eyes on me.

It's been a while since I opened up about my dad's death, and I find myself needing a second or two to digest the question. I pull my gaze away from Scott and focus on the large fish tank behind him. Usually the passing of my dad is a subject people like to skim over pretty quickly. Maybe they're worried I might embarrassingly break down in tears in front them. So, I must say, I'm pretty impressed Scott doesn't seem to be scared to approach the subject.

'I definitely feel as if something is *missing*,' I say, bringing my attention back to Scott.

I wait a second to see if he interjects, but he doesn't, allowing me to continue.

'After he died, it was as if all the pieces of our family never fitted back together again properly. I often wonder how different things might have been if he was still here. Like, would me and my mum get on better? Everything changed so much after he died. Like, we were never well off by any means, but we got by okay. And then my mum, she had to go from being this stay-at-home mum to a mum on her own with these two little kids, having to work two different jobs and all the hours god sent just to keep us all from drowning. And because she worked so much, she wasn't around that much and so she relied on me a lot to take care of my brother and help out in the house, and whenever she was around she was exhausted and short- tempered *all* the time.'

I pause for a second and take a sip from my drink.

'It must have been really tough on her,' says Scott, his words spoken with great understanding.

I nod in agreement.

'Yeah, it was. It really was ... I think now, looking back on it all these years later, that she never really took the time to grieve for him properly. She worked all the time and bottled a lot of it up and all that hurt and anger she felt just got projected onto us. I mean, she's always been in my life, we've never been estranged or anything, but we don't have the best relationship ... I find her difficult to be around. God, sorry, I didn't mean to make everything so depressing,' I say, a little worried I may have darkened the mood.

'Don't be sorry,' says Scott, shaking his head gently at such a notion. 'I like learning about you.'

Our eyes meet across the table and he raises a reassuring smile, which I match, and I'm surprised at how easy it was to open up to him.

'Your turn now. Tell me a story about your family. Something that's not depressing,' I say, drawing my attention back to my plate of food.

As Scott proceeds to reminisce about the time his sisters used to pin him down and force him to wear lipstick, my mind wanders to my own family and to Mum in particular.

Only now, after the loss of my own husband, do I truly understand the kind of pain she must have felt. I take some pride in the fact that I haven't allowed myself to be eaten up by bitterness and anger in the way she has, but it seems my own coping mechanisms are just as shoddy.

So far I've lied my way through all my hurt. Bottling everything up and hiding it away, not allowing anyone to see the crippling level of sadness and shame I feel around Steve's death. I shudder in my seat, disturbed at just how similar Mum and I might be.

Standing outside my street door, I casually rummage through my handbag for my door key, feeling a little saddened that my evening with Scott is slowly drawing to a close. It's been such a long time since I've been on a first date that I'm a little out of touch on the goodnight protocols.

Do I invite him up? Is that a little slutty?

'I hope you had a nice time tonight,' says Scott and I feel my heart melt a little at how goddamn lovely he is.

I did. I really, really did, I want to gush, but I don't, keen to play it cool.

'I had a lovely time. I'm sorry the exhibition was a bit weird,' I say, finally retrieving my door key from my bag.

'Porn on a first date. No need to apologise for that!' says Scott, making us both laugh.

I open my street door and note Scott doesn't seem to be making any move to leave and the truth is, I don't want him to.

'Would you like to come up for a coffee?' I ask, instantly feeling foolish, worried I've just read everything incorrectly. 'That's not some cheesy metaphor, I was just wondering if you fancied a coffee ... or a tea? The choices are endless!' I add, fully aware I'm making myself look more daft by the second.

'Sounds great,' says Scott, displaying a confidence I'm struggling to find.

'Great,' I say, inserting my key and pushing open the street door.

We climb the short narrow stairway and quickly reach my front door.

I fidget with my key at the lock. Scott is standing close to me, mere millimetres between us. Our bodies almost touching. I'm unsure if it's raw primitive lust or something more meaningful but all I can think about is what it would feel like to kiss him, to have his lips on mine and to be held in his arms. Feeling a little overwhelmed, I just about manage to turn the key and open the door on ajar.

'It was a metaphor,' I say, turning to look at Scott.

He narrows his eyes and looks at me quizzically.

'I don't have any coffee. I ran out about a week ago and I haven't bought any more. I *really* want to kiss you,' I say, slightly concerned about desperation radiating from me.

A smile spreads across Scott's face and like a greyhound out of the trap I as good as leap on Scott, pressing my lips against his, taking us both by surprise. To my sheer delight he kisses me back, skilfully slipping his tongue into my mouth, then almost as soon as our kiss begins, I feel him pull away.

'I thought you wanted to take things slowly,' he says breathlessly, leaving me unsure if he's flattered or horrified by my boldness.

'Yeah, I know,' I say, dismissing my earlier doubts and pouncing back onto him like a woman possessed, but he doesn't protest, reciprocating my kiss.

Every, single, thing about him feels amazing. His stubble on my chin, the taste of his mouth, the way he pulls me into him closely with his strong arms. The sheer sensation of his body next to mine making my insides sparkle and glisten.

I slip my hand into the back pocket of his jeans, getting a cheeky feel of his toned behind as his hands move up into my hair. Utterly consumed by each other, we get ever closer, when suddenly I feel myself falling backwards as the door I'd left ajar and completely forgotten swings open. Still attached to Scott, I let out a small yelp, but Scott keeps firm hold of me as we as good as fall through the doorway. Undeterred by our clumsy entrance we continue to kiss, lost in each other.

We're both startled by the sound of a loud throaty cough coming from inside. My eyes flash open and meet Scott's. He looks a little panic-stricken.

'Who's that?' he asks, possibly worried we're about to be met by an intruder, but I know without any visual confirmation that that throaty cough can only belong to one person.

'That's my mum,' I utter, closing my eyes in dismay.

Scott stands aside, giving me full view of Mum perched in the middle of my tiny sofa, looking less than impressed.

'What are you doing here?' I ask, my annoyance palpable.

'You didn't answer my call. I was worried,' she says, glaring at Scott, trying her damned hardest to turn him into stone.

'I was busy,' I say, doing my best not to lose my temper.

'So I see,' she says, issuing me her default look of disapproval and taking a sinister slurp from her mug of tea, her watchful eye on Scott.

'Well, I should be going,' says Scott, understandably keen to get away. 'Lyd, I'll give you a call,' he says, reaching for my hand and giving it a firm shake, the less intimate form of contact maybe too little too late.

'Lovely to meet you—'

'Sue,' barks Mum, looking at Scott as if he were something she stepped in.

'Right. Bye, Lyd,' he says. Forgetting himself he leans towards me, I'm assuming to give me a kiss, but suddenly remembering Medusa behind him he quickly changes his mind and instead heads straight out the door and down the stairs.

At the bottom stair he turns round and looks up at me as I stand in the doorway.

'Sorry,' I mouth.

Scott rolls his eyes and smiles in good humour, looking a little smug, happy he's the one that gets to leave. He makes a phone gesture with his hand and mouths something which I'm sure translates as *I'll call you.* I'm relieved he doesn't seem too traumatised. We wave each other goodbye and I step back into the flat.

'Who's he?' asks Mum before I've even had the chance to close the door.

I know she's just dying to know all the details, but first I want my own questions answered.

'How long have you been here?' I ask, making my way over to the sofa. I plonk myself down, trying to sit as far away from her as I can, which unfortunately is only about a foot.

'Few hours, I fell asleep. Not long woke up. Just made a cuppa. Who is he?' she asks once more, like a dog with a bone.

'He's a friend,' I say, refusing to let her muscle her way into the more intimate details of my private life.

'He looked like more than a friend,' she says, taking another loud slurp from her tea.

I exercise my right to remain silent. I'm an adult, and who I choose to snog outside my own front door is no one's business, least of all hers.

I can tell my silence is aggravating her. She purses her lips, shuffling in her seat.

'The problem with you ...'

Here we go.

'Is you don't care who loves you,' she says, taking another slurp from her tea.

'What?' I ask, shaking my head, intrigued as to what horrible thought she's conjuring up.

'Your father was the only man I would ever love. After he died, there was *no way* I could ever let another man in again. But you. You're so desperate for someone to love you, it don't matter who it is. As long as it's someone.'

I sit silently for a moment absorbing her

words, unsure as to why my own mother would deem it okay to be so cruel. I'm determined not to cry in front of her, desperately wanting to stand my ground in my own home.

'I loved Steve, and I miss him, more than you know. And I feel so sad, all the time. But I don't want to feel like this for ever. I don't want to be on my own for ever … and I don't think that makes me a bad person,' I say, proud of the way I'm managing to stick up for myself.

She looks at me with a blank stare.

'Well, you keep telling yourself that,' she says flatly.

I should have known not to expect anything in the way of approval, but even so her low opinion of me still stings.

'I think it's time you left,' I say, wanting her to leave before I say something I'll regret.

She doesn't protest.

Satisfied that she's fully succeeded in ruining my evening, she places her tea mug down on the floor by the sofa and stands up, gathers her things and heads for the door.

'Leave the key,' I order before she opens the front door, determined never to have a repeat episode of tonight.

She does as I ask, pulling my door keys from her bag and placing them down on the kitchen counter.

'Handsome bugger though, I'll give you that,' she says.

I wonder if that's her way of trying to lighten the mood between us, but I know her well enough to know that she doesn't have a conscience.

I don't respond and I think she knows it's time enough for her to leave.

She opens the door and walks out, closing the door behind her.

Relieved to see the back of her, I sit silently on the sofa chewing over her words. Is it a crime to move on? I ask myself. I'm sure the answer is no. I know how much I loved Steve, and how much he continues to mean to me, but it seems her words have had the desired effect.

I drop my head into my hands and cry on my sofa, wishing I had been a better wife to my husband so maybe he might still have been here.

CHAPTER 13

My alarm sounds, quickly waking me from my deep slumber. Although last night ended on a bit of a low, my first thought as I wake is of kissing Scott at my front door, the memory causing a feeling of happiness to lightly bubble inside me, and I realise that I really can't remember the last time I was happy to get up in the morning. I reach over to my night stand, still with my eyes closed, and slowly pull my phone into the bed with me. I prise my eyes open and swipe my phone to silence the alarm and see that I have an unread message. I tiredly tap into my messages, squinting at the bright screen, and I see the message is from Steve.

My happiness is instantly zapped from me and replaced by a feeling of shock, which causes my hand to start shaking. I quickly sit up in the bed, staring into the screen and tapping into the message to read it. The message is completely blank, with just the name Steve at the top. My eyes scan around it as I try to comprehend why I would've received a blank message from Steve's number.

I never did delete him as a contact from my phone. Maybe the phone company have sent it in error? But I'm sure I cancelled the contract? His bill certainly hasn't been paid in months.

A million different explanations race through my mind, and as I sit in my confused state, I feel a strong urge to pee, the urge quite a normal one for this time in the morning, but the feeling to go is overpowering; with my bladder feeling as if someone has their hand tightly gripped around it, telling me this is an extremely urgent situation. I hurriedly pull back my bedcovers and am met with the shocking sight of Steve's corpse.

I scream a blood-curdling scream.

Steve's body is next to me in my bed, the top half naked, revealing pale white skin covered in a maze of thick blue lines. His lifeless crystal-blue eyes hauntingly stare up at me and I can do nothing but stare down at him and scream, and it's while I'm screaming I feel a warm sensation and it's then I wake up.

I am in my bed, in the same familiar state, with my heart racing and my limbs flying about. I frantically throw off the covers to confirm the bed is indeed empty, with no sign of Steve's corpse, but to my disgust, I discover that I have wet my bed.

'What the ...' I say out loud, quickly jumping out of bed.

'EEEUUURGGGGHHH!' I shriek, dropping my head into my hands in the silent darkness of my lonely flat.

'Enough. Enough now,' I say quietly to myself.

I take a couple of deep breaths in and out and stand still for a moment, waiting until I calm down. Dressed in nothing more than a pair of soaked white knickers and a plain white bra, I pull my knickers down over my legs and step out of them. I pick them up from the floor and toss them onto the wet mattress. I then lean over the bed and tug at the top corner of the bottom sheet to remove it.

'Enough,' I say again to myself as I continue stripping the bedclothes.

'Enough.'

I have work today, and thanks to another night of interrupted sleep, I've been awake since 4 a.m. Wrapped comfortably in my white fluffy robe, I'm sitting on my tiny sofa with my legs crossed eating a bowl of Shreddies. It's now 5.30 a.m. Not wanting to climb back into my pissy bed, I've been on the sofa watching the *Emmerdale* omnibus with some woman doing sign language in the corner for the past hour or so. I'm not really paying much attention to the show, only vaguely aware of the shapes and colours on the screen while lost in my own thoughts.

I keep thinking about last night.

Although Mum's presence was a fantastic passion killer, I had a great time, and a great kiss …

I lift my bowl to my lips and drink up the last of the milk, then unfold my legs from under me and stand up from the sofa. I walk slowly over to the sink and place my bowl down gently in it. Feeling tired, I rest my hands on the edge of the sink and lean my head back to gaze up at the low ceiling and l let out a deep sigh.

To say I'm getting sick of this is an understatement.

Sleeping pills aren't working, the dreams aren't getting any easier and today, in my bed; well that's got to be a new low if ever I've known one!

I turn round, lowering my head, and catch a glimpse of my handbag in the corner, by the front door where I dumped it last night. I wander over to it and sit myself down on the floor beside it. I open the bag and start to rummage about inside, when I soon find exactly what I'm looking for. I pull out the purple leaflet that had made its way to the very bottom along with an empty box of Tic Tacs and some old shopping receipts.

The leaflet doesn't contain an overwhelming amount of information. *Have you lost a loved one to suicide*? it asks. *We're here for you,* it reads. *Group discussions held every week.*

There's a number to call, or an email address I can use to make contact. The idea of attending such a group still fills me with dread, not to mention pure embarrassment, but enough really is enough now.

I don't want to feel like this anymore. Tired,

panicked, lying to people about my husband's death and waking up in my own piss.

Maybe it was last night?

Maybe having human feelings all over again for someone new has made my mind shift. I want to feel normal again, and maybe speaking to people, people who can relate to my nightmare situation, might just help that process begin.

I peel myself from the floor with the leaflet held tightly in my hand and make my way over to my night stand and pick up my phone. I perch myself down on the edge of my bed with my phone in my hand and tap through the screen.

It's certainly too early to make a phone call to anyone; but I feel like if I don't do this now, I'll lose my bottle, and it won't be until I wake up in a wet bed again that I'll be willing to do something about it.

So I decide the best thing I can do at this early hour is to pen an email.

Compose New Email? Compose myself, more like!

I tap in the email address from the leaflet into the address line: Lacey@support.co.uk, then stare down at the blank white screen underneath, wondering where on earth to begin.

Dear Suicide Club ...

Unsure that's really the angle I should to go with, I delete and start again.

Hi ...

Nothing wrong with that. It's easy-going, informal, and so I carry on typing.

Hi

My name is Lydia Green.

This morning I woke up in a puddle of my own piss and I would like some help ...

I look down at the screen and chuckle at the sight of my words, fully aware of how inappropriate my sentence is, and so I tap to delete and start again.

Hi

My name is Lydia Green.

I lost my husband earlier this year to suicide and I was thinking of attending your group.

Kind regards

Lydia

I scan over the email to check it reads okay. It might not contain a huge amount of detail, but it is just the amount I feel comfortable with, and so I hit send, surprising myself at my complete lack of hesitation. Feeling rather proud of myself for taking charge of my disturbing situation, I rise to my feet and gently patter back over to the sofa and slump myself down across it, feeling somewhat more relaxed than I did only half an hour ago. I reach for the TV remote and start switching through the channels, and I let my mind wander into a different direction. Away from sleep incontinence, away from bad dreams and Suicide Club, and over to Scott.

I wonder if it is too soon to be thinking of

a future with another man; my mum certainly thinks so. However, the more I think about him, the more I find myself relaxing as if just the mere thought of him fans away all the worry and sadness that constantly festers inside me.

Gradually I feel my eyes become heavy and I don't resist, letting myself drift back to sleep.

***

'Wow. I mean, I had no idea what a dark horse Steve was. So, all this time the bank was a cover story for the SAS?' says Ruth, shaking her head in despair.

Frankly I'm not sure I appreciate her tone.

I worked at the pub today and as I finished at the more human time of 7 p.m., I decided to swing by to see Ruth after work, keen to fill her in on the details of the night before, but now, as she stares at me with disapproval from her kitchen sink, I'm starting to wonder if it was such a good idea after all.

I had no intention of telling Ruth about Steve's 'army career', but it seems Ben had other ideas, informing Ruth on the more peculiar details of my evening as soon as he got the chance.

I don't say anything, instead I let out a loud huff before dropping my head into my arms at the kitchen table, wishing I could escape her interrogation.

'Why didn't you just tell him the truth?' asks Ruth, unable to comprehend my behaviour.

'I don't know. It was just easier—'

'Really?' questions Ruth, and I notice her screwing up her face as I lift mine from her kitchen table.

'I'm just not ready to talk about it yet,' I say, wishing we could change the subject.

Before Ruth has the chance to impart any wisdom, we're interrupted by the sound of Ben bellowing down the stairs from the bathroom.

'Ruth, where's my razor!'

'It's in the bathroom cabinet!' Ruth bellows back.

'No, it's not. I looked there! Did you use it on your legs again?'

'No, of course not! Hang on, I'm coming!' shouts Ruth, scurrying out of the kitchen and up the stairs.

Happy to embrace a short break from Ruth's Q and A session, I pick up my phone from the table. Having worked all day, I'm a little behind on my updates and our conversation has prompted me to see if there is a reply from my earlier email to 'Suicide Club'.

I tap my screen into my emails and scroll through the circulars from Wowcher and Ticketmaster, when I see it, a reply from Lacey@support.co.uk. Feeling a little nervous, I tap into the email, curious to know where I go from here.

Hi Lydia
Firstly let me start by saying how sorry I am to hear

of your loss.
My name is Lacey and I manage, as well as facilitate, support groups for people like yourself who have lost loved ones as a result of suicide. We run groups where you can come and share your story, or simply listen to the experiences of others.
I run a group every Thursday – 8 p.m. at the Royal British Legion Club, 25–26 Somerset Street, Manor Park.
You don't have to do anything other than show up, but if you would like any more information, you can call me on the number below or reply to this email.
I hope to meet you soon.
Kindest regards
Lacey

In spite of everything, I'm not sure if I'm ready to 'share my story'. However, I am slightly taken by the idea of listening to others; in the hope that maybe there can be some comfort to be found in that.

'Honestly, that man couldn't find the nose on his face without me,' says Ruth, breezing back into the kitchen. 'So, you planning on seeing him again?' she asks, sitting herself next to me at the kitchen table.

'Yes. I am,' I say, pulling my attention away from my phone, greeting Ruth with a sweet smile.

'In all seriousness, you really should think about speaking to someone,' says Ruth, a look of anguish creeping onto her face.

As tired as I am of her nagging, I know it comes from a good place, and I am grateful she cares.

'Trust me, I'm working on it,' I say, placing my hand on top of hers and giving it a small squeeze, trying my best to reassure her that I'm not a complete train wreck.

She smiles back. I'm not sure she's completely convinced, but she doesn't push me any further, and for that I'm grateful.

'Now what's a girl got to do around here for a cuppa?' I say, standing from the table and heading for the kettle, happy to have something in the way of a productive outcome from today.

CHAPTER 14

So far, today has been an ordinary day like any other. I arrived at work, collected glasses, loaded the dishwasher, emptied the dishwasher, poured drinks, did my level best to dodge Larry who bored me senseless about the state of his Alsatian's worms and now, I'm counting down the minutes until the end of my shift.

Tomorrow I'm meeting Scott for what I guess is our second date. I'm not sure as to what the plan is, and although I'm excited to see him, I can't seem to shake off the knot of anxiety tying itself up inside me, brought on by my own stupid behaviour.

Why on earth did I tell him Steve was in the army?

I know I need to come clean with Scott, but do I really want him to know I'm a compulsive liar with questionable mental health problems this early into our relationship?

'Lydia girl, do us an empties lap, will ya, I'm running low 'ere,' says Jon, snapping me out of my worried trance.

Keen for the time to tick by as quickly as possible, I lift the bar top and make my way out onto the main floor, picking up glass after glass on my way. With glasses of all different shapes and sizes balanced in between my hands, I spot one last empty pint glass sitting all on its lonesome on a table in the corner. So far my personal best is nine glasses, not a great number, but I'm determined to improve. I decide here and now will be my moment to achieve my new personal best of ten glasses.

With my eyes firmly on the prize, I make my way over to the glass. Determined to include one last empty into my small collection, I awkwardly pick up the glass from the table, and just as I'm about to stack it for my record-breaking feat, I feel a pair of hands land firmly, not to say with force down on my shoulders.

'Don't drop them, whatever you do!' shouts a voice into my ear.

Scaring the absolute life out of me it makes me drop my glasses, all my progress smashing to the ground in one loud dramatic crash.

'Oi, who's the comedian!' Jon shouts from the bar, ready to spring into action at the slightest sign of any harm coming to a member of his staff.

I turn round, and my mouth drops open.

He beams at me with a smile so happy and wide it's as if sunlight is radiating from him.

'All right, sis!' he says, and just the mere sight of him sends a surge of love and relief straight into my heart.

Without a second thought I fling my arms around him and hold him tightly with the shattered glass at our feet.

'I take it you know this clown?' I hear Jon say, unimpressed, meandering his way over with a broom in hand, checking all is okay.

Reluctantly I let him go. I look into his cheeky face, drinking him in, confirming the young man before me is indeed my little git of a younger brother. His dark hair is longer than I remember, it sitting a little flat on his head. His chin displays a dusty shadow, his attempt to grow facial hair still showing little success, the meagre hair growth making him seem younger than he is, but he looks well, really well. Putting my mind at ease that he's being taken care of in all the ways he should be.

'Jon, this is my little brother, Nick. He's in the army,' I say proudly.

'I hope they taught you how to use one of these in basic training,' says Jon, thrusting a broom and dustpan into Nick's hands.

Accepting his orders from Jon, Nick gets to work on the floor while I head back behind the bar and gladly fetch my little brother a drink.

Technically I still had another hour left on my shift when Nick arrived, but Jon being the wonderful boss he is has allowed me to spend it catching up with Nick, huddled at a table in the corner.

'I'm sorry I couldn't make it back for the funeral,' says Nick remorsefully, taking a sip from his bottle of beer.

'It's okay. I know you would've been there if you could.'

'How've you been?' he asks, not in the generic way you might ask a friend during a giggly catch-up, but seriously, as if he needs a solid confirmation of my well-being.

'I'm okay. I have a job, a place to live. Things could always be worse,' I say, keen to reassure him I'm coping. 'So, how long are you home for?' I ask excitedly.

'I'm flying back again tomorrow night.'

'What? Is that all?' I say, disappointed to hear his visit is so short, his answer banishing all the fun plans I was yet to conjure up.

'But I should have a solid fortnight off next month.'

'That's great, so you'll be home for two whole weeks,' I say hopefully.

'Er, not quite. That's actually what I wanted to talk to you about. I've already kind of made plans to spend it with someone,' says Nick, a coy smile pulling at the corners of his mouth.

'Nick ... do you have a girlfriend?' I ask, gleefully teasing him.

He nods his head, the smooth skin on his cheeks colouring.

My brother has never been much of a ladies' man. He's always been very confident around other men, able to stand his ground and never afraid to throw or even receive a punch, but he's never had much in the way of suave around the opposite sex, always striking me as a little awkward. So, needless to say, this is exciting news.

'What's her name? What's she like? Is she Polish?' I ask, bursting to hear all about the girl who makes my brother's cheeks turn pink!

Nick shuffles in his seat and places his hand into the pocket of his jeans, first pulling from it his wallet, which he places on the table, then his phone.

'Yes, she's Polish. Her name's Hanna, and she's lovely,' says Nick, not looking at me but down at his phone. He taps through the screen before finally turning it round to show me a picture of a pretty young lady with very long chestnut-brown hair that finishes just before her hips. She has large brown eyes and a lovely warm smile.

'Wow, you are definitely punching above your weight,' I say with approval.

'I know,' says Nick, turning the phone back round to look at the screen himself, his smile widening. 'There's also something else I need to tell you,' he says, placing his phone down on the table and picking up his wallet.

I watch as he opens the wallet, pulling from it a small piece of shiny paper. He hands it to me and I look down at the paper in my hand, a mass of white blurry lines set against a black background, in the centre a black kidney-bean-shaped hole, and I'm no medical professional, but I'm pretty sure the white blurry blob in the centre of it is ... a baby.

'Nick, this is a baby scan,' I say, sure this is some kind of wind-up.

Nick doesn't say anything. His smile fades, replaced with a look of angst I think I've brought on with my reaction.

'Nick? This isn't your baby ... is it?' I ask.

He nods.

'With ...?'

Shit, what was her name?

'Hanna,' adds Nick, filling in the blank for me.

I feel my mouth drop open. I look back down at the photo in my hand and blink hard.

'How far along is she?'

'About three months,' says Nick, the smile creeping back onto his face just at the very mention of his baby.

'How long have you been together?' I ask, unable to fathom how quickly this is all moving.

'About three months,' he replies cautiously, as if bracing himself for some kind of telling-off.

An involuntary laugh escapes from my mouth as I shake my head in disbelief.

'I know it's happened fast,' says Nick, correctly predicting my shock.

'Fast! I've seen light travel slower!' I blurt out.

'But I love her. I really do. And she loves me too,' says Nick, that smile returning to his beardless face.

'Does Mum know?' I ask.

Nick shakes his head.

'No, I'm going to tell her later. I wanted to tell you first,' he says, and I feel a wave of supreme smugness that he should want me to be the first to know.

I look back at the scan in my hand, at my teeny tiny niece or nephew, finding it utterly bizarre how the young man in front of me who can't even grow a proper beard can be capable of making an actual person.

I look at Nick. He's starting to look angsty again, his eyes looking a little worried, and it's then I begin to feel bad. He's done nothing wrong, nothing at all. He met a girl, fell in love and made a baby. Or maybe made a baby and fell in love, but either way, he's my little brother and he deserves to be showered with love and support in response to what really is wonderful news.

'Congratulations!' I beam with an animated smile, standing from my seat.

A look of relief washes over Nick, as he too stands up.

I wrap my arms around him, holding on to him tightly.

'I just can't believe it,' I say, still in a state of shock.

'I know. Me neither,' says Nick, his words followed by a small chuckle, and I get the distinct feeling he's utterly relieved to have shared his news to much less of a bollocking than he expected.

I feel him trying to let go, but I don't let him, holding on to him for a little longer, enjoying a rare cuddle from him as I try to wrap my head around his life-changing news.

Finally ready to call it a night, I'm out the back of the pub, readying myself to head home, retrieving my bag and coat from the brass hooks. Nick has already skedaddled, dashing off to visit some friends on his whistle stop tour before heading to Mum's. I wonder how she'll react to Nick's news. I shall brace myself for the phone call.

'I understand congratulations are in order, Auntie,' Jon says, walking in behind me and wandering into the corner to fetch another cardboard hanger of peanuts.

I look at Jon quizzically, wondering how he's privy to my news when I'm yet to tell another soul.

'Told you before, girl, amateur spy,' he says, correctly reading my thoughts.

I nod my head and slip on my jacket.

'Yeah, I suppose so,' I say with a small shrug, feeling a little deflated.

Jon narrows his eyes and frowns at me, sensing something's a little out of alignment.

'Is it not good news?' asks Jon, doubting

his spy skills, worrying he's read the situation incorrectly.

'No, it is,' I reassure him, unable to raise the appropriate level of conviction, when as if completely out of nowhere, as if finally being allowed to show itself, a feeling of pure and utter sadness tears through me.

'I just always thought I'd be first,' I say, my voice almost inaudible, coming out a mere squeak as tears flood my eyes and quickly pour down my cheeks, my sadness unable to be contained for a second longer.

Displaying an understanding smile, Jon nods his head gently.

Feeling embarrassed, I hastily wipe my tears away with the back of my hand.

'There's a time for everything, girl. Yours too will surely come,' says Jon, his poignant words causing my flowing tears to crank up a gear to a full-blown wet and sloppy devastated sob.

Jon places down the cardboard peanut hanger on the floor by his feet and engulfs me in a much-needed hug.

Feeling far too emotional to be embarrassed I place my head on Jon's shoulder and cry. Grieving for the baby Steve and I never had the chance to make, and the news we never had the chance to share.

I'm feeling tired, more so than usual, quite possibly a result of my emotional breakdown before I left work. I still feel a little out of sorts and the last thing I want to do right now is head back to my empty flat to spend the night alone.

I'd quite like to pop to Ruth's. To plonk myself down at her kitchen table and tell her all about my day, and although I know she's far too kind to ever turn me away, I must remember her life doesn't solely revolve around me.

I could call Mum, but then I quickly remind myself that's probably the very last thing in the world I'd like to do. Looking for any kind of detour, I decide to head to the 24 hour off-licence opposite the pub, seizing the opportunity to top up on a couple of essentials.

I walk into the brightly lit shop and say hello to Adnan behind the counter who greets me with a welcoming smile. I stroll the isle, heading to the back of the shop, and grab a four-packet of loo roll and a tin of baked beans.

On my way to the till at the front of the shop, I pass the sugar and the tea bags before spotting the coffee. There isn't a huge selection, and although none of the instant stuff looks particularly appealing it does trigger a rather appealing idea.

I reach for one of the jars, balancing it between my loo roll and baked beans, and reach for my phone.

I open my camera and snap a picture of the jar of coffee before tapping through the screen to my messages. *Fancy that coffee?* I type under the

picture.
I hesitate before hitting send. I have no idea if he's awake or asleep or even if I'm about to make a desperate fool of myself, but I do know if there is even a remote chance of not having to spend the entire night alone, I would like to seize it.
Before I have a chance to talk myself out of it, I tap send.

I walk to the till, placing down my items and paying, and as I step out of the shop I hear my phone alert me to a message. I look down at the screen. *See you in half an hour,* it reads. I smile to myself, heading straight home with an extra spring in my step.

CHAPTER 15

I'd be lying if I said I didn't run home like a fat kid into a cake shop. Feeling a little out of breath and sweaty I made a quick pit stop to wash under my arms and brush my teeth.

I'm not feeling quite as fresh as I might like to, but there's no more time to worry about it, because Scott is here. I walk over to my buzzer and press the button, allowing Scott entry before heading over to open the front door. I pop my head out and to my delight and joy he's climbing the stairs to my flat, armed with a small white plastic carrier bag.

'Can I be honest with you?' he says on approach.

'Of course.'

'I hate coffee. Always have.'

'And yet you still came!' I say with a small chuckle as Scott climbs the final step and walks into my flat.

'I came prepared with other options,' he says, placing his hand into the bag and pulling from it a small box of tea bags – the good Twining's ones.

It's a cute move, one I think quite worthy of a kiss, but I'm of the belief that I should try and play it cool, so I divert my energy elsewhere.

'I'd better get the kettle on then,' I say, excited to see how the next couple of hours unfold.

Relaxed on my small sofa, Scott and I sit chatting whilst sipping our way through our drinks.

'You're going to be an aunt!' says Scott with a smile, and I'm a little ashamed that his reaction to such news is far more enthusiastic than my own. I force a tight disingenuous smile.

'You don't seem very happy about it,' says Scott, sensing my reservations.

'I am,' I say reassuringly. 'I think I'm just in shock. Nothing about the last few months has panned out the way I imagined,' I say with a small sigh.

'Lots of big changes.'

I nod, not quite able to verbalise my feelings, maybe out of exhaustion, or shock, or maybe I just don't have the energy to process another wave of overwhelming emotions.

'How long were you married for?' asks Scott, his question taking me by surprise, but I guess the nature of our conversation invites such a question. After all, it does seem we are in the midst of our 'getting to know you' phase.

'Nine months. We were together for eight years, but we were only married for nine months.'

There's a pause in the conversation. Feeling uncomfortable with the sombre topic, I decide to revert to my trustworthy method of switching the conversation back to the other person.

'What about you? Ever been married, kids?'

Scott takes a sip from his tea and pauses before answering.

'I was with someone, for a while. We really tried to make it work, but in the end we both realised it wasn't meant to be.'

Scott speaks with some sadness in his voice. I guess as we go through life things aren't all rosy all the time, not for any of us. Although his story may not be as traumatising as mine, I guess we all have our own tales of woe.

Happy with the attention being on Scott, I begin to relax and lean myself back a little in my seat.

'You must be scared for your brother. After what happened to your husband.'

Oh Christ, we're back onto me!

I know it's now or never. If I want to banish this lie and come clean, now is the time. It's an intimate moment, just me and him. *Tell him, tell him now.*

'Yeah, of course, but Steve was in the Special Forces, so it's a little different.'

I'm screaming inside out of sheer frustration. I want so badly to be honest with him, just like he was with me, but it's as if something's blocking the way, stopping the truth from freeing itself from me.

'He was always in the forces, from when I first met him, and it was always a worry, you know, that something would happen to him, it never goes away. And then one day I get this phone call. "Is that Mrs Green?" says some man at the other end, and I just knew ... he'd only been out there a couple of weeks at that point ... and that was it, my whole life ... just fell apart. Everything changed. It's like I don't even know that person anymore, the person I was before,' I say with enough emotion and conviction for an Oscar nomination, but it's not all untrue. My last sentences being the only honest thing I've said in my whole pathetic monologue. My life did fall apart, and I really don't know who I am anymore. I never lied, not like this. I'm embarrassed at how easily the lies have poured out of me and I look silently down at my lap trying to hide my blushes.

'You okay?' asks Scott, mistaking my silent shame for sadness.

'Yeah,' I say, pulling myself back into the moment. 'I feel like I'm always bringing the mood down,' I say, my subtle way of implying I'd *really* like to change the subject.

'Not at all. It's all a part of your story. No use pretending it didn't happen.'

I look into his hazel eyes and I feel horrible. Simply awful, feeling undeserving of the sympathy and understanding of the man next me.

I watch as he drinks from his mug of tea, tilting his head back slightly, seemingly finishing up the last drop.

'Would you like another drink?' I offer.

'No, I'm good, thanks,' he says, loosely holding the empty mug in his hand.

I sense he's about to start readying himself to leave; and I'm not sure if it's because I feel sad or lonely or because I'm so attracted to him, but I don't want him to go.

I want him to stay here. For him to hold me in his arms and kiss me on the lips. I want to feel his hands in my hair and for him to tell me everything will be okay.

I casually take the mug from his hand and place it on the floor. With our eyes on each other I place my hand into his and move myself in closer.

I feel Scott place a hand down on my thigh as our bodies press gently against one another. I keep my eyes on him as his lips lower onto mine and we're kissing, soft gentle kisses, each one making me yearn for another. I feel his hand drift from my thigh up towards my waist before gently settling under my boob.

Our kissing becomes more passionate, our tongues entering each other's mouths, and I feel myself pulling him in closer, my hands stroking the stubble on his face, wanting him even more with every kiss and with every passing second. Consumed by one another, we sink back on the sofa until eventually I'm lying down with Scott's body placed deliciously on top of mine.

Scott starts diverting his kisses elsewhere, along my cheek until he reaches my neck. The touch of his lips, his breath against my skin, the sensation the most erotic I've had in months, I'm wanting him so badly it's almost painful.

I slip a hand between us and let it wander, down past his firm stomach until I reach his crotch, and I stroke my hand over the hard bulge in his jeans.

'Stay,' I whisper into his ear, 'stay the night.'

He lets out a little moan, his kisses coming to a gradual halt. He lifts his face from my neck and looks at me with sorrow in his eyes.

'I have an early start. I'll never get up if I stay.'

'You don't seem to have any problems getting up,' I say, my hand still resting on his crotch.

He gives an amused smile and plants a soft kiss on my lips.

'I need to go,' he says, pulling himself up and climbing to his feet.

Worried I might have come across as desperate, I make an effort not to seem too disappointed.

'Do you always do that?' I say, climbing to my feet, casually brushing my hand through my hair.

Scott looks at me quizzically and stays silent, permitting me to finish.

'Leave them pining for more,' I say jovially, hoping to mask my embarrassment.

He doesn't say anything, but raises a smile, looking awfully pleased with himself.

He moves in closer, placing his hands around my waist, and kisses me on the lips.

'I'll see you tomorrow, when we'll have all the time in the world,' he says, gazing into my eyes, his words spoken softly and sincerely.

Before Scott leaves we kiss one last time by my front door. A long lingering tease of a kiss that makes me yearn for him all over again, but I don't let it get the better of me.

I wave him goodbye as he descends the stairs and goes out through the street door. Once he's gone I step back into my flat. Closing the door behind me I stand and ponder for a second, intrigued and excited as to what tomorrow has in store.

CHAPTER 16

In a few short hours from now my little brother will be boarding a flight back to Poland. I have no real clue when I'll see him next and by the time I do he may well be a father.

Before Nick leaves for the airport he and Mum have swung by the pub for a farewell drink. As pleased as I am to spend a last few precious moments with my brother, I'm willing him and Mum to be gone within the next twenty minutes. Scott is due to meet me as soon as my shift is over and I'm not sure every date we go on requires a guest appearance from a family member.

Having had some time to absorb yesterday's news, I've almost convinced myself to feel pleased, if not a little excited about becoming an aunt. However, a feeling I can't quite put my finger on is still gnawing away at me, which I'm sure isn't being helped by Mum's constant gloating.

'A father! Your dad would be so proud of you, son. A career and now a family. I just wish I could say the same for both my kids,' she says with a menacing smile, happily reminding me of what a disappointment I am to her.

'Oh, if only I'd let a foreign solider get me pregnant the moment I met him,' I muse, not completely convinced Nick deserves the level of praise she's piling on him.

Nick rolls his eyes, choosing not to say anything, and I get the sense he's more than ready to get back to a life that doesn't involve our constant bickering.

'Don't listen to her. She's just jealous,' says Mum, rubbing Nick's arm affectionately.

Unfortunately, she's not wrong.

I can't seem to shake off the notion that Nick has swooped in and stolen my life. I'm aware that jealousy is a very unattractive trait, and so I force my best false smile and pretend to be happy.

'I can't wait to come out and visit you and Hanna. Maybe I can stay with you and help out when the little one arrives,' says Mum, excitement building in her voice, and as if by magic any jealously or self-pity melts away as I watch Nick's face drop in sheer horror at the idea of Mum moving herself in with him and his family.

'We wouldn't want to put you out. Hanna's family are nearby so...' says Nick and it takes all my will power not to laugh in his face.

'I think that's a great idea,' I chip in, much to Nick's dismay.

'You're gonna need all the help you can get, son. Honestly, it'll be no bother. I'll fly out and stay a week or two, god knows I deserve some proper time off!' says Mum, taking a swig from her Bacardi and Coke.

I gleefully watch Nick angrily chew down on his bottom lip.

Suddenly feeling ever so slightly better about myself, I notice the door to the pub swing open and Scott walk in.

Pleased as I am to see him, I feel a little anxious that my family are still here. I smile at Scott as he approaches and issue a small wave, which causes both Mum and Nick to turn to see who has grabbed my attention.

'Who's that?' asks Nick, looking back at me with a frown, his tone unnecessarily aggressive.

'That's Lydia's boyfriend,' says Mum, just as Scott pulls up beside her at the bar, an awkward look flashing across his face confirming that he most definitely heard her.

'We haven't really put a label on it yet,' I say, trying to sound casual as I feel myself squirm.

'What else do you call the bloke snogging your face off?' says Mum, the snark in her voice palpable.

'You never said you were seeing anybody,' says Nick, looking directly at me, totally ignoring Scott's presence.

'You never said you were impregnating people!' I say to Nick, before finally turning my attention to Scott.

'Hi,' I say.

'Hi,' says Scott, sheepishly looking between me and my relatives like he's a little unprepared for the spontaneous get-together.

'This is my little brother Nick,' I say.

Scott turns to Nick, displaying an easy smile.

'Hi, Lyd told me all about you. I hear congratulations are in order,' says Scott, reaching out his hand to shake Nick's.

Nick stares blankly at Scott. Unsmiling, he keeps his hands firmly to himself whilst sizing Scott up like a cat stalking its prey, waiting for its moment to pounce.

'And you remember my mum,' I say, swiftly moving on.

Mum manages a small, strained smile in Scott's direction, but doesn't offer any further pleasantries.

''Ere you are, girl,' says Jon, coming up behind me and thrusting a sheet of white paper at me.

I don't need to look at it to know it's the shift rota for the week ahead. I look down at the rota in my hand and notice that, as usual, I've been put on for the long shift on Thursday, from lunch until closing.

Before Jon has a chance to move too far away from me, I call out to him.

'Oh Jon, sorry, I forgot to mention, I er, I can't work Thursday nights.'

'Why?' asks Jon, taking me by surprise. I wasn't expecting to have to explain myself.

'I have plans,' I answer.

'Oh right, with this one, is it?' Jon gestures towards Scott, who now along with Mum and Nick is casually listening in to my and Jon's conversation, which I'm guessing is a far better alternative than them having to talk to each other.

'Um, no, actually…' I say.

I have no fear of telling Jon that Thursday is the night I was planning on attending Suicide Club, but I don't particularly want to announce it here behind the bar, and especially not in front of Scott.

'I've joined that *club* … you know, the one we spoke about.'

'A club? What kind of club?' asks Mum, her interference most unwelcome.

'Well, it's more of a group, a class actually. A … yoga class.'

'Since when do you do yoga?' asks Mum, turning her nose up.

'Since next Thursday,' I snap, wishing her to go away.

'Okay. So, is that going to be every Thursday?' asks Jon.

'I'm not sure yet, I've never been before. But if I find it *helps*, I might make it a regular thing.'

'Right …' says Jon slowly with a gentle nod, gradually joining the dots together in his head. 'So what time does *yoga* start?' he asks, and I feel frustrated at his constant questioning.

'I dunno, eight o'clock, I think,' I say, desperate

for the conversation to come to a close.

'Okay, well give it a go, and let me know if you find it *helpful*, then I'll make arrangements for future Thursdays. Norma's been asking for more shifts anyway,' Jon says calmly, before walking off to serve a customer.

I breathe a deep sigh of relief, proud to have made it over a Suicide Club-related obstacle.

'So, Scott, what are your intentions with my sister?' asks Nick, finally willing to acknowledge Scott.

Scott frowns and I notice his back stiffen, the primitive energy building between the two of them nothing short of laughable.

'Don't you have a plane to catch?' I interject, and I feel my heart ache, wishing the annoying little git standing opposite me didn't have to leave tonight.

Doing well to mask my sadness I decide to fetch Scott a drink while Nick takes it upon himself to interrogate him.

CHAPTER 17

Saying goodbye to Nick was harder than I thought it would be. I really have no idea when I'll see him again, and I know that by the time I do, whenever that is, his life will be so different. He will be different. Needless to say, I am grateful to have a distraction in the form of a date with Scott to take my mind off things.

It's a hot and sticky summer evening, the sun only just starting to set in the light dusky sky. Scott has brought us to St Katharine Docks. We're at a small Turkish restaurant and sitting outside at a little iron table. The restaurant overlooks the wide marina where moored boats bob gently on the still, bottle-green water.

Only yards away from us there's a small yacht, named *The Lady Madeleine*. On the deck we can see a grey-haired couple sitting peacefully, enjoying a cup of tea while relaxing aboard their pride and joy. The waterside pavement is busy, with lots of people doing the same as us. Sitting down to eat outside at one of the many packed restaurants.

Our small table is cluttered with our empty used plates and glasses. I feel relaxed, with a full belly and good company, the conversation between me and Scott easy and flirty.

'So, which family members do I get to meet next?' asks Scott, giving me the distinct feeling he's most relieved it's finally just the two of us.

'Ha, I think that's pretty much everyone ... although I do have an uncle and some cousins I haven't seen in a while. Do you want me to check when they're free?' I tease, lifting my glass to take a sip from my drink.

'Only if they're more friendly than your brother,' says Scott. I know he's joking but I sense a little resentment at the way Nick behaved towards him.

'I'm sorry he was cold towards you. He's very protective ... and aggressive and really quite rude, but mainly he's just protective. His heart's in the right place.'

'I'm sure it is,' says Scott, not quite convinced.

'That's the problem with working in a pub, family members can just turn up whilst you're working and stay for hours. If they'd done that at my old job it would have been weird. Like grounds for dismissal weird.'

'What were you doing before you worked at the pub?' Scott asks.

I look up at him and smile realising just how few genuine facts I've disclosed about my old life.

'Nothing exciting. I worked as a receptionist for an advertising company. Actually, the day we met on the train, that was my last day working there.'

'Did they sack you?'

'No. But why does everyone keep asking me that?' I say, making no secret of my offence.

'Sorry. It's just I remember you, that day on the train. I noticed you, before you passed out, and I remember you looked a little upset,' says Scott, putting my mind at ease, and I feel flattered that he noticed me that day, even if I might not have been at my best.

'So, if they didn't sack you, why did you leave?' asks Scott, reaching for the last black olive in the glass dish and popping it in his mouth.

'That day, it was my first day back after ...' I pause, taking my time to navigate my answer.

Scott nods his head.

'The whole thing, going back, I guess it was more overwhelming than I thought it would be. I think after everything that happened I just needed to be somewhere different. I couldn't go back and pretend nothing had changed,' I say, feeling reflective.

'The pub is certainly a change.'

'It certainly is. It doesn't pay that well, but Jon's been great. I'm grateful to him for the gig.'

'Likewise, I'm grateful he gave you a job too,' says Scott, giving me a smile that lights up his eyes, causing me to beam back at him.

'You know, I only go to that pub to see you.'

'Ha, what a line! You so don't, you were already going there before I worked there!' I laugh, at which Scott laughs too.

With my right hand resting on the table, I notice Scott move his hand over to mine and he starts to gently trace invisible lines along my hand with his index and middle fingers.

As we continue to sit and chat, a middle-aged couple walk past our table. They're looking over towards the marina and stop for a moment while the man points to one of the small yachts on the water. They have their backs to us, but are standing in the middle of the narrow walkway, not leaving much room for others to get by. They soon realise they are in the way of the foot traffic, and take a few steps back, the woman walking straight into the back of Scott's chair.

'Oh my goodness, I'm so sorry!' she says with an awfully middle-class accent. She seems a little flustered.

Scott looks behind him and up at the lady, a little bemused.

'That's okay,' he says, forgetting the incident almost immediately.

She's dressed very well in a floral maxi dress, the print fuchsia and blue on a white background, and has long thick wavy red hair that flows past her shoulders.

The man she's with looks a little embarrassed. He is really rather tall, with a mop of thick, long, salt-and-pepper hair swept back. He's wearing a light pink polo shirt and navy-blue tailored shorts. He looks over at the two of us to apologise once again on his partner's behalf, and I see him take a double glance at me.

His gaze stays on me for a second longer than it should and my mouth drops open when I realise who the man is, Steve's old boss Richard. It's been a while since I last saw him and almost four months since I falsely informed him that Steve had died in a car accident.

'Oh goodness, it's Lydia, isn't it? Lydia Green?'

Oh shit!

I pull my hand away from Scott's, as if I've just been caught doing something I shouldn't. My initial instinct is to play dumb. I can't pretend I'm not Lydia Green, but I can pretend I have no idea who he is.

'Yes ... sorry ...?' I squint at Richard, pretending to be terribly confused as to how he knows my name.

'Richard, Richard Williams, Steve's—'

'Oh god yes, oh yes, of course, Richard!' I interrupt before he has a chance to finish his sentence. I enthusiastically rise from my chair and shake his hand as if I'm so unbelievably happy to see him.

As we shake hands, Richard places his free hand on top of our handshake, pausing the movement.

'How are you, Lydia?' he asks quietly in a very sympathetic manner while giving me a look of genuine concern.

'You know, Richard, I'm good! Really, really good. It's a lovely evening, and I'm out at this lovely place, and I'm here with my lovely ...'

Friend? Boyfriend?

'And I'm here with my Scott,' I say, making myself, and all around me, feel uncomfortable.

I look over at Scott and it's safe to say he looks confused as to why I should have given the most animated and overenthusiastic answer to the most sympathetic and simple of questions.

Richard also looks a little dumbfounded by my reaction, but has the good grace not to squirm.

'Er good. This is my wife Lisa, I believe you met at the—'

'Yes, Lisa, of course, nice to see you again!' I interrupt once more, before Richard has a chance to say 'Christmas party at the Gherkin', surely giving away the fact that Steve was never in the army and blowing my whole cover story.

To be honest I don't remember her at all!

There were so many people at that Christmas party, I'm not sure she and I were ever introduced, but I'm willing to play along as if I remember her.

I release myself from Richard's hold and eagerly shake Lisa's hand.

'Yes, well, we'll leave you two to it,' says Richard as Lisa and I let go of each other's hands.

I smile widely at Richard, silently willing him and his wife to leave.

'Okay, well, it was lovely to see you,' I say, getting myself ready to sit back down at the table, but before I get the chance Richard takes hold of my hand once again, sandwiching it inside both of his.

'I really am so very sorry, Lydia, about Steve, and really if there is anything I can do, if there's anything you need, give me a call. You have my number.' His voice is low and his tone so sympathetic that it makes me realise he must know I lied to him.

As Richard's words slowly sink in, my eyes fill with tears, not tears for Steve as such, but for myself.

So many people have said those exact words to me over the past few months, and other than Ruth and Ben, not one person has really meant them, not even Steve's parents, who I barely hear from these days.

I look away from Richard and over into the distance at the pub across the marina that's heavily decorated with vibrant hanging baskets and window boxes. I nod my head, still looking away, and I mouth the word 'Thank you'.

Richard lets go of my hand and returns his attention to his wife.

'Nice to meet you, Scott,' Richard says as he and Lisa turn away.

I watch them walk away and finally sit back down at the table, trying to force the tears that have formed to stay in my eyes.

'Who were they?' questions Scott, glancing behind him to check Richard and Lisa have gone.

'He was just an old associate of my husband's,' I

answer, my voice a little croaky with emotion.

'You okay?'

'Yeah, I'm fine,' I nod. 'Actually, I'm just gonna pop to the loo,' I say, and I rise to my feet once again, keen to take a breather.

Feeling a little fresher, I return from the loo to see Scott paying the bill. I sit myself back down just as the waiter hands Scott his receipt from the card machine.

'Are we leaving?' I ask, a little worried that my odd encounter with Richard has caused Scott to call time on our evening together.

'Yep,' says Scott, pushing back on his chair and climbing to his feet.

I do the same, feeling a little disappointed to be leaving so soon.

'I thought we could try somewhere else for dessert,' says Scott. 'I know a place.' He leads the way along the bustling pavement and I notice him pull his phone from his pocket and tap through it gently; looking between the screen and our surroundings.

We walk towards the pub with the vibrant hanging baskets and window boxes and I feel Scott reach for my hand, gently holding it in his. Our fingers lace together; my hand feeling small but safe inside his. I look up at Scott and smile, but he doesn't look back at me, seemingly more focused on locating our next destination, which remains a complete mystery to me.

We walk past the large pub with hordes of people loitering outside and begin to walk away from the main buzz of the docks. After a few minutes we hit a dead end, at what looks like a block of flats. Scott stops in front of the building and turns to me.

'This is it!' he says with a wide grin spread across his face.

It's not a glamorous block of flats, just a simple concrete block, about ten or so floors high.

'This is dessert?' I question, at which Scott leads us inside, not put off by my obvious lack of enthusiasm.

The lobby is spotlessly clean, if rather bare, the floor tiles beneath our feet are small black-and-white squares like a chess board. There isn't much in the way of furniture, just a large mahogany desk along the wall with two large potted white orchids placed at either end and dare I say, not a single dessert in sight.

Scott walks towards the set of metal lift doors in front of us and pushes the button.

The doors to the lift open and we walk inside. Scott pushes the button for the tenth floor, which I notice is the top floor.

'Where are we going?' I ask as the doors shut and my curiosity gets the better of me.

'All will be revealed,' says Scott, giving nothing away.

The lift stops and the doors slide open into a long sparse corridor with the same white walls and black-and-white floor tiles as the lobby.

'This way!' says Scott as he turns left out of the lift, walking us a little further down the corridor, and then taking us round a sharp corner.

We come to a metal fire-escape door. Scott pushes down on its long green bar along the middle, it opening out onto a black metal-stair fire escape that runs along the outside of the building. Scott continues to lead the way, climbing the stairs of the fire escape. The stairs don't feel overly secure beneath my feet with large gaps of fresh air in between each step. With only a thin black handrail to hold on to, I keep a tight grip, deliberately taking my time, keeping my head down all the while, careful not to miss a step.

I fail to notice when we finally reach the top, bumping into Scott who has stopped right in front of me.

I step back slightly to straighten myself up. As I do so, the purpose of our climb becomes clear. 'Oh my god! What is this?' I exclaim in a voice full of shock and wonder. I have been brought to the roof terrace of the ten-storey building and it's absolutely stunning.

The terrace must be triple the square footage of my entire flat with the whole area covered in greenery that's twinkling with clear coloured fairy lights. The entire surrounding wall of the terrace is draped in berried ivy and another plant that has small white flowers with a purple centre. I take a quick glance at the back wall and it's lined with tall bamboo all the way along. In the left corner is an L-shaped black rattan sofa with clean white cushions, a glass-topped coffee table positioned in front of it.

In the middle of the terrace is a long black iron table with iron chairs surrounding it. On the table sits a silver champagne bucket, the gold neck of the bottle on display, and next to it there are two empty champagne flutes and a silver plate of strawberries. I think the nicest touch are the tea lights lined up along the middle of the table. Their light flickering gently under the evening sky.

'What is this place?'

'Essentially it's someone's back garden,' says Scott walking further into the terrace and looking out at the view, which without a doubt has to be the terrace's most breath-taking feature. From where we are facing we have a direct and clear view of Tower Bridge all lit up, the dark blanket of river running beneath it. Over to the right in the distance I can see the Tower of London, and also the Shard further on. I look down below and I can see the marina where we were just eating with its sailing boats bobbing on the water and the people bustling around.

'Are we allowed to be up here?' I ask, concerned that our being up here is technically trespassing.

'Don't worry, my mate Gaz manages this

building and he owes me a favour or two. The owner's working away in the States at the moment. He says it's fine, as long as we don't break anything,' Scott says confidently, drawing his gaze away from the view.

I look at Scott curiously. He seems very at ease in our surroundings and I wonder how many others he may have frequented this most glamorous 'back garden' with.

'Have you been here before?' I ask, running my hand along the foliage-covered wall.

'Only with Gaz. It wasn't very romantic. He fell asleep and got sunstroke ... I'm hoping you'll be better company.'

'I'll certainly try my best,' I say with a small chuckle.

Scott makes his way over towards the table harbouring the champagne. Lifting the bottle from the silver bucket he pulls out the cork with a pop and I watch as he fills the two glasses.

He walks back over to me, a glass in each hand, handing me one before pulling his phone from his jeans pocket.

'Now, if I remember rightly ... I should be able to connect my phone to the speakers.'

After a few seconds the sound of Coldplay's 'A Sky Full of Stars' rises from the speakers hidden somewhere in the foliage. With the speaker system in full working order, Scott slips his phone back into his pocket.

'Cheers,' he says.

'Cheers,' I repeat as we clink our glasses together.

We each take a sip and put down our glasses and it's then Scott takes my hand in his and twirls me around so I'm facing him and before I know it, we're dancing along to the music. Scott lifts my hand so my arm is waving in the air and feeling just a little bit silly I start to giggle. I notice Scott's smile, an easy lovely smile of pure happiness, joy even, and I realise just how long it's been since I let myself be silly and happy with another person.

We dance for a few moments like two giggling idiots on our own private dance floor. Scott twirls me around one last time before pulling me into him. He wraps a strong arm around my torso, my back resting comfortably against his chest. He rests his chin on my left shoulder. I can feel the stubble from his face brushing my skin and I can feel him breathing gently against my neck as we lean into each other's bodies, the feeling causing me to develop goose bumps down my left arm.

'What do you think?' he asks as we look out at the view.

'It's amazing,' I gush in pure wonder at such a spectacular scene.

'Glad you approve.'

We stand for a moment in a comfortable silence, each taking in the view before us, this being the first time I've experienced the

London skyline in such peaceful and beautiful surroundings.

With Scott's face against mine, I turn my head and look into his hazel eyes and I can feel my heart flooding with a fluffy warm feeling of sheer happiness and I know it's impossible for me to resist him for a moment longer. I move in ever closer, my lips finding his, and we kiss under the London sky feeling like the only two people in the entire world.

CHAPTER 18

Our time on the roof terrace was simply glorious, with the last few hours spent doing nothing other than drinking, dancing, chatting and kissing. It's now just past midnight and Scott and I find ourselves in the back of a taxi that's just pulled up outside my flat.

I haven't been so bold as to ask Scott if he would like to come home with me, but it seems no such discussion is needed, as he makes the correct assumption and climbs out of the car with me. Walking a step ahead I open the street door and eagerly lead the way up the stairs to my front door. As I fidget with my keys trying to find the right one I feel Scott place his hands either side of my waist. I happily let my body relax in his hold as he places his lips down upon my neck. Planting a small trail of kisses up along my neck until he reaches my ear.

'Your mum's not in there, is she?' he whispers, understandably scared after our previous encounter at my front door.

I laugh loudly at his question.

'God, I hope not!' I say.

I open the front door and step inside and take a quick scan around, happy to confirm we are indeed alone.

'The coast's clear,' I say as Scott gently closes the front door behind him and I slip off my sandals and toss my keys and bag down on the floor.

Scott looks so incredibly sexy, and I can't hide the wide smile on my face. Unable to resist him, I'm the first to lean in and kiss him on the mouth, letting my fingers brush through his short fair hair. I gradually allow my hands to wander south, down Scott's body, until I'm finally able to slip my hands underneath the front of his T-shirt, caressing his skin as I move them upwards, my fingers brushing through the hair on his stomach and chest and pushing up his T-shirt until his whole torso is on display.

I like that he has hair on his chest. It's short and fair like the hair on his head and I can see for the first time just how muscular he is, and I thoroughly enjoy running my hands all over him.

Scott reaches for his T-shirt and pulls it off over his head, then carelessly tosses it onto the floor. Standing in front of me topless, he leans in to kiss me once more and I'm distracted by his wandering hands. With my body backed up against the door, Scott slips a hand up my skirt, and into my knickers. I rest my head back on the door and look up at the ceiling while Scott buries his face in my neck, kissing my skin while fondling inside my knickers, letting his rough fingers tenderly caress me.

'Oh god!' I whisper.

'You're so wet,' Scott whispers. He gives me a quick kiss on the lips, then pulls his hand away and lowers himself to his knees in front of me, leaving me breathless. He slips his hands into the waist of my knickers and slowly pulls them down to my ankles before rolling up my skirt.

He leans into me and gently kisses the inside of my thigh, with his hand gently following behind, the anticipation of what's about to happen filling me with wild excitement. Once Scott's lips have traced up to the very top of my thigh, his mouth begins to explore the most intimate part of me. I lean against the door as my knees start to weaken, leaving me unsure as to how long I'll be able to stand here for. My breathing is heavy as I lean back and enjoy the warm sensation of Scott's mouth on me.

Scott suddenly pulls his mouth away, and trails small kisses up and along my body. Lifting my skirt up further, he trails kisses up towards my stomach and gradually up past my belly button with the gentle touch of his rough hands following each kiss, until his face is just below my bra.

Unable to take the anticipation any longer, I pull my dress off over my head and toss it to the floor to join his T-shirt.

Scott lifts himself up from the floor and kisses me on the mouth. I decide it's my turn to start exploring him. I move my hands down towards the front of his jeans and trail a line along the top of his jeans and along his stomach with my finger, feeling the elastic waistband at the top of his boxers, and I move my hand towards the button on his jeans. As I do so, Scott places a hand in his jeans pocket and pulls out his black leather wallet.

He opens it up as I undo his jeans and unzip his fly and pulls out a condom in a red foil wrapper. I run my hands back up Scott's torso, and then make a grab for the foil packet as Scott drops his wallet to the floor. It's been a long time since I had sex using a condom and to be honest I've never been much of a fan of them, but the fact that he's prepared and the one to initiate protected sex is rather gentlemanly and a further turn-on. The wrapper in my hand, our eyes fixed on each other, I push Scott's jeans down past his hips, with his black boxers being carried down with them in one clean sweep, exposing his erection while his jeans and boxers rest above his knees.

My focus is firmly fixed on Scott's rock-hard cock in front of me, while he stands still and confident in his display of manhood. The wrapped condom is still in my hand, but before I open it, I decide to reach down and take hold of Scott's cock, letting my hand glide from the base to the tip. Scott groans with pleasure, and makes a grab for my arse, pulling me closer to him. I toy with the idea of giving him a blow job, but I'm so desperate to have him inside me that I choose not to, and release my hand to open up the foil wrapper. As I do so, Scott loosens his grip from my arse and pushes his jeans all the way down, shrugging off his shoes with his feet, quickly stepping out of his jeans and boxers and pulling off his socks.

I take out the condom and Scott watches my hands as I slowly roll it all the way down his erection. He pulls me to him once again and lowers both my bra straps, and I reach my hand around my back and unhook my bra myself, but we are standing too close for my bra to fall to the ground. Scott pulls my face towards his, and we kiss as I stroke my hands through his chest hair. We gravitate over to my messy unmade bed, still tangled together, and fall onto it, lying horizontally across it, seemingly too overcome with desire to care that we're lying the wrong way.

Scott places a leg between mine, spreading my legs apart, and while we're still kissing he enters me. It's been months since I last had sex, and my body knows it, my insides feeling a little tight, sore even. Scott slips himself inside me, finding his rhythm and teasing me. I pull his face onto mine, and I kiss him hard on the lips and once our short kiss comes to an end, Scott picks up the pace.

Any feelings of tightness quickly disappear, the sensation of him inside me feeling amazing. Scott's hands continue to explore my body as our hot sweaty bodies rock against each other in my stuffy flat. I gently kiss Scott's neck. He tastes a little salty, and even the raw smell of him is turning me on. I gradually feel myself building, and I soon choose not to hold on any longer. I allow myself to climax, letting out all the built-up stresses and frustrations from the past few months.

Moans of pleasure follow while I enjoy the sensation taking over my body. Scott then takes the cue from me and, knowing that I'm spent, picks up his pace. I feel his body tense, before crumbling completely on top of mine. I stroke the back of his head, gently letting my fingers brush through his hair, while my other hand gently strokes his back with the tips of my fingers. We lie still for a short while, both breathing heavily as our bodies wind down.

Scott slowly raises his body up and he looks into my eyes while gently brushing my hair away from my face.

'You okay?' he whispers in a hoarse voice.

I nod my head, looking into his hazel eyes, smiling up at him with genuine happiness skipping around inside me.

'Yeah,' I whisper back.

He lowers his face and kisses me on the lips,

then raises himself up further and gently pulls himself out of me.

He gets up from the bed but I stay lying on my back, completely exhausted, and watch him walk naked towards my small kitchen area. I watch from the bed as he peels off the condom and throws it away before picking up an empty glass from my draining board and filling it with water from the sink. He stands and drinks the glass of water all in one go. I lift myself up and move up the bed, sitting up with my back leaning against my headboard. Scott refills the glass, walks slowly back to the bed and hands the glass of water to me.

I notice the duvet is nowhere to be seen. It must've fallen onto the floor, but it's so hot and stuffy in here so I can't say I need it.

'How you feeling?' Scott asks me, still sounding a little out of breath while displaying a very knowing smile on his face.

I take a much needed gulp of water before answering.

'Extremely satisfied,' I say with a smug smile.

'Ha, pleased to hear it!' says Scott, and he leans into me and plants a small kiss on my forehead.

I take another large gulp of water before leaning over the side of the bed to place the glass down on my bedside table. I pull myself down the bed so I'm lying on my side, at which point Scott follows my actions and lies down beside me, pulling me into his embrace for a naked spoon cuddle. I feel his body relax around mine and him breathing softly onto my neck.

As we lie on the bed with our naked bodies folded into each other, Scott tucks his arm under mine, and as I glance down at his strong arm wrapped around my body, I catch sight of my hand that is still wearing my wedding and engagement rings. I look down at my rings in complete shock, as if I'd completely forgotten they were there. I stare down at my hand as guilt surges through me. I've just had sex with a man who wasn't my husband, while wearing my rings. I feel ashamed, as if I've just been unfaithful somehow. I play back the past half-hour in my head and I don't recall Steve entering my head at any time, not once, and I was wearing the symbolic commitment to him. I slowly spin my rings with my thumb while a painful feeling of sadness builds up causing my eyes to fill with tears. They start to run down my face and onto my pillow. I bite down hard on my lip to stop the crying as it dawns on me for the first time that never again will I have a moment like this with my husband. That thought is the most painful of them all. As I cry silently to myself, I'm startled by the motion of Scott jerking his leg downwards kicking the air beneath him. I quickly lift my hand to wipe my eyes and turn my head to look at Scott. He's asleep, completely out of it. He looks really peaceful and I watch him for a moment as he breathes in and out gently, then moves unconsciously onto his back, freeing me from our hug, and it's only then that another troublesome thought enters my head.

What if I have a nightmare?

The kind that causes me to wake up screaming and kicking, or worse?

Should I wake him? Ask him to leave?

I can't.

That in itself would raise all kinds of questions that I'm not willing to touch on.

I pull myself off the bed and walk towards my bathroom and spot the duvet in a heap on the floor and decide to pick it up and place it over Scott, covering his modesty, folding it just up to his hips. I stand and watch him for a moment. He looks gorgeous asleep, and I stand and think back to the night that we've just shared together. I feel disappointed with myself that such a great night has been tarred by feelings of guilt and sadness and I wonder if it's possible to be falling in love with someone new, while still grieving for my husband. I wonder if everything that's happened to me was already written. What if Steve dying was the universe's way of bringing *this* person into my life?

Was it was meant to be Scott all along?

I shake my head, the never-ending cycle of thoughts feeling really quite torturous.

I shrug my shoulders and patter my way into the bathroom.

I've been lying awake in the darkness of my flat for the last three hours, too scared to fall asleep for fear of experiencing an unpleasant dream. I feel tired but more than anything else, I feel bored. With Scott still sound asleep beside me, I decide to climb out of the bed and slowly drag myself into the bathroom to use the toilet, simply for a change of scenery. I walk into the dark bathroom completely naked and sit myself down on the toilet. As I take my seat facing my shower cubicle, I freeze in horror at the sight of Steve inside, slumped naked against the glass screen.

His face is exactly how it was the last time I saw him. His blue eyes rolled back in his head and his mouth dropped open. I watch as his slender body slowly slides down the glass screen and falls to a heap on the shower floor, the sight causing me to scream out in terror. I try to pull myself up from the toilet to run out of the bathroom, but I can't move due to a great pressure pushing down on my wrists restraining me, preventing me from fleeing.

'Lyd! Lyd!' I hear a familiar man's voice call out, causing me to open my eyes.

Scott's lying next to me, his eyes wide and his face displaying a look of grave concern. My eyes dart around the room as I try to confirm my surroundings. I'm in my flat and Scott is still here. We're lying on our sides facing each other in the bed with Scott gripping tightly on to both my wrists as if trying to restrain me.

'It's okay, it's okay,' Scott says calmly and softly, slowly letting go of my wrists and rolling me gently onto my other side so I'm facing away from him.

My heart is racing and I feel sick at the sudden realisation that my worst fears for tonight have come true. That I couldn't get through one single night without Steve haunting my subconscious.

Scott tucks his naked body in behind mine, keeping an arm wrapped around me. I feel his other hand in my hair, brushing through it gently to expose my neck, and I feel him plant a small kiss on it.

'I'm sorry,' I say, my voice shaky as I try to suppress my humiliation and fear.

'It's okay. It's okay,' Scott whispers reassuringly, folding my body firmly into his.

Scott nestles his face into the nape of my neck and I can feel him breathing gently against me, the feeling of him so close calming me down. I feel tired and vulnerable, but safe as I close my eyes, allowing myself to rest in his arms.

CHAPTER 19

My eyes open, the morning sunlight having already burst in through the flat's window. I turn my head resting on my pillow and I'm met with the view of Scott's broad back as he sleeps soundly on his side. I turn my head to the high ceiling, trying to recall the various scenarios of last night.

I remember the restaurant. I remember the roof terrace. I remember the fun we had in this bed and I also seem to recall a particularly disturbing dream. I remember the dream vividly, as I always do, but the piece of the puzzle I'm struggling with is the part where Scott came in holding on to my wrists, and I wonder for a moment whether that was part of the dream. Knowing that life couldn't possibly be that kind to me, I'm all too aware that Scott was never part of my dream, but a witness to it. Now likely to have a whole host of questions and concerns as to what goes through my head while I sleep and why.

I hear Scott begin to stir a little, letting out a small groan in his sleepy state. I roll back onto my own side to face Scott's back once again and place my hand on his shoulder, letting my hand stroke from the top of his shoulder over to the other, then letting it wander towards the middle of his back. I stroke my hand all the way down, widening my fingers and enjoying the soft feel of his skin. Scott starts to stir a little more, my touch waking him, and so I bring myself in closer and softly kiss the area between his broad shoulder blades. My kissing finally wakes him completely and he turns onto his back still with his eyes closed but with a naughty smile spread across his face.

'Morning, beautiful,' says Scott almost in a whisper, his voice a little hoarse. His eyes slowly open and fix on mine. He wraps an arm around me, pulling me closely into him, his fingertips gently caressing my back.

'Morning,' I say and Scott gives me a short kiss on the lips.

'You okay?' asks Scott.

'Yeah, you?'

'Yeah,' replies Scott before placing another kiss on the crown of my head. 'You had a bad dream last night,' he adds.

I feel my heart begin to race and my stomach sink. I should've known there was no way of avoiding this discussion. I try to remain calm as I think of the best way to explain what happened. I wonder if now, as we lie lovingly in each other's arms, this might be the moment to be honest about all that's really happened to me over the past few months.

'Sorry if I scared you,' I say in a small voice, as I try to build myself up to approaching the uneasy subject.

'What were you dreaming about?' Scott asks, sounding a little concerned.

I shrug my shoulders.

I want to be honest with Scott. I don't have to give the full story, but I can tell him what I dreamed about, surely, while still keeping the details to myself.

'I can't remember,' I say, trying to keep my tone light, and I look up to the ceiling in frustration as I brush my fingers through his chest hair.

'Really?' says Scott, unconvinced by my answer.

'What? You've never woken up with no idea what you dreamt about the night before?' I say. The words so easily flowing from my mouth, as if to lie is my default setting, as if I'm unable to speak the truth, no matter how badly I want to.

'Of course, but I've never woken up like that.'

I shrug once again, wanting to know exactly what kind of state Scott saw me in, but feeling too scared to ask.

Did I hit him? Did I cry out or scream?

'I ... I'm starving,' I say, trying somehow to navigate the conversation into an entirely different direction. 'Would you like some breakfast?' I offer.

'Yeah, we could have some breakfast

afterwards,' suggests Scott as he leans into me and kisses my neck and his hands begin to wander across my body.

Happy as I am to use sex as a distraction, to say I feel frustrated with myself is an understatement.

I wonder if there's maybe something psychologically wrong with me, lying being so much easier for me than telling the truth. I feel disappointed with myself. I worry Scott will never know the real me, not the whole me, for I'm unable to be honest about the one life event that defines me more than any other.

CHAPTER 20

Today is a beautiful summer's day. There's not a cloud to be seen in the bright blue sky, the sun burning so high and bright it's simply impossible to imagine doing anything other than heading to the park, lying back and soaking up some rays. That being exactly the mood I found myself in until Ruth and Gavin thought it a good idea to hire out a giant swan-shaped pedalo on the park's small lake.

As our swan elegantly glides along the dark waters, I offer little in the way of help with the boat. Instead I choose to sit at the back and work my way through a rocket-shaped ice lolly whilst filling everyone in on last night's date with Scott.

'So, am I right to assume you slept with him?' asks Ruth, a maternal concern in her voice.

'Why would you automatically assume that I slept with him?' I say, attempting to defend my reputation.

'Oh, please! You possess all the signs of a woman who's just been on the receiving end of a good rogering!' says Gavin; self-appointed captain in charge of steering.

I laugh at Gavin's comment, wondering what might give away such a fact, unable to deny the seemingly obvious.

'So, how was it?' asks Gavin, keen to get right down to all the smutty details.

'It was good ...great in fact,' I say, my downcast tone not quite matching my words.

I notice Ruth and Gavin look at each other, Ruth frowning and Gavin narrowing his eyes, both sensing something is a little out of alignment.

'What's wrong?' asks Ruth, looking back at me from her co-captain's seat.

'Nothing, really. He's lovely, the sex was great ... it was just afterwards. I felt really guilty, as if I'd been unfaithful, and then I had this really horrible dream and ... I dunno ...' I trail off, unable to accurately summarise everything I'm feeling.

'Maybe it was too soon,' suggests Ruth. I sense she's starting to feel a little guilty for persuading me to date Scott in the first place.

'Too late to worry about that. He's been inside her, there's no going back now,' muses Gavin, his vulgar description making me grimace.

'You know she still hasn't told him about Steve,' Ruth informs him.

'Oh, for goodness' sake!' gasps Gavin, with a frustrated eye roll. 'He still thinks Steve died on some secret war mission? Why hasn't she told him?'

'I think she's still having trouble processing everything that's happened.'

'I am here!' I interject.

'You need to tell him. He's not just some customer you flirt with, you're involved with one another. Trust me, the longer you leave it, the harder it will be,' says Gavin in the utmost seriousness, taking his eyes off 'the road' to issue me his most sober face.

'He knows Steve died, are the details really that important?' I say defensively.

'We all know you're smarter than that,' says Gavin, holding eye contact.

'Gav, the bank, the bank, we're getting too close!' barks Ruth in a panic, causing Gavin to concentrate on the job in hand and steer the boat back towards the centre of the lake.

'What's happening with the support group thing?' Ruth asks curiously.

'I contacted them,' I say, my voice small.

'And do you plan on attending?' Ruth follows up.

'I do. They run it on a Thursday evening. I've already asked for the time off to go.'

Ruth nods with approval.

'Do you want me to come with you?' she asks.

One half of me would love the moral support, but the other half of me knows that if Ruth comes with me I will definitely have to go and I'm still a little uncertain if the whole Suicide Club thing is something I really want to commit to.

'No, I'll be okay. But thank you,' I say, sincerely grateful for the gesture.

'You should go. Meet other grief-strickens. Shed a tear over the custard creams. It'll be great,' adds Gavin, turning round to issue me a wink, making me smile. I love how he's able to add an element of fun to even the darkest of subjects.

'Gav! The bank, the bank!' yells Ruth, her outburst followed by a crashing sound and a jolt so forceful I lose hold of my ice lolly and drop it straight into the water.

'Mayday! Mayday!' shouts Gavin, comically throwing his arm into the air, calling out to no one in particular, our shipwrecked swan smashed into the grassy verge causing all three of us to laugh hysterically.

CHAPTER 21

It's Thursday evening. I've had a shower, applied my make-up, dressed myself, and I have officially decided that I do not need to join Suicide Club!

I have even gone so far as to compile a list on the back of my credit card bill.

1. I don't feel the need to discuss my private business with a group of strangers.
2. I don't want to make new friends.
3. I should only join clubs that will bring an element of fun to my life.
4. It is doubtful this will be fun.
5. I will not be gaining any worthwhile skills.
6. I don't have any money for subscription fees.

Alone in my flat, I've been pacing the floor for the past half an hour with my list of very viable reasons held tightly in my hand. I walk towards the large window at the back of the flat and stand and stare out. I wonder if I should call Ruth and ask her to come with me.

I could?

But in truth I don't really want to. I feel like

I've used Ruth as an emotional crutch one too many times these past few months, and maybe dragging her along to this is too much.

I'm startled out of my pondering at the window by the sound of my mobile ringing and I follow the sound towards the kitchen counter.

I see it's Jon calling.

I pick up the phone and swipe the screen to answer.

'Hello.'

'You in there, girl?' bellows Jon.

'Eh? Jon? I'm at home. Where are you?'

'I've been standing outside your flat for the past five minutes pressing this buzzer to no avail.' The annoyance in his voice makes me chuckle.

'That buzzer doesn't work. Stay there, I'm coming down!'

I hang up the phone, and make my way downstairs, baffled as to why Jon has turned up at my home.

I open the street door to a slightly disgruntled-looking Jon. 'You wana get that looked at!' he says, pointing at my broken buzzer, which I'm struggling to take an interest in, rather more concerned as to why Jon is here on my doorstep on my night off.

'What you doing here?' I ask bluntly.

'I'm here for yoga!' laughs Jon, holding out his arms as if addressing a crowd.

I stare at Jon blankly, unable to come back with

any kind of witty response as my heart sinks, knowing that he has come all this way to escort me to something I've already decided I'm not going to.

'Eight o'clock, you said? It's 6.50 now. I'm guessing it can't be that far away. Shall I wait here while you grab your things?'

I shake my head.

'Jon, I'm so sorry, but you've had a wasted journey. I'm not going, it's decided. I don't want to do it!'

Jon gives me a tight understanding smile.

'Listen, girl, I was exactly the same as you are right now, but, trust me, once you give yoga a try, you'll never look back!'

It's impossible not to be touched by the kindness shown by Jon in coming all the way down here, but I still can't bring myself to budge on my decision.

'But what about the pub? You can't just walk out and leave it to run itself!' I tell Jon, trying to panic him into running back to work.

'The pub will be fine, my dear. Norma's got it covered.'

I look up at the overcast sky, hoping for some kind of divine intervention that will prevent me from having to follow Jon to this group.

'So what, you've done this before then? You did this group thing when your wife and daughter died?' I blurt out in the hope that plain old rudeness might just make him go away.

'Not when my daughter passed so much, no. But let's just say, my wife and your husband weren't so different.'

I look at Jon in complete shock, my eyes wide open.

'Your wife? Really?' I say quietly.

Jon doesn't respond and instead reaches for his shirt pocket and pulls out a green lighter and his box of Benson & Hedges, opening it and taking out a cigarette. He quickly lights up as I stand silently and watch him. Jon takes a hard pull on his cigarette, and I wonder if this particular cigarette is his form of some much-needed stress relief, if he's preparing himself for the experience of opening up some old wounds.

'Come on, girl, I've not got all day. Go get your things, I'll wait here.' Jon points towards the stairs behind me, indicating I should go and get ready, then turns away from the street door to blow the smoke out of his mouth.

I'm still in shock, having had no idea that Jon's wife ended her own life. I stand and look at Jon for a second too long, causing him to turn his head, and seeing that I still haven't moved he points at the stairs once again.

'Lydia, go, come on, we don't want to be late!'

Jon's snapping quickly brings me back round, and I do as I'm told and make my way back upstairs to get my things.

After an awkward bus journey jammed full of

stifling small talk and a slow walk, we finally arrive at the British Legion on Somerset Street with ten minutes to spare.

The Legion sits at the corner of a quiet side street, just off the busy main road. It's exactly how I had imagined it, a little shabby and run-down. Above the doors the words *Royal British Legion* read proudly on the dirty white cladding.

Jon walks slightly ahead of me, nearing the building ready to make a confident entrance, but I find myself pulling back. My walking pace slowing right down, before coming to a complete stop.

I watch Jon as he opens one of the heavy wooden doors, and I wonder: If I turn round now and start running, what are the chances of him catching me? But it seems I don't put my plan into action soon enough. Before I have a chance to run, Jon is looking over his shoulder to check I'm still with him.

'Lydia! What you doing, girl? Get over here!' he yells as I stand a good ten feet away from him. Jon's waving his arm through the air to beckon me over, but it's no good. I'm glued to the spot, unable to move due to the nervous fear that's taken over my entire body.

'Lydia! Come on!' Jon calls out, becoming impatient.

'I can't, Jon. Please, can we just go home?' I call back, a little worried I might just burst into tears right here in the street.

Jon lets go of the door, letting it swing itself to a close, and slowly walks over to me.

'Look, girl, if you really don't want to go in, then we won't,' he says softly.

I breathe a sigh of relief at my small victory, and instantly feel all fear and anxiety leave my body.

Jon reaches into his shirt pocket for his box of cigarettes.

'You think you're bad? You should've seen me!' Jon chuckles to himself as he pulls a fag from the box. 'There was no way on God's green earth I would've given something like this a go. But things were bad, girl, I mean you know the routine all too well, I'm sure. I weren't sleeping, weren't eating, weren't talking to nobody about nothing.' Jon pauses to light his cigarette and takes a long pull from it.

'I think it all came to a head when I threatened to knock out some punter after I gave him the wrong change!' says Jon, laughing a little as he reflects on the troubling memory. 'That's when Norma stepped in. Brought me to a place much like this, some run-down working men's club. Fed me some tale about them closing down and wanting to sell me some cheap booze.'

Jon rolls his eyes in disbelief that he could've fallen into the trap so easily. 'But I'm grateful that she did. I know it's scary, girl, the idea of saying all that's in your head out loud, but it's gotta be done, or it'll for ever eat away at you.' Jon takes another long pull on his cigarette, then throws the hardly smoked fag to the pavement.

Any relief I felt a moment ago has quickly evaporated, as fear welcomes itself back into my body. It sinks in that Jon really is going to make me go through with this, and I feel sick with nerves.

Jon steps behind me and places his hand on the top of my back, slowly guiding me along the pavement until we reach the wooden doors. I'm biting on my thumbnail as I'm led inside the building.

Much like the outside, the inside is a little shabby and run-down with scuff marks on the lemon walls. Immediately to our left is a door labelled *Toilets* and straight ahead is another set of doors with a large glass window offering a view into a bar area. I can see the lights of a fruit machine flashing and a few heads bobbing and I'm filled with hope as I wonder if we've come to the wrong place.

Jon looks just as dumbfounded as I am, and just as I begin to get excited at the prospect of turning round and going home a smiley lady walks through the dark wooden door on our right. Unlike the door straight ahead, there's no window; perhaps that's why Jon and I paid no attention to it on entering the building.

'Hello, are you Lydia?' asks the lady in a very friendly manner.

'Er, yes, hi,' I say in a nervous splutter.

'Nice to meet you, Lydia, I'm so pleased you made it. I'm Lacey, I facilitate the group here.' She reaches out her hand for me to shake.

Lacey is younger than I imagined, around my age, possibly in her early thirties or so. She's taller than me with wavy dark blonde hair that rests delicately on her shoulders and pretty green eyes. She's a little bohemian-looking, wearing cotton trousers decorated with a black-and-white zigzag pattern, black flip-flops and a tight plain black T-shirt, showing off her ample bosom.

'I see you've brought a friend with you,' says Lacey addressing Jon.

'Hello, Jonathan Briggs, nice to meet you, dear,' says Jon, giving Lacey a firm handshake.

'Hello, Jonathan ... Well come on through, both of you,' Lacey says.

She says *come on through* with the kind of positive energy I would use when welcoming someone into my house for a barbecue. I guess this is her trying to make us feel at ease, but I think it's all a little odd.

Lacey walks ahead and she holds open the door for us. Jon walks through first and I nervously follow. Lacey lets the door swing shut behind her and stands beside me.

'I know this is all a bit daunting, but there really is no need to be nervous. You're going to be fine, everybody is really friendly,' says Lacey reassuringly, and I smile nervously at her.

We're standing in the entrance of a long wide hall, the kind of hall that can be found in any number of working men's clubs around the country. The first thing I notice is the people, not as many as I had imagined, only five. A number I feel comfortable with.

Everybody is gathered around a brown fold-away table littered with tea- and coffee-making paraphernalia, as well as a plate of biscuits. Everyone is standing around rather casually chatting as if they were at some kind of WI meeting, the gentle hum of light conversation filling the room.

There's a small unmanned bar at the end of the room, and the centre of the floor is a light wooden laminate, the area likely doubling up as a dance floor on happier, more uplifting occasions. In the middle of the dance floor red chairs are arranged in a large circle, the sight of which makes me feel nauseous once again.

'Make yourselves a tea or a coffee if you like and then we'll get started,' Lacey tells me and Jon.

Jon nods and quickly makes his way over towards the fold-away table, leaving me behind.

'Do you not have anything stronger?' I ask.

'Ha ha, I'm afraid not,' laughs Lacey, who clearly thinks I'm joking, but I was in fact quite serious.

'You two are the first newcomers we've had for a while,' says Lacey, interrupting my thoughts of panic and anguish, and I flash a tight awkward smile.

'We

usually start with tea and coffee. I find it's a good way to get everybody to relax a little, then we have a sit-down, and just chat. There's no agenda, it's all very free-flowing, just whatever you want to discuss,' explains Lacey.

I nod and smile once more, unable to think of any kind of response.

'Really, don't worry, you're going to be fine,' says Lacey, reassuring me once again, this time wrapping her arm around me and giving my upper arm a soft brush with her hand. I notice a wedding band and a sizeable diamond engagement ring on her finger. I bet she has a happy marriage with some caring hipster type, holidaying by the coast in their VW minivan with their scruffy dog and perfect kids.

Jon walks back towards us, looking quite proud of himself, holding two white polystyrene cups of hot coffee whilst balancing two digestives between his fingers.

''Ere you go, girl, get that down ya,' says Jon, handing me one of the cups and a biscuit.

'Cheers,' I mumble.

'Okay, everyone, shall we take a seat!' Lacey calls out, causing the group over by the table to look round and slowly meander their way over to the circle of chairs on the dance floor.

Jon and I are standing the closest, and I hesitate, realising there's no 'back row' for me to hide in, and so I follow Jon, who plonks himself down on the first chair he reaches. I sit myself down next to him, clinging on to my coffee and biscuit while nervously watching the rest of the group making themselves comfortable. Next to me sits one of the men. He has spiky salt-and-pepper hair and is dressed casually in jogging bottoms and a casual T-shirt. He looks relaxed and at ease, the complete opposite to me.

'So, we have two new faces joining us tonight, so shall we go round and just quickly introduce ourselves? Just your name and any other information you'd like to share?' Lacey asks the group who give her their approval with gentle nods and smiles. 'I'll start. Hi, my name is Lacey, and I facilitate this group, offering support to those who have lost loved ones as a result of suicide.' Lacey's tone drops slightly from upbeat to soft and more understanding, as if she's offering her condolences to a room full of people all at once. Lacey turns her head to the left, gesturing for the next person to say their hello.

'My name is Pauline,' says a middle-aged black lady with an African accent. She has long braids that go past her shoulders and thick square glasses. 'I've been attending this group for, ooh, about six months or so, since the loss of my son.'

Next to Pauline is a young lanky boy with floppy black hair and bad skin.

'Hi, I'm Gareth. I live nearby in Stratford and I'm a student studying English Literature.' Gareth's voice doesn't match his appearance. I was fully expecting someone awkward and uncomfortable, but I'm in fact left feeling surprised by his eloquence and confidence.

Next is the guy sitting beside me.

'Hi, Martin. I also live not too far away in Manor Park, and I work for a security company in town. I lost my father to suicide about ten years ago, but I only started coming to this group a few months back.'

Now it's my turn, and all eyes are on me. My mouth is dry from worrying about how much information I'm expected to give. I decide to quickly moisten my mouth, taking a large gulp from my coffee. Almost instantly I feel the hot coffee burn my tongue and the inside of my mouth. Trying to resist the urge to spit my coffee back into the cup, I swallow it down, causing further burns to the back of my throat.

'Lydia!' I blurt out with a cough, fighting through the scorching pain in my mouth. Everyone looks on, waiting to see if I would like to add anything more, but after my introduction is followed by complete silence, Jon does the kindest thing he could possibly do, and steps in.

'Jon Briggs,' he says, looking up from his cup of black coffee, his spontaneous introduction occurring mid-sip. He then takes a bite from his biscuit, signalling he's also unwilling to share any more at this time.

Next to Jon sits a white lady, rather tall and thin with long thick brown hair. She's dressed smartly, her black heels and Mulberry handbag making me wonder if she's come straight here from her City job.

'Hi, I'm Kim, I'm thirty-five and I've been coming to this group off and on for the past year and a half.'

I'm left a little baffled as to why Kim felt the need to reveal her age. I wonder if she realises this is Suicide Club, or does she think she is at a singles event?

Lastly is an older lady.

'Hello, I'm Maura, I've travelled here today from the people's republic of Ilford and I'm a retired teacher.'

I like Maura straight away, her confidence and humour making me feel at ease. She's wearing a mismatched outfit – a baggy orange T-shirt, light blue cotton trousers and dirty, no longer white trainers. She's certainly not going in for a best-dressed award, but I find the unapologetic nature that oozes from her refreshing.

'Lovely, so, as I say, there's no agenda for tonight, so who would like to kick things off?' says Lacey, her eyes surveying the group.

It's then I notice from the corner of my eye Jon raising his hand slightly. Jon still has a small bite of biscuit in his hand, which he quickly shoves into his mouth. 'I'm happy to go first,' Jon says to the group with his mouth full, taking me by complete surprise that he would be so brave.

'Yes, okay, go for it, Jon,' says Lacey, looking

really chuffed that one of her newest members should be so keen.

'Ah ... well ... yes, okay ...' I notice a slight stutter in Jon's voice, making me second guess just how confident he really is.

He places his polystyrene cup on the floor by his feet, then sits up, resting his hands on his thighs, transforming himself into the showman I've become used to seeing at the pub.

'It's been a while I must say since I've attended one of these things. I'm really here today to support me ol' china Lydia 'ere ...' Jon slaps me on the side of the arm with the back of his hand, just to make all aware of who Lydia is. '... who has her own story to tell, but I'm happy to go first and show her how it's done. So let's see ... I met my wife Val at a house party thrown by my mate Andrew Fletcher, whose brother at the time happened to be seeing her mate Norma. We all got chattin' and fast forward, a couple of years later me and Val got married, and after we married it became apparent that we didn't have two pennies to rub together. I'd worked as a barman all me working life, and so we got a job together managing a pub, which worked well for us cos it meant we could live in the flat above, see. Well, you know, the pub game was hard work, still is, and we never did have much time for all that newlywed stuff, so no one was more surprised than we were to find out about ten years into our nuptials that she had a bun in the oven.'

Jon chuckles, causing the rest of the group to laugh lightly.

'Oh but don't get me wrong, on top of the world, we were, we just never thought it was gonna happen to us. Always just thought that kind of thing ... that was for other people. So we're just going about life, and Val's getting on fine, but you see, it all took quite a dramatic turn when Val went into labour seven weeks early. So Sarah comes along, tiny, she was, and it was touch and go for a while there, but you see what had happened was Val had pre-eclampsia. Well, as tiny as Sarah was, she did well and made good progress, and eventually she was allowed home, but my Val, well the baby came home, but not my Val. She had to stay in the hospital for weeks after Sarah came out. She got ever so poorly, and she had a terrible case of the blues. So you see, we never had any more after that. Not that we didn't want to, mind, it was just, Sarah coming into the world had been so traumatic, for all of us, that we couldn't really bear the idea of ever doing it again. So needless to say, our Sarah was very, very precious to us.'

This is the first time I've ever really heard Jon talk about his daughter, and to hear him speak so lovingly of her when I know she is no longer alive brings a lump to my throat.

'Then, when Sarah was seven, she got very ill, she had leukaemia. Of course we were just devastated.' Jon's voice drops quite dramatically as he reflects back to that time.

I look around the group, and all the faces that were alight with the jolliness in Jon's storytelling have now become sombre and silent as he continues.

'... an awful lot of time spent in and out of hospital, back and forth between this doctor and that consultant, we thought it would never end, but for a while it did. She got better, the all-clear, and we were overjoyed. But then a year later, it all started again. I remember she kept falling asleep at school, couldn't keep her eyes open for love nor money. We took her to the doctor, and well, long story short, it had come back.' Jon pauses, taking a long moment to compose himself as the sadness within him begins to surface.

'Sarah passed away one week before her tenth birthday. That day we lost our only daughter, and I can honestly say, that was also the day I lost my wife as well. My Val, she was never the same after that. We still had the pub to run, a business in fact, we were owners by this point.' Jon pauses and looks blankly into the space in front of him. He inhales a deep breath, composing himself before carrying on.

'You know, it was as if Val walked around in a permanent state of shock, as if the news of Sarah's death had never really sunk in. You know she only ever cried twice, at the hospital on the day, and the day of the funeral. Other than that,

I never saw her cry. I think it was safe to say that she just bottled all of it up inside her. She never wanted to speak about nothing, she never wanted to ask how I was coping, because you know, I lost me daughter too. She just wasn't my fun-loving Val anymore. She'd work in the bar, and do her best with the punters, but her sparkle, it had all gone.' Jon looks down to the floor, shakes his head and lifts his hands up slightly from his knees, before patting them back down again, showing his feelings of hopelessness as to his wife's sadness.

'I remember the night Val ended her life. I can see her face now, clear as day. She said she had a headache, that she was gonna head on upstairs and have a lie-down, and before she left, I said to her, "Rest well, love," and she grabbed hold of my face and gave me a kiss on the lips. I'll be honest, I thought at the time maybe I was on to a promise!' Jon laughs, breaking up the sadness in his voice a little.

'... it was all very out of character though. I let her rest and a few hours later, once the bar had closed for the night, I went up to check on her, and there she was, game over. Next to her was a bottle of Gordon's and two empty boxes of paracetamol.' Jon's voice sounds as if it's going to break, and so he pauses once again, this time lifting his round glasses and rubbing his face, possibly trying to suppress any tears.

'You know, for a long time, I just, I couldn't

get me head round it, and like I say, it's been a while since I done anything like this. But now I think about it, all these years on, I feel at peace with it. No one knows more than me how much my Val suffered after losing Sarah. It's like when people die of cancer, and people say, oh well at least they ain't suffering no more, and that's sort of how I feel. At least my Val ain't suffering no more, cos grief, you see, that was her cancer. Just ate away at her until there was nothing left, but not no more, now I just think, well, at least the two of 'em are together now. No more pain, no more suffering. I mean, Christ, I'm not saying it's what I'd prescribe, but that's just the way I look at it, it's a way of looking at it that brings me some kind of peace is all.'

Jon finishes speaking and the room falls silent.

I notice Pauline opposite me lift her glasses and wipe her eyes with her hand.

Jon looks spent. His face is red and he lifts his glasses again and rubs his face and head, the exertion of opening so many old wounds all at once taking its toll on him. He leans back down and picks up his coffee from by his feet, and takes a large gulp from it.

'Thank you so much for sharing that with the group, Jon,' says a very compassionate Lacey.

'I like what you said, Jon, how you've since been able to find some comfort in Val's choice,' says Maura.

'You know, I've sat in many a room like this

over the years, spoken it through, gone over and over things in me head, and you know what the conclusion I've come to is? I choose to accept her choice,' says Jon, who seems relieved that his storytelling is over, for now at least.

'Well it's certainly very brave of you to be so honest, Jon, especially in front of a group of complete strangers,' replies Maura, clearly impressed by Jon's fearless approach to sharing his experiences.

'This isn't my first rodeo, my dear! Like I said, I'm really just 'ere for my friend Lydia 'ere!' says Jon, pointing his thumb towards me. 'Who I know would like to share a few things!'

What. The. Fuck!

I'm absolutely horrified. The whole group looks at me in anticipation, willing me to be as open as Jon and share my story with them.

'Of course, Lydia, please, by all means,' says Lacey, inviting me to take command of the room with my own tale of woe.

I can feel my cheeks burning up. I look at Jon, in the hope that he will extinguish the situation he's just landed me in, but he looks away, back out towards the wider group, leaving me stranded, with no choice but to talk my way out of this dire situation.

'I mean ... I don't know what to say ...' I splutter nervously, not addressing anyone in particular.

'Just whatever you feel comfortable with sharing, Lydia, really, anything at all,' Lacey tells me, still with her default look of compassion on her face.

'Um, okay, so yes, okay …' I mutter, trying my best to compose myself, while gripping on to my coffee cup.

'My name's Lydia, and I lost my husband to … I lost my husband a few months ago,' I say.

I pause for a second, thinking of what to say next, looking down into my polystyrene cup.

'His name was Steve. He was thirty-three years old. He was five ten, with dark brown hair and blue eyes. He, er, he actually had gorgeous sparkling blue eyes … I used to look at his eyes and think, if we have kids someday, I really hope they get your eyes.' It's then, as I describe Steve, the man that was my lovely sweet kind husband, that I feel my defensive exterior gradually soften. I'm finding an unexpected comfort in talking about him in a way that I haven't since he died.

The thought of him gives me the confidence to look up from my cup, and out towards the wall behind Lacey, as I continue to describe the man I loved so very much.

'He was really funny … well, he used to make me laugh a lot. He was never the type to take himself too seriously,' I say, lowering my gaze from the back wall to the people surrounding me. They're all listening intently, and the respect they're showing me as I waffle on about some bloke they've never met makes me feel at ease, safe in the presence of strangers.

'He worked in the City for an American investment bank, but he was really down to earth, like a really genuine person. He had friends from all walks of life, he wasn't at all judgemental, and he was really sporty. Football in the winter and cricket in the summer. He was really popular, just one of those people that people gravitated towards ... everybody wanted to be his friend, myself included!'

I smile to myself as I remember just how loved Steve was, not just by me, but by so many others, and it's then that I feel a tightness develop in my throat as I try to understand why somebody who was seemingly so happy and loved would end their life the way he did.

'I loved him so much ... and I really thought we were happy. And that's why I still can't quite believe it, that he would just up and leave me the way that he did!'

I can't hold it together anymore. I feel my eyes prick with tears, and so I let them flow.

'Because that's how I feel. I don't feel like he died, I mean I know he died, but to me, it just feels like he left. When times got tough, rather than coming to me and talking to me, he just scarpered! He left me, in this huge mess with a ton of unanswered questions, and if I'm honest, I feel really angry with him because of that. And I know that sounds so selfish, and that in turn makes me feel guilty, because then I think, well, what kind of wife was I?'

I notice Lacey pass a box of tissues to Pauline, who then passes them on to the next person, and the next, until they reach me. I place my coffee on the floor by my feet and accept the box from Martin, pulling out a tissue to wipe my face before carrying on with my emotional outpouring.

'I mean, what kind of wife has no idea that their husband has lost his job and has all this worry and strain on his shoulders? Because that's what I would think, if this had happened to someone I knew. And so I don't tell people. If I'm asked how he died ... I just lie! I tell people he died some other way, like a car crash. I've even told this guy I've been seeing that he was in the army and died in Iraq!'

Jon turns his head sharply and fires me a look of utter bewilderment, seemingly having been unaware of that particular piece of information.

'And I know that's complete madness, but to be a widow to a car crash victim or brave soldier, it's just an easier part to play than having to deal with the ugly truth. The reality being that my husband died because he chose to. That he was too weak a person to stick around and sort his shit out. That he chose a coward's way out ... because you know the truth is, I still love him. And I don't want people to think that way about him, you know? It hurts me to think that that's the opinion people would have of him. Because as angry as I am at him, I still want to protect him, because he really was a good person.'

Although I'm a sobbing mess with a wet face and a stuffy nose, I'm surprised at how much better I feel, almost euphoric. A freeing feeling of finally releasing all that's in my head out into the atmosphere maybe beginning the process of banishing some of my uncomfortable thoughts.

'You okay?' Jon asks me quietly, placing a comforting hand on the top of my arm.

I nod while still dabbing my face with a tissue, a little conscious that my make-up has been damaged by my tears, and Jon nods back and places his hand back on his lap.

I notice Martin, the guy sitting next to me, raise his hand slightly, gesturing that he'd like to speak, and Lacey gives him a gentle nod, giving him the green light to go ahead.

'No one here thinks you're mad, lying about Steve's death.'

I frown at Martin, curious to know where he's going with this. He gives me a light smile and continues.

'My father, he ended his own life. He hung himself. And the only people that know that, well, other than the people in this room, are me, my mum and my brother. Even my own wife, my brother's wife, our kids, they all believe that he had a heart attack. That's what we told them, that's what we decided as a family to tell people.'

'Really?' I say, shocked by Martin's blatant admission.

'People often fear the stigma that's attached when losing someone to suicide. You're really not alone with that, Lydia,' interjects Lacey.

'It's not an easy thing to say out loud, that the person you loved took their own life,' says Martin.

'It's really not! I have no issue at all with telling people that I'm widowed, that my husband is dead, but you're right, I can't bring myself to say it out loud, that he killed himself, I just can't bear to say it,' I say, my sobbing subsiding nicely.

'So where does your missus think you are every Thursday night?' asks Jon.

'The gym!' laughs Martin, looking down at his gym-like attire.

'You think that's healthy, you know, keeping such a big secret from your family?' asks Jon, avoiding using a judgemental tone, something he's perfected after many years of working behind a bar and providing an unbiased listening ear to many a troubling tale.

'No I don't. But you know, some men have affairs, some gamble or have a drink problem. There are worse secrets a person can keep,' answers Martin.

Although I know I am just as guilty as Martin when it comes to fabricating the details around my own loss, I find his situation has left me feeling a little uncomfortable. For ten whole years he has been lying to his loved ones about something so tragic. I wonder how a person can have enough energy to sustain such a lie for such a long period of time?

As the discussions continue to stir around me, I find myself lost in my own thoughts, imagining myself ten years from now, still attending 'yoga' every Thursday, and still researching the SAS online, trying to feed convincing tales to strangers, who could go on to become loved ones, tying myself into a web of lies that becomes impossible to untangle, making me no better than Steve himself; and what if, like him, I dive so deeply into my own fabricated tales that there's no way out?

By the time Jon and I take our seats to commence our bus ride home, it's nearly 10 p.m. The bus is almost empty, with only us and three others on board. Although crying hysterically isn't out of the ordinary behaviour for me these days, I feel exhausted! Unaware that the act of honest confession could be so tiring!

'So, shall I tell Norma she can have the Thursday night shift for a bit or what?' Jon asks me.

'Yeah, I suppose so.'

'You know, for what it's worth, I'm proud of ya, girl,' says Jon, causing me to laugh.

'For my husband killing himself, or for lying to people about it?'

'Ha ha. I'm proud you went through with it tonight, I know it wasn't an easy thing to do, but while we're on the subject, what's all that about? So ol' Scotty Boy thinks your old man died fighting in the desert?'

I suppose I should be grateful that Jon seems to see the funny side, but I do feel embarrassed that he is now privy to that piece of information.

'Yeah, something along those lines. You're not gonna tell him, are you?' I say quietly, unable to hide the shame in my voice.

'What did I tell you before, girl? Keeper of the secrets, that's me! It's not in my interests to tell nobody nothing, it's bad for business. But you … you know you can't keep lyin' to him for ever, don't ya?'

'I don't know … Martin seems to be handling it quite well,' I laugh, causing Jon to laugh too.

'No I know. I will tell him, I *will* … it's just hard for me to tell other people a truth that I'm still struggling to come to terms with myself,' I say, feeling anxious just thinking about how on earth I'm going to explain to Scott that I've been lying to him all this time.

'I know, girl. But keep at it, the group thing, I think it'll help.'

'Thank you for coming with me tonight. It was really decent of you,' I say to Jon, who I think has maybe had more than enough emotional chit-chat for one night and turns his head away from me to look out of the window, unwilling to engage in any soppiness.

'Ah look at that, they're opening up a KFC next

to the Aldi on the high road,' says Jon, pointing out of the window.

'Up you get, this is me,' I say, pressing the red button on the handrail whilst getting up from my seat.

'Want me to walk you back, girl?'

'No, don't be silly, I'll be fine,' I say, holding on to the handrail waiting for the bus to come to a complete stop.

'Get back safe, girl. See you tomorrow,' says Jon as the bus slowly comes to a halt.

'And you. See you tomorrow,' I say as the bus doors open and I hop off, beginning my short stroll back to my flat, feeling happy and relieved that the night I had been dreading is finally over.

CHAPTER 22

I've just hopped out of the shower and with my hair dripping wet and wrapped in my white fluffy robe, I'm standing barefoot at my front door watching Mum climb her way up the stairs to my flat. As usual she's popped round unannounced, but at least these days she can't let herself in.

She looks her usual self, tired and worn out, but there's a lightness in her step that's most unusual and if I'm not mistaken it looks as if she's smiling.

'You just got out the shower?' she asks.

'No, I got a lift home in a fish tank.'

Usually a comment like that would see her scowl at me, but instead she walks on into the flat and, she is ... she's definitely smiling.

I close the front door as the jolly woman disguised as my mother places her shopping bags down on my kitchen work surface.

'I was just on my way home, but I wanted to show you what I bought,' she says, positively giddy. 'Now I know they don't know yet if it's a boy or a girl, but I couldn't resist,' she says, pulling from her shopping bag a three-pack of tiny white socks decorated with tiny teddy bears along with a brown fluffy baby jumpsuit with a hood and bear ears.

I smile.

While Nick's baby news may have come as a shock to us, it seems the pending arrival of her first grandchild has brought out a side in Mum I never knew existed. For the first time ever I'm seeing her display excitement and joy, and I have to admit, it's nice. Maybe this baby might just be the tonic she needs to finally be a nicer, more cheerful person. I even wonder if maybe it could see the start of the two of us finally getting along a little better.

'Very cute,' I say, picking up the fluffy jumpsuit and running my hands over the soft material.

'I loved having babies,' she muses. 'Shame you'll never have any,' she adds with a sideways glance, and just in case I was worried Mum's meanness was about to disappear for ever, I'm left reassured as it bounces straight back.

'I'm not even thirty. There's plenty of time.'

She doesn't respond, but looks dumbfounded, as if I've just told her I'm going to run away and join the circus, as if the idea of me having a family one day is the most ludicrous thing she's ever heard.

'Anyway...' I say, handing her back the jumpsuit. 'I'm heading out shortly, so ...' I nod towards the door, firmly indicating it's time for her to leave.

'But I only just got here,' she says, annoyed I should want shot of her so soon.

I shrug, having nothing more to say.

Agitated, she shoves her purchases back into her shopping bag.

'Off to meet your new boyfriend, I presume,' she says with a strong air of disapproval.

'Amongst others. Ruth's invited us along to a gig she's doing,' I say, sure I don't need to explain myself, but nevertheless feeling I should.

'I barely left the house after your father died, let alone contemplated seeing another man,' she adds, her voice becoming raised as if she's bothered by my plans.

'Okay, I won't go then. I'll call Ruth and Scott, and I'll tell them my mum said I can't go. And I'll lock the door and I'll stay in this flat and I won't talk to another soul or laugh or smile for the next thirty years. Would that make you happy?' I rant, my own voice becoming raised, and I'm annoyed with myself at how quickly my temper has flared.

'I don't care what you do, Lydia,' huffs mum, refusing to be pulled into such pettiness.

'Really? Because you seem to have a lot to say on the matter! Are you jealous, is that what it is?'

Mum looks at me with such disgust and pure anger, I'm a little worried she might actually slap me around the head, just like she'd do when I was growing up. If we gave her lip or stepped too far over the line, without hesitation she'd whack us around the back of the head. Her wide-open slap issued with inexcusable force, the rings on her fingers always adding to the impact and sting.

'Jealous? Of you? Of all this!' she says, almost laughing as she darts her eyes over my tiny flat. 'Do me a favour,' she adds, close to snarling as she heads for the front door and yanks it open.

Granted, it might not be the most impressive of homes, but it's *my* home, so I dig deep and find the confidence to stand my ground.

'You are. You're jealous. Because I'm not letting my life disappear down a dark empty hole like you did,' I yell at her, frustrated at how the mere presence of her can take my mood from happy and content to fuming in less than five short minutes.

'No, it's true I didn't go to carnivals after my husband died. But unlike yours, my husband didn't have a choice,' she tells me, a sickening smirk creeping across her face.

Her words cut through me. I feel my bottom lip tremble. I will myself not to cry, mystified as to why my own mother would take such glee in being so hurtful.

'I wouldn't be so sure. If I was married to you, I'd throw myself off a roof!' I say, initially quite proud of my comeback, but as soon as the words are spoken aloud, I realise what's coming.

Without a second's hesitation, Mum abandons her position by the front door and storms over to where I am at the kitchen counter. I cower, and in an instant flashback to my youth, she raises an open palm and strikes me, not once but twice on the back of my head. It hurts more than I remember, the thud impacting all her force, the pain blunt, leaving the back of my head throbbing.

Mum quickly straightens herself up and with no great urgency makes her way back towards the front door and storms out of the flat, slamming the door behind her.

I stand motionless by the kitchen counter, cradling the back of my head with my hand, shocked but by no means surprised by what just occurred. I really don't want to cry; to let her get the better of me, to let her ruin my evening before it's even begun.

Feeling undignified in my bathrobe, my hair wet, I can't help desperately wishing she could be more like other mums; and our relationship didn't have to be this hard.

CHAPTER 23

Gavin and I have manged to secure a picnic table in London's Hyde Park. The park is bustling with people this evening. Joyous screams can be heard from those enjoying a ride on the dodgems and the waltzer, the smell of popcorn and fried food lingering nicely in the air. But this isn't just any fun-filled event held in London's Hyde Park, this is the annual summer event of some fancy blue-chip company.

I've already managed to drag Scott along for a quick spin on the big wheel with me and indulged in some free candyfloss, the fun atmosphere in stark contrast to the intensity of only a couple of hours earlier.

Although neither I nor anyone I know works for the company hosting tonight's festivities, we've managed to score ourselves an invite to the private event courtesy of Ruth and The Dancing Shoes, who will be taking to the stage any minute now for the evening's 'Dance-a-thon!' finale.

As is the case with any self-respecting blue-chip do, the booze is free, a perk I'm determined to take full advantage of after my earlier encounter with Mum. I'm already a few vodkas in and beginning to feel their effect, my head feeling a little on the fuzzy side as I bore Gavin about how horrible my mother is.

'Who the hell is she to say I'll never have a baby? I can have a baby if I want a baby. I'm in the prime of my life,' I say, my words a little slurred and spoken louder than necessary.

'Of course you can, darling. You can do anything you want. If you want a baby you can have a baby,' says Gavin reassuringly.

'What's this?' asks Ben curiously as he appears at our table with Scott, placing down more free drinks.

'Lydia. She's going to have a baby!' says Gavin triumphantly, reaching for his red wine.

'What!' exclaims Scott. His mouth drops open and a look of sheer panic flashes across his face, the sight of him so shocked aided by the alcohol making me cackle with laughter.

'Hypothetically speaking. Horrible row with Mum. Don't worry, darling, no need to purchase a pushchair,' adds Gavin, clearing up any confusion.

'Okay,' nods Scott, looking a little baffled as the colour quickly returns to his cheeks. He takes his seat next to me, wrapping a strong protective arm around me, and I gleefully lean into his body.

'I just had to try and convince some jobsworth at the bar that I worked in the accounts department. These might be the last freebies we score,' Ben informs us, a look of grave concern on his face.

'Nonsense, we're with the entertainment, we're entitled to our drinks as much as anyone else,' says Gavin.

'I'm not sure that's entirely true, but I'm certainly happy to milk it for as long as we can,' I say, taking a sip from my vodka and Coke.

'Ruth was saying if this gig goes well they're hoping to get the booking for the Christmas do, so we should all keep our calendars open,' Ben jokingly informs us, keen to attend another fun-filled event a few months from now.

'Actually, Benjamin ... I'm afraid I won't be here at Christmas,' says Gavin, his tone so mournful I'm genuinely worried he's about to tell us he's dying of an incurable disease. 'I have some news,' Gavin continues.

He pauses for dramatic effect before a huge smile spreads across his face.

'I've been made an offer in Brighton. Compering a cabaret show!' chirps Gavin, clearly very proud of the opportunity he's been granted.

'Wow, that's amazing! As Orgazma?' I ask, referring to Gavin's travelling drag queen alter ego.

'The very one!'

'That's fantastic, Gav. Lucky you. Your job is so glamorous.'

'Oh it's really not, darling! It might seem all

glitter and hairspray, but trust me, it's really just a lot of drunken people, long nights and sore feet!' says Gavin, shaking his head to dismiss any glamour and taking a sip from his wine.

'How long will you be gone for?' I ask.

'Six months. Maybe longer if all goes well.'

'Wow, that's a really long time,' I utter, feeling sad to hear of Gavin's departure.

'But you'll visit, all of you. It'll be wonderful,' says Gavin hopefully.

'Does Ruth know?' asks Ben, sure he would already know such news had Ruth been privy to it.

'I'm going to tell her tomorrow. I didn't want to cast a shadow over her gig tonight,' says Gavin.

A sombre silence hangs between us for a moment, no one knowing quite what to say, feeling unprepared for another change to the regular dynamic of the group.

'To Brighton,' says Scott, breaking the silence and lifting his bottle of beer.

'To Brighton!' we say in unison, all lifting our drinks to toast Gavin and his good news.

'Well done, mate,' says Ben just as the opening chords of 'Better the Devil You Know' blare out across the park.

We turn to see Ruth and The Dancing Shoes have taken to the stage. Ruth looks amazing. Emerging from a cloud of artificial smoke, she's wearing a green-sequined playsuit, showing off a lovely pair of long legs. All teeth and big hair, she smiles broadly to the adoring crowd that's gravitating towards the stage.

As the musicians play, Ruth beckons everyone to their feet to join her in dancing the night away. With my insides absorbing nothing but vodka and sugar, I take little persuading, dragging Scott along with me towards the stage, ready to let my hair down and dance the night away.

An orange glow stick around my neck and with confetti stuck in my hair, I'm singing along with Scott an inebriated version of 'Mumbo Number 5' as we get to the front door of my flat. Between us we can't decipher which order Jessica, Rita or Mary feature, throwing in a Mabel and Mavis to fill in the blanks.

Although we have both taken full advantage of tonight's free alcohol, it's certainly fair to say one of us has taken a greater advantage than the other, that person being me! I as good as fall through my front door in a scattered mess of hilarity. With alcoholic fumes radiating from my every pore, Scott chivalrously holds me in his arms and guides me over to the bed.

I plonk myself down, only managing to stay upright for a mere two seconds before my upper body slumps onto the mattress, leaving my legs dangling over the edge.

I close my eyes and hear the sound of the front door closing. A few seconds later I feel the rough skin of Scott's hand upon my ankle.

I open my eyes and see him kneeling in front of me.

'You are ... so handsome.' I say with a small hiccup, momentarily panicked I might vomit.

'You are *very* drunk,' he says with a small laugh, gently removing my sandals from my feet.

'Are you going to make love to me now?' I say, stretching my arms out over the bed and arching my back, my best attempt at seduction while I'm unable to raise my own head.

Scott lifts my ankles and moves my legs onto the bed so I'm lying down in a more conventional position and although my head isn't quite on the pillow, I feel a lot more comfortable.

'Not tonight, beautiful. You need to sleep it off,' he says, leaning over and kissing me on the lips.

I pout, feeling disappointed.

I watch Scott remove his jeans, then pull his T-shirt over his head, revealing his muscular physique. I'm so transfixed by the sight of him, it's only when he climbs onto the bed and lies down beside me that a feeling of horror sets in. My mind flashes back to the last time he stayed. To the night we spent in this bed, when I woke up terrified in the night with my limbs flying about.

Scott can't witness me like that, not again.

'You can't stay,' I say, rolling onto my side to face him, my words spoken with great seriousness.

Scott frowns, looking a little confused.

'Why not?' he asks, his face centimetres from

mine.

'What if I have a bad dream? Like last time,' I say, my voice small. I'm almost on the verge of tears.

Scott looks at me, his eyes searching my face. He raises a small smile before lifting his hand, his fingers gently brushing the strands of hair from my face.

'Do you have a lot of bad dreams?' he asks.

'Yeah,' I say with a small nod.

'What do you dream about?' he asks gently, his voice soft and quiet.

I look into his warm hazel eyes and reach for his hand that's by my face, holding it in mine.

I want to tell him everything. I want to lie here and be held in his arms while I pour out my heart to him and am honest about everything that's happened in my life. I feel my lips part, the words ready to leave my mouth.

'I can't ... I want to tell you, but I can't,' I say.

'Because you're bound by the Official Secrets Act?' says Scott, the light humour in which his words are spoken making me feel all the more pathetic, reminding me just how ridiculous the situation is.

'It's not that ... I just can't,' I say, as a single tear falls from my eye and rolls down my cheek. Feeling physically and emotionally exhausted, I close my eyes, hoping in some vain hope it will disguise my vulnerability.

'It's okay, baby,' says Scott.

I sense he's realised the topic is a far more delicate one than he ever imagined. Holding my hand inside his, he pulls me into him and I can feel his heart beating through his chest.

'If you have a bad dream, I'm here. Nothing bad will happen,' he says reassuringly, before planting a soft kiss on my forehead.

I keep my eyes closed, and I feel my upset starting to subside. Allowing myself to relax, I feel myself drift off to sleep, safe in the knowledge that while Scott is beside me, everything will be okay.

CHAPTER 24

My eyes feel sticky, the residue of last night's make-up practically gluing them shut.

I rub my hand over my face, as the faint tinkling of a teaspoon stirring brings me back to life. I groan as I manage to peel my eyes open and am greeted by the sight of Scott standing topless at my kitchen counter, tending to two steaming mugs in front of him.

He looks over at me and smiles.

'How you feeling?' he asks.

'Awful,' I moan.

I sit my aching body up and I feel a whole new depth of depravity when I realise I'm still fully dressed in last night's clothes.

Scott places the teaspoon in the sink. Armed with the two mugs of tea he makes his way over to my side of the bed. He sits himself down next to me and kindly hands me one.

'What's the time?' I ask.

'Nearly nine.'

I groan aloud again, knowing I have to be at work in an hour from now. I silently contemplate pulling a sickie, but I know I simply can't afford to.

'Did I sleep okay?' I ask Scott, looking into my mug, a simple, yet loaded question, one I dread hearing the answer to.

'You were out like a light,' says Scott.

I wonder for a second if he's just being nice. However, I don't recall anything terrifying happening last night. Usually, my dreams are so vivid it's impossible to forget them.

'So, I didn't ...' I ask, needing clarification.

'No,' says Scott, shaking his head and taking a sip from his tea.

'Hmm, maybe I should get blind drunk more often,' I quip, lifting my mug.

'Ha, I wouldn't recommend it,' laughs Scott.

A short silence hangs in the air between us. I notice Scott fidget a little, and I sense there's something he wants to say.

'Look, I know ... it's a lot. And I know maybe you're not quite ready yet, but whenever, if ever you want to talk about things ... I'm here,' says Scott, looking relieved to have said the thing he's wanted to say.

His words make my heart melt. I realise the time has well and truly come for me to be honest with Scott. He's sleeping in my bed, he's witnessed me at my worst, and all the while he's still here, asking for more, asking for all of me; and who am I to deny him that?

However, as I sit here in last night's clothes and with a raging hangover, I can't help feeling right now might not be the best moment for a tell-all. I need to get to work, and I also need to navigate how I'm going to logically explain all the lies I've spouted over the past few months without coming across as an absolute nutcase.

I lean into Scott and rest my tired head on his broad shoulder.

'I know,' I say, touched by his sweetness and understanding. 'I need to get in the shower.'

'Actually, I could do with a shower too. Mind if I join you?' asks Scott, kissing my neck and sending goosebumps down my arm.

'You'll make me late. I have to get to work,' I whisper.

'I can drop you off. I promise you won't be late,' Scott whispers, and continues to kiss my neck, tracing a line with his fingers down my back, his advances impossible to resist.

CHAPTER 25

I was late for work, about twenty minutes late, and I would feel bad if it wasn't totally worth it! The activities that took place in my shower have certainly put an extra spring in my step, although the after-effects of last night are still raging strong.

As if working a double shift today isn't crippling enough, aided by this monster hangover it's going to be nigh on torture, but I'm determined to power on through even if it kills me.

Unfortunately for me the pub has been fairly busy so far, providing little opportunity to slump over the bar and silently regret last night's decisions, which would be my preferred way to spend my shift until home time.

Digging deep, I summon the strength to stay upright and pull open the door to the dishwasher, the escaping steam hitting me like a smack in the face as Norma squeezes her way past me.

'You all right, Lydia love? You look a bit pasty, you coming down with something?' she asks, Norma's diplomatic observations welcome as ever, confirming I do indeed look as awful as I feel today.

'Coming down with something, my eye! She's hungover! Good night, was it?' mocks Jon, finding great amusement in my agony.

'Yeah, a bit too good,' I groan, rubbing my forehead as I pull out the top rack.

Taking out the glasses, I bend down slightly to place them under the bar top in uniformed rows. My little army of glass soldiers all standing clean and ready for action.

When I re-emerge from under the bar, I'm startled by the sight of my mother standing on the other side.

'Bloody hell!' I gasp.

'Hello, Sue love, what you having?' asks Jon, issuing a more polite welcome than I'm capable of.

'Oh, I'm not stopping, I was just wondering if I could have a word,' says Mum, giving me her serious eyes.

'I'm working,' I say bluntly, royally not in the mood for her today.

'You're allowed a break, aren't you? I'll only be five minutes,' she says, the slight desperation in her voice almost making me feel sorry for her.

'No, not really. I was late today, so I need to make up the time,' I tell her, already turning on my heels, ready to walk away.

'Go on, girl, take a break, god knows you could do with it,' says Jon, his sympathy for my mum stretching a lot further than mine.

I let out a frustrated sigh, knowing she won't budge until I give her what she wants.

'Five minutes,' I tell her, reluctantly making my way out from behind the bar.

We go outside to the only vacant picnic table in the concrete beer garden.

'You look rough,' she says as we sit down, and I quite literally have to bite my tongue to stop myself saying something that might anger her.

I lean my elbows on the table, resting my tired head in my hands, and silently stare at her.

She looks a little uncomfortable, shuffling in her seat, unable to settle. She opens her mouth, but no words escape.

I widen my eyes and glare, willing her to spit out whatever it is she came here to say.

'About yesterday … I shouldn't … I'm sorry,' she utters, and although her apology isn't issued with the utmost conviction, I know her well enough to know that for her to come here and say such a thing has taken a huge amount of courage, or maybe guilt, but either way, the gesture is still appreciated.

I feel tears prick at my eyes, an emotional reaction brought on by pure exhaustion. Not in relation to the late night and raging hangover, but to us. This toxic relationship of ours.

'Is there anything you want to say?' she says sternly, ignoring my upset.

I dab my eyes with the tips of my fingers,

breathing a jiggered breath before I answer.

'I'm sorry for what I said,' I say, looking up at the sky, my voice tight and small. I release a tired sigh.

She lets out a large huff, then starts rummaging in her bag, pulling out her box of cigs and her lighter.

'Well, sorry I'm not the world's best mum,' she says, removing a cigarette. She sticks the end of it between her lips and flicks the lighter. 'But I'm the best mum I know how to be,' she concludes, and takes a long hard pull on her fag.

I know I should feel touched by her words in some way, by the frank admission of imperfection, but in truth, they fill me with horror. Is this as good as it's ever going to get? Is this version of her the very best I can ever ask for?

'But you weren't wrong ... maybe I am a little ... envious,' she says, blowing smoke out the side of her mouth.

'What? Why?' I ask, genuinely dumbfounded as to how anyone in their right mind could be envious of my current situation.

'Because you got something that I didn't. A chance to start afresh. No ... baggage,' she says, looking me up and down and pointing at me, just in case I was in any doubt as to what 'baggage' she was referring to.

'So sorry to be the reason for all your unhappiness,' I say, shaking my head, ready for this interaction to be over.

'You're not. You weren't. You were planned and wanted, both of you,' she says, tapping ash onto the ground. 'But what can I say? Suddenly finding yourself on your own with two little-uns. It's a very different situation to the one you're in,' she says, reflecting on her hardship.

'Yeah, well, it's no picnic on your own either,' I say, unable to describe to her just how alone and angry I've felt these past few months. In some respects envying her; often wishing I had a little piece of Steve left behind in the form of a child of our own.

She looks at me with a soft smile, her eyes a little sorrowful, and I wonder if she's about to display something in the form of sympathy, but instead she places her fag back between her lips and takes another long pull.

'Right ...' she says, climbing to her feet, and I get the distinct impression she would like to remove herself before she breaks and says something resembling kindness or understanding. 'We good?' she asks.

'As good as we'll ever be,' I say, also climbing to my feet.

Satisfied, Mum nods, flicking more ash onto the ground. She places her hand on my shoulder, giving it a gentle squeeze, and without saying goodbye she turns to leave.

I stand and watch her for a moment as she stomps away, the canvas shopping bag swinging from her arm, and I wonder if things will ever get any easier between us. I'd say the odds are pretty bleak, but we've managed to clear some of the fog between us, for today at least.

CHAPTER 26

It's Thursday evening and tonight I'm back at the British Legion with a polystyrene cub of instant coffee in my hand, here making my second visit to Suicide Club. Now Jon is confident in my willingness to attend, he's trusted me to put on my big girl pants and left me to go it alone tonight.

Sitting between Martin and Kim I feel a little nervous, unsure what to expect exactly; hoping things won't get quite as heavy as they did last week.

As everyone gets themselves comfortable, Lacey kicks things off.

'So, welcome everybody, thank you all for coming this evening. Now, I see we don't have any first-timers with us tonight, but I am sorry to say that it is the last time we will be seeing one of you for a while.'

The group look around at each other, all of us intrigued as to who our departing member could be, when we spot Gareth smiling coyly, the eyes on him causing him to blush.

'Ah, you're returning to university?' assumes

Pauline with interest and a keen smile.

'Er, no. Actually, I'm taking a break from uni and I'm going travelling, to South America.'

Pauline leans back in her chair and looks away in confusion and concern.

'Is that such a good idea?' she asks. 'Abandoning your studies?'

'Probably not,' laughs Gareth, taking Pauline's reaction in good humour. 'It was a trip me and my brother were meant to make last year, which never happened because he ...' Gareth pauses. He draws in a deep breath and looks down at the floor and I notice him anxiously lick his lips.

I'm sure it would be wholly inappropriate to ask, but I can't help but wonder how Gareth's brother ended his life. He must have been so young, with a whole life of experiences waiting for him. I'm sure everyone here already knows the details, so I swallow down the urge to say anything that could see me ostracised.

'Anyway, it's been almost a year now, and it just felt right. Everyone thinks I'm mad, but I just know if I don't do it now, I never will.'

'Then you must go, you must. See the world! Go to parties, get drunk, have passionate sex with beautiful women,' says Maura, enthused by Gareth's plans, her words making us all laugh.

'And make sure you come back and tell us all about it!' adds Martin.

'I wish my mum and dad were as enthusiastic,' says Gareth, looking a little forlorn at the mention of his parents.

'Are they not supportive of the trip?' asks Lacey.

'They're worried. I know I would be,' says Pauline with a sideways glance, not so approving of Maura's advice.

'Maybe, but I think it's more than that. They've been pretty suffocating. As if they're terrified to let me out of their sight. They think it's still too soon and I should be crying up in my room for another year, but honest to god, I need to get out of that house ...' says Gareth shaking his head, a desperation in his voice.

'I can relate to that,' I say, surprising myself as the words fall out of my mouth.

'How so, Lydia?' asks Lacey, her head tilted to one side, graciously offering me the chance to share, and suddenly the eyes of the room are on me.

I sit open-mouthed for a second, silently regretting having spoken. Everyone's waiting for me to elaborate, leaving me with no choice but to say what's on my mind.

'My mum ... she likes to make me feel bad about things,' I say, fully aware of how vague my response is.

'What kind of things?' asks Lacey, pushing me for more.

'I er, think I might have mentioned last week that I've started seeing someone. And my mum, she thinks it's too soon, and you know, maybe it is, but I really like him and I know he really likes me and I know it's early days, but I'd really like to see where it goes,' I say with a small shrug, feeling very unsure of myself.

'You're moving on,' says Maura with a reassuring smile.

'Do you ever feel guilty about that, though? Moving on? Like you're disrespecting their memory somehow by being happy without them here?' I ask.

'That's an interesting subject area, Lydia, and not an attitude exclusive to suicide loss. Lots of people, after suffering a bereavement, worry that moving on is wrong,' says Lacey.

'I think it's other people that expect you to stay still,' says Maura, looking straight ahead at no one in particular. 'I remember after Alf, my husband, took his own life, that very same day I started clearing out his things. His clothes, his toothbrush and razors, I just started bagging them up, getting them ready to take to the charity shops and whatnot. And I remember his sister telling me I was the most uncaring witch. But I just didn't see the point in hanging on to it all. He wasn't coming back! I certainly don't think you should beat yourself up for allowing yourself to move forward,' says Maura, turning her head slightly and bringing her attention back to me.

Maura's words resonate with me. I remember having to sort through Steve's clothes and personal possessions a lot sooner than I would have liked to on account of the house having to be sold. I can only wish I didn't have to rush that process at that point in my life, but I had no choice.

'Exactly, grief is a very personal journey. The human body and mindset is very adaptable. We learn, we adapt and we cope. I personally would be very disturbed if I had a group that couldn't move past those first stages of grief. Learning to move on is just as important a process as grieving. You and only you get to decide when and how you do that,' says Lacey in her usual calm and compassionate voice, addressing the group as a whole.

Although I completely agree with what Lacey is saying, I'm still struggling to shake the uncomfortable feeling inside me. I know moving on with my life is a positive process, but I still feel so incredibly guilty that I've let another man into my bed so soon and worse still, a man that I'm quickly falling in love with.

'Is this the same guy that thinks your husband died in Iraq?' asks Kim, who up until now has been concerningly quiet. I'm so pleased now is the time she's chosen to find her voice.

I nod, regretting having shared that piece of information.

'You gonna tell him the truth?' Kim asks.

Dressed smartly in her office attire, Kim crosses her legs and casually sips from her polystyrene cup of coffee, as if we're just two girls from the office gossiping on our lunch break, the interaction reminding me of a time gone by. Except, this isn't my lunch break, and this isn't idle gossip about Martina from the marketing department. This is the sorry excuse of my life.

Everyone looks at me with eager eyes, awaiting my response.

'I want to. I think I'm ready to. I just— '

'Don't know how to?' Kim interjects.

I nod.

'Hmm, my family lied to me. They told me my mum died of cancer, and twenty years later I found out she was actually a manic-depressive that threw herself in front of a train. Finding out the truth, after all that time, almost killed me. That lie did nothing but cost me a fortune in therapy and made me very distrusting of people.' Kim takes another sip from her coffee and looks a little too proud of herself for my liking.

While I know I should be grateful to Kim for her candour, I feel a little put out by her harsh comparison.

'I'm not entirely sure that's the same situation,' I say, trying my best to disguise my annoyance.

'A lie's a lie. I'm just saying, how do you think he's going to feel when he finds out you've been lying to him all this time?' says Kim, homing in her point nicely and making me feel like the most awful person in the entire world.

'So, Gareth. Where's the first stop on your

big trip?' asks Martin, interrupting the tension and shifting awkwardly in his seat, Kim's words possibly having shaken some uncomfortable truths for him also.

While Gareth happily shares his plans with the group, I find myself disengaging slightly. I sit silently, chewing over Kim's words, wondering how on earth I'm going to explain myself to Scott. I worry that once the truth is out there he'll hate me, and the very thought of that is nothing short of terrifying.

CHAPTER 27

I'm fast approaching the final throes of today's shift at the pub and I'm excited for it to come to an end. Rather than heading home tonight and burrowing myself down in bed, I'm heading out to join the gang for Gavin's farewell drinks ahead of his departure to Brighton.

In a short while from now Scott will be meeting me here and joining me for fun and frolics in London's Soho. I love how he's slotted in so nicely with my friends and I can't wait to see him and for our evening to begin.

Between Scott's work schedule and mine it's been a couple of weeks since we've managed to spend any real time together, but tonight after our evening he'll be staying at mine, and tomorrow we have the whole day to ourselves to spend doing whatever we like.

Another reason I'm excited for my shift to come to an end is so I can finally see the back of my mother. For the past hour she's been here propping up the end of the bar and droning on about her work and her bunions and the fact Nick never answers her phone calls.

'Lydia, this Coke's not diet,' she moans, taking a sip from the drink I've just placed in front of her.

'You've just eaten three packs of crisps. I wouldn't worry whether or not the Coke's diet,' I tell her.

'I hope you're not that friendly to all our customers,' says Jon, coming up behind me to issue a subtle telling-off for my customer-service skills.

Just when I'm about to walk away, I notice the pub door open and my insides light up at the sight of Scott stepping over the threshold.

He looks lovely. Dressed in a dark shirt and jeans, looking all clean and delicious. He spots me at the bar and issues me a handsome smile, walking right over.

'Hello, beautiful,' he says, leaning over the bar to greet me with a kiss on the lips.

'Oh, don't mind me,' interjects Mum.

'Oh, hiya, Sue. Sorry, I didn't see you there,' says Scott, looking a little embarrassed.

'Ignore her. She's allergic to loving displays of affection,' I tell Scott.

'Charming,' says Mum, looking away from me and diverting her sights over to Scott, looking him up and down.

'You're looking rather dapper,' Mum says to Scott, and I'm rather taken aback. Mum doesn't dish out compliments to just anybody, but then again, Scott does look undeniably gorgeous, and I guess she's a red-blooded woman like any other.

It seems the compliment isn't wasted on Scott either. I notice him smile and relax a little.

While he and Mum make easy small talk, I take it upon myself to fetch Scott a drink.

'Don't you have work tonight?' I ask Mum, trying to hurry her along.

Mum looks at her watch as I place Scott's drink down on the bar for him.

'I've still got half an hour,' she says, taking a small sip from her drink.

'Right ...' I nod, disappointed by her answer. 'Okay, well I need to get changed. Are you gonna be okay?' I ask Scott, reluctant to leave any poor soul in my mother's company but I need to get ready.

'What on earth do you think I'm going to do to him?' says Mum, clearly insulted.

'I dread to think,' I say. 'I'll be as quick as I can,' I tell Scott, trotting out from behind the bar.

'I'll be fine,' Scott reassures me as I disappear into the ladies' loo to freshen up.

There really is only so much a girl can achieve in a pub toilet, but I think I've done a pretty decent job.

After a quick spritz, an outfit change and a top-up of my make-up, I re-emerge a slightly fresher and more glamorous version of my previous self. Tonight, I've opted for my favourite LBD, a sexy little number with long sleeves that shows a lot of leg and just the right amount of cleavage, matched with a killer pair of high-heeled sandals.

It's been a really long time since I got this dressed up and I feel really good, as if a small part of my former self is starting to work her way back to me, and I'm pleased; feeling ready to start letting that girl back into my life again.

I strut towards Scott, still exactly where I left him.

'Hiya, handsome,' I say, wrapping my arms around his waist, excited for him to see me looking so glamorous.

Scott turns to face me and it's fair to say he looks surprised, shocked even, but not in quite the way I was expecting. He certainly doesn't look pleased to see me, his face unsmiling and his manner cold, unreactive to my touch. He looks at me in a deathly silence, issuing nothing in the way of a compliment. Instead, he stares at me as if I'm someone he recognises but can't quite place.

I release myself from his person and straighten myself up, sensing something is seriously out of alignment.

'Everything okay?' I ask, feeling decidedly awkward, trying my best to plaster on a smile.

'He ... killed himself?' utters Scott, looking at me in utter bemusement.

I feel my lips part and a sick feeling instantly hits my stomach, Scott's words knocking me for six.

'What?' I mumble.

Fearing the worst, I turn and look at Mum. She takes a cautious sip from her glass of Coke, glancing between me and Scott, looking just as bemused as him.

'I need a breather,' says Scott, marching his way past me and out the pub.

'What have you said to him?' I ask Mum, urgently needing an answer.

'What have *you* said to him, more like,' says Mum, and I can hear the concern in her voice, realising she's stumbled into a maze of lies and confusion without any prior warning.

Not waiting for Mum to elaborate, I turn on my heels and run as fast as I can out of the pub and after Scott.

Outside I spot him across the road by the off-licence. He's standing with his back to me, straight and upright, his hands clasped on his head. I can't see his face, but I can tell from his stance that before me is a perplexed and angry man.

'Scott!' I call out, clattering my way across the road in my heels, desperate to speak to him.

He turns round and as I suspected he looks annoyed. He looks at me for only a second, shakes his head, turns back round and begins to walk away as if desperate to get away from me.

'Scott! Scott! Please don't go!' I call out.

I pick up my speed and feeling out of breath I finally catch up with him.

'You shouldn't listen to her. You know what she's like,' I say. Desperate to speak to him I reach out and manage to grab his arm.

Sensing my building hysteria he stops and turns round.

'So, it's not true then? Your husband didn't kill himself?' says Scott, looking me sternly in the eye.

'Why … why were you even talking about that stuff?' I ask, a surge of embarrassment crashing into me, my mind a whirl, I not having imagined for one second that ten minutes of small talk with my mum would result in the unearthing of such traumatic truths.

'Because you won't tell me anything!' shouts Scott, at his wits' end trying to get a straight answer out of me.

'So, you thought you'd ask my mum instead?' I snap back, insulted he should go behind my back.

'Lyd, I get that you don't want to talk about it, I get that now. But to make up a whole story about the army and Iraq. What sane person does that? She looked at me like *I* was crazy,' yells Scott, and I sense he's just as angry about looking foolish in front of my mother as he is about anything else.

I don't know exactly what Mum has said to him, but I know that time is up on the lies I've told and there really is no point denying it for a moment longer.

'You don't get it!' I say, shaking my head, annoyed he should think that one conversation with my mum makes him some kind of expert on my life.

'You don't know the half of it! What did she tell you? Did she tell you how he lied to me for months? That I found him hanging in our bedroom? Did she tell you about the nightmares? Once they were so bad that I wet my bed? Did she tell you that?' I yell, my lip trembling and tears pricking at my eyes. Everything I've tried so hard to keep hidden from him rushing up to the surface.

Scott exhales loudly. He runs his hands through his short hair and I notice his face soften, his eyes that were full of anger only a moment ago suddenly flooding with pity, now that he's privy to the more disturbing details of my life.

'My husband died in a horrible and ugly way … maybe I am insane,' I say, allowing myself to succumb to the general assumption. Struggling to finish my sentence as I begin to weep, tears streaming down my face. 'Because I hate talking about it … I hate even thinking about it.'

'Lyd …' Scott utters sympathetically.

He reaches out his hand to me and steps forward, ready to embrace me, but I step away.

'Lyd …' he says again, repeating his actions, but I'm not interested.

Feeling embarrassed and vulnerable after such a tense outpouring and with my emotions fraught I want nothing more than to be left the hell alone. I push Scott away and turn round. Wanting to get away from him, I storm my way back down the street.

'Lyd, come back!' Scott calls, but I ignore him, desperately wanting to abandon tonight's plans and head home.

I reach the off-licence opposite the pub. With Scott only a step behind me I look up the street and see a white Audi about to turn out of a side road. Not wanting Scott to catch up with me, I make a quick dart across the road before the car turns into the street.

My feet land on the pavement and just as I'm about to head into the pub to gather my things I hear the sound of car tyres screeching, then a loud dull thud, like a sack of potatoes hitting the ground at great force.

I turn round sharply as a blood-curdling scream echoes in my ears.

I look across the road, at where I was just standing, and where I fully expect Scott to be, but he's not there, all physical sign of him disappeared. It takes me a second to register the white Audi stationary in the middle of the road. A young Asian woman is sitting behind the wheel, screaming whilst frantically trying to get out of the car. My eyes wander downwards, over the bonnet of the car, and it's then I see him, Scott, lying in a heap in the road right in front it.

I run straight over to Scott, collapsing on my knees next to him.

'Scott, Scott!' I yell, searching his hazel eyes, desperate to see signs of life, already fearing the worse.

'What's happened?' I hear a panicked voice say.

I look up and see Adnan from the off-licence standing over me, a look of shock plastered onto his face.

'He's been run over. Call an ambulance!' I scream at him, but Adnan doesn't react. In shock, he stands opened-mouthed, his eyes darting between the car and Scott on the ground.

'Adnan! Quickly!' I scream, becoming hysterical.

Adnan finally snaps back to earth, nods his head and slips his phone from his shorts pocket.

'Scott, Scott, talk to me,' I say, gently placing my hands either side of his face, his cheeks drained of their usual colour.

His eyes meet mine and in that instant I feel an overwhelming sense of relief.

He can see me. He's alive.

Scott's lips move, he's trying to say something, but I can't hear him. I place my ear closer to his mouth and I feel him clear his throat before he tries to speak again.

'My leg,' he says, his words spoken distinctly, albeit very quietly.

'Your leg?' I confirm, lifting his head gently from the concrete and resting it on my lap.

'Is my leg okay?' he asks.

I look down at Scott's legs. One looks perfectly

fine, the other does not. The lower part is twisted at an unholy angle, his foot about ninety degrees the wrong way, leaving me pretty sure something is seriously wrong.

'It's fine,' I lie, pulling my eyes away from the gruesome sight and looking back at Scott's ashen face.

'Really?' he says and I can see the strain in his eyes and I worry about the amount of pain he must be in.

'Yeah, it's fine. I promise,' I say, painting on my most convincing smile. 'Just sit tight. The ambulance will be here soon, and they'll sort everything out,' I say, looking up the street, wishing they'd hurry up.

I stroke my hands tenderly over his hair, trying to keep us both calm.

'I don't think I'm going to make it to Soho tonight,' says Scott.

'That's okay, I don't really fancy it now either,' I say, and I hear a small laugh come from him, the gentle banter between us reassuring me he's okay.

I look over towards the pub and see a large crowd has formed in the beer garden. I spot Jon and Mum standing together looking worried, both anxiously puffing on cigarettes. Next to them stands a very emotional Asian lady. Her body's shaking and I can see tear stains on her face. She keeps nervously running her hands through her long black hair and I realise she's the driver of the car.

I see Jon place a kind hand on her arm, trying his best to comfort her. Mum offers her a cigarette which she declines.

Finally, after what feels like an absolute age, I hear the faint sound of a siren. As the sound becomes louder I look down the road and feel a surge of relief at the sight of an ambulance heading our way.

'Scott, they're here. The ambulance is here,' I say and I feel my voice starting to crack. Not wanting to break I decide to distract myself by lifting my arm and waving down the ambulance, as if they might not be able to spot the carnage in the middle of the road.

The ambulance pulls up a few short yards away. The siren stops but the flashing lights continue, casting a flashing blue shadow over Scott's face, illuminating the strain in his eyes.

A paramedic, carrying an enormous bag over her shoulder, hops out of the vehicle and calmly makes her way over to us. She looks around Mum's age, late middle age, with short blonde hair and a semi-serious expression.

'Okay, darling, we'll take it from here,' she says to me, placing her bag on the ground, her words sending a grave level of panic through me.

'No, no. I can't leave him,' I say, desperate to stay by Scott's side.

'I need you out the way so we can treat him,' the paramedic says sternly, and I know she's right, but I'm as good as rooted to the ground, terrified by what could happen to him in my absence.

'It's okay, Lydia. I'll stay with you,' says a gentle voice and I feel a hand rest on my shoulder.

I look up and see it's Adnan from the off-licence.

He offers me a hand. I gently move Scott's head from my lap and with Adnan's help awkwardly lift myself up from the road.

'I won't be far, Scott, I'll be right here, just over here,' I reassure him, pulling myself away from him.

Adnan graciously moves me out of the way, and stays by my side, only a few short feet from where Scott is lying helplessly on the ground. I look around and absorb the surrounding commotion. The abandoned car in the middle of the road, the gathering crowd, the staring eyes, the flashing blue lights, and I'm unable to fathom how, yet again, life can propel from happy and carefree to a heart-breaking mess in just a few short moments.

I feel my body begin to shake, possibly out of shock, or fear. As I watch the paramedics tend to Scott, tears surface in my eyes. Unable to compose myself a second longer, I stand at the roadside and break down in tears. Adnan from the off-licence wraps his arms around me and kindly allows me to cry out all my worry and fear onto his shoulder.

CHAPTER 28

It's past midnight and I'm sitting in the back of a minicab with Mum on our way home from the hospital, the last few hours spent anxiously by Scott's side. Mum was insistent she came with us to the hospital, and I didn't feel strong enough to protest against it.

Most of her time was spent outside the building chain-smoking, but I guess I should be grateful that she stayed long enough to escort me home. Scott's injuries don't seem to extend too far beyond a fracture to his leg, the doctors reassuring us just how lucky Scott is to have only maintained one serious injury.

We won't know the full extent of things until the morning, but with the doctors confident all is okay, we've finally called it a night and decided to head home; leaving Scott to rest for the night.

'You'll wanna clean those up,' says Mum, pulling my attention away from the window. I look at her and she's pointing at my grubby knees, red and sore from kneeling in the road.

I nod and rub my tired head. I feel exhausted, the panic and worry taking its toll.

I look at Mum. She looks pretty at ease, the complete opposite of me, as she gazes out the window again, and even though it's late and I'm beyond exhausted, I have to know exactly what she said to Scott earlier at the pub.

'What did you say to him?' I ask, my voice quiet.

She looks at me, shakes her head and exhales, annoyed she was unable to dodge the inevitable conversation, a look of frustration sweeping across her face.

'He was asking about Steve, asking if I knew what happened to him. It was weird … like it was some big conspiracy or something …' she says, baffled, screwing up her face and looking away from me before continuing, as if trying to retrace her steps.

'..and I thought, okay, well I know Steve killing himself isn't something you might have shouted from the rooftops, but it's not *that* unusual. And then he said something about the army and I thought he was confusing Nick with Steve, so I dunno … I just … put him straight,' she says, as if she's done me some massive favour.

If I wasn't so tired and confined in the back of this car I'd most certainly have walked off.

'This is all your fault,' I say, unable to contain my anger at her interference.

'My fault? I wasn't driving the car, Lydia!' says Mum, raising her voice, offended by my accusation.

I look forwards and see the cab driver lift his head, his eyes cautiously checking us in the rear-view mirror.

'If you hadn't said anything he wouldn't have stormed out and we wouldn't have rowed,' I say, my frustration all too clear as I lean my head back on the head rest and peer up at the low cab ceiling in despair.

'Has what happened to Steve taught you nothing? Lies, Lydia, they don't stay hidden for ever. They always come out in the end. He deserved to know the truth.'

'But that wasn't your call to make,' I snap, looking back at her, raising my voice, unable to keep my emotions in check.

'I know it wasn't. And airing your dirty laundry really wasn't my intention. But it's done now. You should be thanking me,' says Mum with the utmost seriousness

'Thanking you! Thanking you for what? You've ruined everything!' I yell, absolutely flabbergasted by her suggestion that I should be grateful for her interference.

'Everything okay back there?' asks the cab driver, looking at the back seat once again in the rear-view mirror, not wanting any bother.

Neither Mum nor I respond.

We sit silently for a few moments, the atmosphere tense. I stare ahead, seething, feeling too angry to look at her, her comment probably the most ludicrous thing she's ever said to me.

'Here?' asks the cab driver as we pull into Mum's road.

'Just up here, please, the second one on the right,' instructs Mum, gathering up her bags on the seat next to her as the car comes to a stop. She reaches for the door handle, pulling it open, but before she climbs out she pauses and looks at me.

'You should thank me ...' she says, unable to drop the matter. 'For taking care of something you were too scared to do yourself.' She holds eye contact with me and I think she seriously believes she acted kindly out of motherly duty.

'Please just go,' I say quietly, too tired to row and unable to offer anything in the way of gratitude.

I hear her let out a tired sigh, the evening's events having caught up with her also.

She climbs out of the car and walks under the dark night sky towards her front door.

As the car begins to pull away and I'm finally alone in the back seat, I feel tears form in my eyes and fall down my cheeks.

Exhausted and emotional, I cry silently in the back of the cab.

I cry out of worry for Scott, out of anger at Mum's interference, and for the person I once was, when worry and sadness were problems for other people.

CHAPTER 29

It's been a couple of days since the accident and I still feel severely out of sorts.

I've hardly slept and barely eaten, the stress and upset the situation is causing me giving me a constant sick nervous feeling in my stomach, not too dissimilar to the way I felt when Steve died.

I'm starting to wonder if I am in fact cursed, every good man in my life being struck down. Maybe I did something terrible in a past life and now I'm paying the price for it.

When I expressed this concern to Ruth, she assured me it was just sleep deprivation making me overthink things. I'm sure she's right, but even so, I can't help but wonder.

I'm back at work today, which has been a welcome distraction, but it hasn't stopped the urge to check my phone every ten seconds, desperate as I am for any kind of news on Scott's welfare.

For the four thousandth time today I slip my phone out from my back pocket and check my messages, and yet again I'm met with disappointment.

'You check that screen anymore and you'll end up with square eyes,' says Jon, placing a small stack of used glasses down on the bar top.

'Sorry,' I say, slipping my phone back into my pocket, knowing Jon likes to maintain a 'no checking your phone' policy when his staff are on the clock.

He issues me a sympathetic smile, and I realise he's not telling me off, but speaking out of concern.

'Still no news?' he asks, to which I shake my head.

Any news from Scott has been pretty non-existent.

My phone calls have gone unanswered and the messages I sent him were eventually responded to only in the form of a kiss, which although filled me with confidence that he was indeed alive, didn't tell me anything at all about his welfare, the not knowing slowly killing me.

'I wouldn't take it personal. He's probably off his nut on painkillers and the like.'

'That, or he just doesn't want anything more to do with me,' I say, succumbing to the harsh reality of the situation.

'Nonsense. I've seen the way he looks at you, girl. I'm not so sure he scars that easy,' says Jon, not hearing a word of such self-pity.

'You didn't see the way he looked at me the other night. Like I was clinically insane,' I say, my mind casting itself back to that fateful night.

Scott looking at me as if he didn't even know me. The memory a harsh and painful one.

'I'm sorry, girl. At least the truth's out there now, eh?' says Jon, trying to see some kind of silver lining in such a pitiful situation.

'I suppose,' I say with a shrug, struggling to see the upside.

'Why don't you get off early, pay him a visit,' suggests Jon.

'I would, but the other night they were talking about transferring him to the London to operate on his leg. I don't even know where he is.'

'Have you tried giving the hospital a bell?' asks Jon, refusing to give up on finding a solution to my woes.

'I did. But I'm not family ... no one would tell me anything,' I say, the hopelessness in my voice palpable.

I look down at the floor, worried I might start crying.

'Maybe give him some space, time to heal. He's probably still in shock,' says Jon, finally out of suggestions.

I nod, knowing he's right, but it doesn't stop me worrying and wishing my life wasn't such a constant tidal wave of catastrophe.

'It'll all come right in the end, girl. In the meantime, you can occupy yourself by bottling up. That fridge is looking a bit low on mixers,' says Jon, pointing to the fridge behind me.

I let out a small chuckle, happy for the

distraction of work and grateful for Jon's listening ear.

'Thank you,' I say, the words leaving my mouth silently, but with sincere gratitude.

'Any time,' says Jon, before walking off to wipe some tables.

CHAPTER 30

I'm in Whitechapel, a part of London I'm not overly familiar with. Having just emerged from Whitechapel Station I'm standing outside the main entrance of the Royal London Hospital, feeling very nervous, not to mention overwhelmed. The vast size of the hospital alone is a lot to process, the modern blue towers almost futuristic in comparison to its otherwise run-down and tired-looking surroundings.

As originally predicted, Scott was transferred here the day after the accident for an emergency operation to his leg. It's been almost a week since the accident, and after days of near radio silence, Scott *finally* got in touch last night, arranging for me to visit.

I've arrived about forty minutes earlier than planned, partly because the journey didn't take as long as I'd thought, but mainly out of anxiety, having been unable to sit idle at home a moment longer.

I am excited to see Scott, but I'm also undeniably nervous. I'm hoping Jon was right, and the lack of contact was down to nothing more than Scott being out of it on pain medicine, but I'm still fearing the worst.

I'm worried about everything. That he might blame me for what happened to him, or that he won't be able to move past the lie I fed him for so long. To soften any possible animosity between us, I decided to bring a fruit hamper. Ruth assured me it was the most sophisticated of peace offerings, while the fruit would provide the kind of healing qualities one wouldn't get from chocolate.

My hamper is beautifully wrapped in clear cellophane with a large gold bow, decoration taking firm priority over practicality, making it all the more difficult to keep hold of in my sweaty grasp. In my other hand I'm holding my phone, scrolling through it, trying to find Scott's message containing the information I need on where to find him.

I make my way into the hospital's main entrance and am still no clearer on where I need to be. The space is vast with a lot of people milling around. I catch sight of a sign for the lifts and decide that might be a good place to start.

Standing at the lifts, I'm even more confused, with some of them only going to certain floors and wards. I look back down at my phone, whilst also trying to read the signs on the wall to decipher where I need to be, and just as the lift doors directly in front of me ping open, I feel the fruit hamper slipping from my grip and sliding down my body. Just before it hits the floor, a person stepping out of the lift rescues the hamper from its fate.

'Oh careful!' she says, graciously handing the hamper to me, securing it back in my hold. 'Oh my god, Lydia. Hi!' she says, her voice surprised and a little high-pitched.

Straightening myself up, I realise the woman in front of me is Lacey from Suicide Club, and she's not alone. Lacey is accompanied by a super cute little girl with sunshine-blonde hair who can't be any older than three years of age. I smile at her and she looks up at me with large hazel eyes as she inches closer to Lacey and reaches for her hand.

'Hi, Lacey. What are you doing here?' I ask, feeling flustered.

'We're here visiting my husband,' says Lacey, who also looks a little flustered. Her wavy hair is tied up in a loose ponytail, her complexion shiny. She's carrying a large overnight-type bag, the strap of which has fallen halfway down her arm. Lacey secures the fallen strap back onto her shoulder, then lifts her little girl from the floor, placing her on her hip.

'Oh no, nothing serious, I hope?' I ask. It never really occurring to me that the woman who guides us through all our problems could possibly have any of her own.

'No, no, he's going to be fine. Actually, he should be coming home tomorrow. We're excited for Daddy to come home, aren't we?' says Lacey, drawing her attention to her little girl, whilst not giving too much away.

The little girl smiles brightly and nods eagerly, clearly happy at the idea of her Daddy returning home.

'That's good. So this is your little girl,' I say, dragging the small talk out a little longer.

'Yes, this is Lola. Lola, say hello to my friend Lydia,' says Lacey.

'Hi, Lola,' I say, in the animated way in which you're forced to speak to children.

Lola goes shy and buries her face away in Lacey's shoulder.

'Are you here visiting someone?' asks Lacey, nodding towards my fruit hamper.

'Yeah, my—'

'Mummy, I need the toilet,' interrupts Lola, a flash of urgency sweeping across Lacey's face.

'Oh, sorry, Lydia. I better go,' says Lacey, already beginning to walk away.

'Of course,' I say understandingly.

'But I'll see you at group?' adds Lacey with a hopeful smile.

'Yep, of course,' I say.

I watch Lacey walk away with Lola attached to her hip, before drawing my attention back to my phone and trying to construct the correct route to Scott's ward.

Once I establish the right lift, I make it to Scott's

ward with relative ease.

I walk through the ward and past the large nurses' station, the familiar hospital smell of overcooked vegetables and disinfectant hanging in the air.

Finally, I make it to bay C, and I see him. In the bed at the back closest to the large window. He doesn't see me, his gaze fixed on what is actually a very impressive view of the high-rise towers, including the Gherkin and the Walkie Talkie Building, on the London skyline, especially on such a bright and clear day.

I walk gingerly into the silent bay. A middle-aged man nearest the entrance with a bald head and grey beard sits in his own visitor's chair and issues me a small smile as I pass him. The scrunching sound of cellophane draws Scott's attention away from the window and I'm relieved when he smiles at me, filling me with confidence that he is pleased to see me.

'Nice view,' I say, nodding towards the window, admiring the type of panorama many would pay a lot of money to see from the balcony of a fancy hotel.

'It is. Almost makes up for the terrible food,' says Scott.

I sit myself down in the large visitor's chair tucked behind the bed curtain.

Despite the large blue-coloured cast covering Scott's leg, he looks well; relaxed. Dressed casually in a white T-shirt and a pair of grey shorts, he looks a damn sight better than when I saw him last. The colour has returned to his cheeks and his eyes are focused, no longer processing anything in the way of fear or doom. I notice a large graze on his elbow, presumably from where he hit the ground. It looks sore, but not life-threatening, making me realise how incredibly lucky Scott was that night.

'I brought you a present,' I say, proudly placing the hamper down on the wooden swivel table next to the bed, beside a water jug and Scott's mobile phone.

'Thank you, Lyd, you didn't need to,' Scott says sincerely.

A short silence hangs in the air between us as Scott looks over the hamper, neither of us knowing what to say next.

Desperately wanting to banish any awkwardness, I'm the first to dive in and break the silence.

'How're you feeling? How's your leg?' I ask.

'It's okay. They said it was a pretty clean break, so they're confident it should heal quickly. They told me today I can go home tomorrow.'

'That's really good news,' I say, genuinely pleased to hear the positive prognosis.

Scott nods, and things go silent again, for a second longer than I'm comfortable with, and so I decide to jump straight in and address the elephant in the room.

'I'm really sorry,' I blurt out.

'What for?' says Scott, baffled by my apology.

'For everything. For lying to you for so long and making up that whole story about Steve and the army. I've been so worried about you, and you've hardly been in touch, and I was sure it was because you must hate me. If I hadn't lied, we wouldn't have rowed, and you wouldn't have—'

'Lyd, I could never hate you,' says Scott, interrupting my emotional rambling.

'You don't hate me?' I ask, needing clear confirmation.

'Of course not,' he says, shaking his head in disbelief, as if horrified I should obtain such an idea. 'I'm sorry I wasn't in touch. It's just been a lot with the op and overload of information from doctors and my mum's been here keeping a bedside vigil as if I've got minutes to live,' says Scott with an eye roll and a small chuckle.

'I've really missed you,' he adds.

He smiles warmly at me, the kind of easy loving smile that reassures me everything is going to be okay, and all my pent-up worries of the last few days miraculously vanish. Maybe I shouldn't have underestimated the power of a few days spent apart. Maybe it's given Scott the time he needs to think things over, to gain some perspective on things between us.

'I've missed you too,' I say.

Scott offers me his hand, and just as I'm about to place my hand safely inside his, springing from nowhere, a toddler with sunshine-blonde hair comes bounding in and climbs onto the bed, her sudden presence scaring the life out of me.

'Lola! What are you doing back here?' says Scott, the shock in his voice clear as the excitable little girl I recognise from downstairs wraps her arms around Scott.

'She waited until we got into the station to tell me she left Candy Floss here,' says a female voice I instantly recognise.

I turn to see Lacey bending to the floor at the foot of Scott's bed and retrieving from under it a grubby-looking pink unicorn soft toy.

'Lydia?' Spotting me from behind the curtain, Lacey says my name as if it's a question. She holds eye contact with me, as if equally dumbfounded.

'You know each other?' asks Scott.

'Lydia's one of my group members,' replies Lacey, her eyes still fixed on me. 'How do you two know each other?' she asks me, taking the words right out of my mouth, for I would like her to answer me the exact same question.

Lacey glares at me, making me feel small and uneasy, and although I'm confident I've not done anything wrong, I freeze, sensing something is very, *very* wrong indeed.

Before I have a chance to answer, Scott jumps in.

'Lydia was the person who called the ambulance, she works at the pub,' he says, answering on my behalf, and making sure to give

Lacey the answer he wants her to hear.

'Right ... small world,' says Lacey, finally pulling her death stare away from me, a small disingenuous smile pulling at her lips.

I wonder if maybe I'm overthinking things. Lacey said she was here visiting her husband. Maybe her husband is elsewhere? Maybe he's residing in one of the empty beds? Maybe the unicorn just happened to slip under Scott's bed by mistake?

'You shouldn't have come all the way back for that. I would have brought it home tomorrow,' says Scott.

Home. Home!

The word screeches through my ears like a car alarm. Scott confirming that *home* is in fact a life he shares with these two people before me. A wife and a daughter I had absolutely no idea existed until this moment.

I look at Scott, his arms wrapped around Lola, her little body tucked comfortably into his as she enjoys a cuddle from her dad, while my mind is racing with a million different questions. Scott looks completely at ease, his cool and collected manner making me wonder just how experienced he is at lying to his family.

'Yeah, well she won't sleep without it, you know that,' says Lacey, the familiar chit- chat between them more than I can bear.

Wanting nothing more than to get the hell out of here, I finally find my voice.

'Maybe I should get going,' I say, trying and failing to climb to my feet, my shocked body unable to move, and I wonder in that moment if I am in fact having some kind of out of body experience, the whole situation so surreal.

'No, stay, you've come all this way ... with your fruit basket,' says Lacey, eyeing it up as if it has personally wronged her. I get the distinct feeling that if earlier she had known the hamper's intended destination, she would have happily let it crash to the ground.

'Come on, Lola, say goodbye to Daddy, it's time to go,' orders Lacey, and I find it beyond strange Lacey should grant me her permission to stay.

Maybe she does believe I am just the girl from the pub?

I honestly have no idea what is going on or what to think.

I watch as Lola and Scott bid each other goodbye. Lacey offers her hand to Lola, helping her from the bed.

Lola jumps down and stands before me. She looks at me with hazel eyes that I can now see are just like her dad's, the sight of them confirming everything. She smiles at me, and I feel my heart break, she having no idea of the kind of man her father is.

'I'll see you tomorrow,' Lacey says to Scott.

And just in case I'm still in any kind of doubt as to who Lacey and Scott are to each other, Lacey leans over the bed and kisses Scott goodbye. It's not a quick peck, but a full-on kiss. Their eyes closed, her hand stroking his face, her diamond engagement ring and her wedding ring gleaming at me, taunting me, the sight of them as good as a kick in the gut. Lacey sensually presses her lips to Scott's in such a way that I begin to feel uncomfortable. I look away, worried she might be about to slip in her tongue, the spectacle nothing short of sickening, Lacey firmly marking her territory for me to see.

Finally, she pulls herself away from Scott, takes Lola's hand, and without offering me anything in the form of a courteous goodbye walks straight past me and exits the ward.

I sit silently in the visitor's chair, unable to comprehend what has just happened.

'Lyd ... Lyd ...'

I hear my name, it taking me a few seconds to register that it's Scott speaking to me, his voice bringing me back from what felt like some state of hypnosis.

'I'm so sorry. I know what you're thinking,' I hear him say, a note of panic in his voice.

'You have no idea what I'm thinking,' I utter, unable to look at him, worried if I do I might actually hit him.

'It's not what it looks like,' says Scott.

'Are you taking the piss? Just how stupid do you think I am?' I laugh, absolutely flabbergasted Scott should try and brush off what's just happened as a simple misunderstanding.

I turn to look at him. There's an angst on his face, the ease he seemed to have possessed only a few moments ago vanished.

'You're *married*. You're married with a kid, and you didn't think to mention that!' I say, my voice becoming raised, my anger beginning to surface, and I'm not sure if I'm more angry with Scott, or with myself for being so unbelievably stupid.

'Things between us have been bad for ages. It's been awful. We sleep in separate rooms. We haven't even had sex since before Lola was born,' says Scott, starting to lose his cool. He places a hand on his head like I saw him do the night he got hit by the car, the tension starting to get to him.

'Oh well! I'm so happy I could be of service!' I yell, every word coming out of his mouth angering me further.

Scott covers his face with his hand, realising his explanation probably didn't come off as well as he had hoped.

I notice the middle-aged man who smiled at me on entry glance over. He looks annoyed as he climbs from his chair and hastily leaves the ward, our raised voices starting to cause a scene and a nuisance to others.

'It's not as if I'm the only one that's been dishonest,' Scott hisses at me, throwing my own shortcomings back in my face.

'Fuck you!' I hiss back. 'I might have lied, but I lied about something awful that happened to me that I didn't want to be defined by— '

'Exactly. That's *exactly* what I'm saying. Just give me a chance to explain,' says Scott, raising his voice, desperate to make me see his point, but I'm not interested, unable to comprehend any viable way for him to explain his way out of this.

Too angry to sit by a moment longer, I stand from my chair.

'No, there's no way this is the same. I might have fudged the details a little, but the bottom line remains the same. My husband did die, and I am a widow. You have a wife and a child! You're leading a double fucking life!' I scream, no longer able to suppress my anger and humiliation, beyond caring who can hear me or who I might be disturbing.

'I'm going to have to ask you to leave. You're upsetting the other patients.'

We each turn to see a nurse standing at the end of Scott's bed, addressing me with steely eyes and a no-nonsense manner, her presence I'm sure the result of the middle-aged man reporting us.

'Don't worry, I'm going,' I tell her.

I pick up my fruit hamper, Scott no longer deserving of my efforts or its expense. I turn my back on him and storm past the nurse.

'No, Lyd, please don't leave. Not like this. Just let me explain. We can sort this,' pleads Scott, unable to chase after me with his broken leg.

I turn round to look at him. He looks sad,

pathetic even. A look of pleading devastation etched onto his reddening face as if he's desperate for us not to part ways so bitterly. In any other circumstance I might feel sorry for him, but right now the only thing I feel is undiluted anger.

'I already had my own lying husband. What makes you think I want someone else's?' I tell him before turning on my heels and walking away.

I hastily walk back the way I came, past the nurses' station and the other bays until I make it to the double doors at the ward's entrance. I hit the large green exit button, swing open the door and step into the main corridor and before the door has even had a chance to swing shut behind me, I break down.

There are plenty of people milling around, but I'm in too much emotional turmoil to care. With my fruit hamper held securely in my arms, I collapse to my knees and cry my heart out right there on the floor in front of all to see. Everyone around me carries on with their own affairs, looking on, but not stopping to ask if I'm okay, for I'm just another in a long line of visitors to this building to receive devastating news.

I'm sitting alone on a wooden bench outside Tower Hill Station, people going about their business all around me, heading to and from the busy underground station blissfully unaware of the trauma I've endured today. I've spent the past hour aimlessly walking the streets of London with no destination in mind. I made a stop at a newsagent and finally succumbed to the urge to buy a packet of cigarettes and a lighter, desperately needing some kind of relief from my troubles.

Once I saw the recognisable sight of the Tower of London, me and my fruit hamper decided to take a seat and light up. The mere sight of the popular attraction evokes such bitter-sweet memories. The last time I took in its view was only a few weeks ago, on a roof terrace with a man who it turns out I never really knew at all.

The sky above me is starting to grey and a strong breeze is blowing through my hair and over my face but I welcome the cold blast of air, finding it refreshing after another day of unexpected events.

I have no idea what to do now, my body unable to do anything other than sit and stare aimlessly into the space in front of me as I puff away on my cigarette. I feel so alone, not to mention so incredibly foolish. I suddenly feel the all too familiar sensation of tears forming in my eyes and I quickly wipe them away with the back of my hand.

I can feel my nose beginning to run and so I open up my handbag resting on my lap in search of a tissue. As I rustle through my bag I start to feel my phone vibrating. I pull it out from where it's buried at the bottom and see it's Nick calling.

How did he know? I wonder.

How did he know that I need him near; to hear his voice and feel the kind of familiarity that I will never find in any other form.

I swipe the screen to answer.

'Hiya' I say, my voice tight and strained as I try and compose myself, wiping the tears away from my face.

'All right, sis,' I hear faintly over the sound of the busy traffic. 'You okay?' he asks, and I can hear a concern in his voice.

'Yeah, yeah, I'm good,' I say as convincingly as I can. 'You okay?' I ask, and take another pull from my cigarette.

'Guess what?' says Nick, and I can hear the bubbling excitement in his voice.

'What?' I ask.

'It's a girl. We're having a girl!' he announces, and I don't think ever in my life I've heard Nick sound as happy as he does right now.

'Wow, Nick. Congratulations. I'm so happy for you both. A girl!' I say, tears falling from my eyes, feeling resentful that such a moment between me and my brother is marred by my own sadness.

'But how are you? How's things?' Nick asks.

'Yeah, all good,' I say, not wanting to burden him with my troubles on what is such a wonderful day for him. 'Tell me more about you. You're having a girl. How're you feeling?' I ask, just wanting him to carry on talking to me so I can just listen while I sit anonymously on a bench in a busy London street. The sound of my little git of a brother's voice never feeling more comforting than it does right now.

CHAPTER 31

Exhausted, I finally switch off the lights and gently patter over to my bed in the dark. I lift the duvet and climb in under it, resting my heavy head on my pillow. I close my eyes and I feel them burn, the result of hours of constant crying.

I lie silently in the solitary darkness of my flat when my sleepy state is interrupted by the sound of an almighty crash. My eyes flash wide open and I spring out of my bed and run towards my large window.

I look down at the dimly lit high street below and I see a white Porsche 911 with a black soft top, just like the one Steve used to own, has crashed through the glass shop window of the all-night mini supermarket on the opposite side of the road. The lights are still on in the shop with the whole front of the car wedged inside it. I can make out the damaged shelves, their contents of tins and jars of food all crashed down onto the floor.

Wearing nothing more than a pair of pink knickers and a plain white bra I turn on my heels and run straight towards my front door.

Unconcerned about my half-naked state, I run down the stairs towards the street door, opening it in a hurry, and with no shoes on my feet I run across the road towards the white Porsche. I can hear the continual sound of the horn and I can see the car's back red brake-lights flashing on and off.

I run towards the front of the car, keeping my head down, watching my bare feet treading on the thousands of small pieces of shattered glass. When I reach the driver's door I look through the window and sitting upright in the driver's seat is Steve.

He looks immaculate without a single scratch or a single hair out of place, dressed in one of his smart work suits, the top two buttons of his shirt undone. I lean forward trying to get a closer look at his face through the window. Steve is laughing hysterically with tears of sheer happiness streaming down his cheeks.

I bang on the window with a clenched fist, trying to get his attention.

'Steve! Steve! Get out of the car!' I yell at him, but Steve simply ignores my pleas and makes no effort to move from his position.

I pull myself away from the window and I look around, desperately trying to find some help, when I notice a body lying on the pavement, just outside the shop window. I lean down to take a closer look. It's definitely a man, his face a mess, covered in deep bloody cuts and scratches, the eyes closed. I squint, trying to bring his face into focus, when I suddenly realise that the lifeless body lying in front of me is Scott's.

I feel a tightness in my chest, I try to scream for help, but no noise comes out and it's then I open my eyes.

I shoot up from my bed in the darkness of my flat. My body following its usual routine with my heart racing and my entire body dripping in sweat. I kick the duvet from my legs and hurry over to the large window, taking a look down at the deserted dark high street below.

I look over at the all-night mini supermarket to see its shop front perfectly intact, its lights on and all its shop shelves exactly where they should be, and breathe a deep sigh of relief. I turn away from the window and slowly make my way back to my bed. I lie back down on top of the messy duvet, looking up at the ceiling into the darkness, feeling concerned at how much trauma is embedded into my subconscious.

I close my eyes again and wait for my body to calm down, hoping to eventually fall back to sleep.

I never did get back to sleep last night. Once awake I lay in bed thinking everything over again and again from around 3 a.m. onwards. Needless to say I feel exhausted. The only plausible way of spending my day I could think of was to head to Ruth's, and offload all the horrible details of yesterday while slumped back on her sofa.

'Wow, and you really had no idea he was married?' asks Ruth, shaking her head in disbelief. She takes a sip from her mug of coffee.

'No, I really didn't ... but now it all makes sense. How I never went to his place and how he wasn't in touch after the accident. I figured it was because he was angry with me, but now I know—
'

'It's because his wife was around,' says Ruth, finishing my sentence for me.

I nod, unable to fathom how I could have been so naive.

'Eurgh, Ruth, you should have seen the way she kissed him goodbye. It was so ... *primitive.* Honestly, she might as well have just peed all over him.'

I drop my tired head in my hands and close my eyes, my mind flashing back to that moment. The very thought of anyone else kissing Scott's lips making me feel sick with jealousy.

'Do you think she knows?' asks Ruth.

'I really don't know ... possibly ... maybe ... surely not,' I say, exhausted by the torturous stream of constant questions running through my brain. 'She didn't accuse either of us of anything. Because you would, wouldn't you? If you thought the woman sitting there with a fruit basket was banging your husband ... you'd say something, surely? I know I would,' I say, trying to rationalise every minute detail.

'Maybe he's got form? Maybe he's done this to her a lot and it's something she just accepts,' says Ruth, her words resting uneasily with me.

As if the idea of being Scott's bit on the side wasn't awful enough, the idea of being one in a long line of extra-marital conquests is too much to bear, and not a possibility I'm willing to accept.

'No. No, that can't be. When we were together, it was never just about sex. It was deeper than that.'

Ruth glares as if I'm trying to convince her the sky's green, clearly disturbed by my naivety.

'The guy's a scumbag,' says Ruth in no uncertain terms. I know she's being a good friend in looking out for me, but I feel offended by her insult to Scott's character.

'He really isn't. He was sweet and kind and when we were together, it was always so—'

'Shit, Lyd. You're not seriously defending him, are you?'

Maybe I am defending Scott. Maybe because I know, as angry and hurt as I am, it doesn't take away the feelings I have for him. I purse my lips and shrug my shoulders, unable to find the correct response to say out loud.

'Lyd, no, come on. He was lying to you the whole time!' Ruth places her mug down on the coffee table in front of us, and looks me in the eye with a serious expression, trying her best to make me see sense.

'I know, but I lied too.'

'True ... I don't know what to tell you, Lyd ... maybe it's for the best. It seems to me neither of you were ready for whatever it was between you.'

'Maybe ... but that doesn't really make me feel any better. I just ... why? Why does it hurt so much? We weren't even together for that long,' I say, rubbing my forehead in frustration, annoyed that I allowed myself to fall so hard for Scott in the first place.

'What are you going to do about Suicide Club?' Ruth asks sympathetically, knowing that Suicide Club was something I was beginning to enjoy.

'There's absolutely no way I can show my face there again.'

'Good, correct answer,' says Ruth, satisfied I've given at least one appropriate response to my issues, just as the doorbell bing-bongs through the house.

'I'm sure there's another one you can join. I'll help you look,' says Ruth, rising from the sofa and heading towards the front door.

While Ruth answers the door I sit silently on the sofa and begin to fidget with my wedding and engagement rings, twisting them around my finger. I've sat here, in this very spot, hundreds of times; drinking coffee, or wine. We've laughed and put the world to rights. We've talked about TV shows and make-up. We've bitched, moaned and occasionally we've cried, but never do I remember, in all those times, the conversation being quite as heavy and sad as it's been these past few months. I miss those days, when life was so much easier and subject matter was so much lighter.

I hear the front door close and look up at Ruth who's heading back to the sofa with a small plate in her hand, a loose piece of kitchen towel covering the top.

'Who was that?' I ask.

'Stacey and Olivia,' says Ruth, and I notice a certain reluctance in her tone.

'Who?'

'They live next door,' says Ruth.

Translation: *The people who bought your old home and now live out your previous life.*

The sale of our old home was such an incredibly painful experience, I've consciously never asked Ruth a single thing about her new neighbours, unable to bear the thought of someone else living in my lovely home.

'What are they like?' I ask, curiosity finally getting the better of me, sure my heart has endured enough pain it's now numb to any further hurt.

'Oh, a vast improvement on the previous neighbours. They never brought me cake,' says Ruth, sitting back down on the sofa and lifting the piece of kitchen towel to reveal four haphazardly decorated fairy cakes, smothered in icing and colourful sprinkles.

'They bring you cake!' I say with a small chuckle.

'It's little Oliva. She's four and likes to bake,' says Ruth, picking up a cake from the plate and handing it to me.

'But don't worry, you're still my favourite. The cakes are sweet, but they're not a patch on your drunken barbecues,' Ruth reassures me.

'The chicken was as red as the sangria!' I say with a small laugh, casting my mind back to a happier time.

'Ha, we're lucky any of us lived to tell the tale!' laughs Ruth, and I sense a small hint of sadness in her voice as we reminisce over a bygone era.

I take a bite from my cake; a cake that was baked in my old oven, in my old kitchen, in my old house, where I lived out my old happy life back in a time where I could never have imagined feeling the gut-wrenching level of hurt and pain I feel right now.

CHAPTER 32

Larry is by far our pub's most dreaded customer. Every day he swings by, around 6 p.m., orders half a pint of bitter and proceeds to give to whichever one of us is unlucky enough to serve him the most detailed account on the most boring subject imaginable to man. These subjects have ranged from fuse boxes, wallpaper, even filing cabinets.

Unfortunately, today it's my turn to be granted the misfortune of serving Larry, who is currently in full flow about his garage door. Usually such a scenario would send me into a deep state of boredom-induced hypnosis, but today even Larry can't bring me down.

In a few short minutes from now, I will be clocking off, heading home and packing my bags ahead of a fun-filled weekend in Brighton. Tomorrow morning Ruth and I will be boarding a train to visit Gavin and I simply can't wait to get events underway.

In the whole time I've been working at the pub, this is the very first time I've been granted a full two-day weekend.

Ruth thinks the sea air will do me good, and I think she's right, a change of scenery being long overdue, even if it is only for one night.

I smile politely at Larry, making sure to 'oh' and 'ah' in all the right places, not allowing the ungodly boredom to dampen my mood.

'Lydia girl, ain't you meant to be making tracks now? You don't wanna miss your train,' says Jon, a little louder than necessary, causing Larry to stop mid-flow.

'Oh, I'm not leaving until ...' I reply, to which Jon holds eye contact with me, urging me not to say any more, not to expose myself and trap myself back into the torture that is a conversation with Larry.

'Right ... yes, sorry, Larry, I'd better be heading off now,' I say, stepping away slowly but eagerly.

'I'll leave you to get on,' says Larry with a nod, before turning to seek out another unwilling victim.

'Go on, girl, you get off,' says Jon, and with that short sentence my weekend has officially begun.

With a spring in my step, I waste no time in heading out the back to gather my things. I return to the bar with my jacket on and my bag over my shoulder, ready to say my goodbyes.

'Right. I will see you on Monday,' I say gleefully, lifting the bar top. 'Don't miss me too much!'

'I shall be counting down the days!' says Jon, followed by a small chuckle.

'Are you leaving?'

The familiar-sounding voice from behind me makes me stop dead in my tracks. I close my eyes. I feel pure elation that he's near but also dread, worried this encounter could become heated.

I turn round and face Scott.

It's been almost two months since I last laid eyes on him and just the sight of him takes my breath away. I find myself feeling coy and unsure as to what to say.

He's dressed casually in shorts and a comfy-looking black hoody but still looks so unbelievably handsome. Even with the addition of a pair of crutches and a black leg-support boot, the only things to suggest there could be anything remotely wrong with him.

My heart absolutely aches for him, for the closeness we shared, for the ease and happiness I felt when he was near. I miss him, more than I could ever have imagined. However, all the longing I have for him sits in a part of my heart that is bruised and crushed by sadness; I'm unable to fathom how somebody who seemed so wonderful could cause me such hurt and humiliation. The conflicting emotions constantly plague my mind, keeping me awake at night as I toss and turn, overthinking every tiny detail of our time together, wondering if there were signs that I missed that could have saved me from all the heartache.

'You sure you should be here, son?' says Jon, his words spoken sternly as he stares daggers at

Scott.

Scott shifts awkwardly on his crutches, having maybe not expected such a hostile reception.

'How are you?' Scott asks me, which I think to be a ridiculous question.

What does he want me to say? That I'm totally heartbroken? That every single day it takes me all my strength not to break down and sob just at the very thought of him?

'What do you want?' I ask nonchalantly, doing my best to mask any signs of emotion.

'You never replied to any of my messages,' says Scott, referring to the many messages I have received from him over the past two months, all of which have taken a hell of a lot of will power to ignore.

'That's generally how break-ups work. The ceasing of all contact is pretty standard,' I say, as if to remind Scott of a blinding fact he's overlooked.

'You want me to get rid of him?' says Jon, making his way out from behind the bar, keeping his gaze firmly on Scott.

'I don't want any trouble,' says Scott.

'Cos I will. I'll march him out that door before he knows what's hit him,' says Jon, now standing next to me and meaning business, ready to spring into action on my command.

'It's fine,' I say, greatly appreciative of the gesture, but not feeling the need to cause a scene.

'I just want to talk,' says Scott, looking at me, a

longing in his voice.

I stand silently, unsure how to react.

I have so many unanswered questions as I'm sure he does too. Although I don't believe he's worthy of my time, I wonder if a chance to talk things through could heal some wounds, or at least help me get a good night's sleep, the opportunity to talk things through not being one I had with Steve, and I would give anything to have had that.

'Please?' says Scott, a pleading in his eyes reminiscent of the last time I saw him. Pleading with me not to leave, to let him explain.

'Fine,' I say, 'But not here.'

I hear Jon sigh, disappointed I should be so easy on Scott in light of everything that's happened.

'We can go to yours. My car's outside,' suggests Scott, eager to speak in a more private setting.

'Can you drive?' I question, looking down at the crutches and giant black boot.

'Yeah, it's an automatic. It's fine.'

'You can drop me home and we'll talk in the car. That's my best offer,' I say sternly, happy to take advantage of a lift, but unwilling to offer a warm welcome into my home, finding it a liberty he should make such a suggestion.

I turn to Jon and smile, grateful for his protective nature. He smiles back at me and rolls his eyes. Shaking his head gently he heads back behind the bar.

I walk out of the pub ahead of Scott, waiting for him to catch up on his crutches.

I'm sitting silently in the front passenger seat of Scott's car, keeping my gaze on the windscreen wipers moving up and down, wiping away the rain relentlessly beating down on the glass.

We've only been in the car a short while and neither of us has spoken a single word. I'm conscious the journey home won't take all that long, and at this rate we're going to be back at mine having got nowhere further forward with one another; so I take it upon myself to cut through the stagnant silence festering between us.

'Where does your wife think you are?' I ask, my words laced with a bitterness I'm unable to mask.

'She's away for the weekend. Gone on a trip to the country with Lola and some mum friends.'

'Are you okay on your own?' I ask sympathetically, looking down at Scott's leg, thinking it a little cruel to leave someone in his condition all alone for days.

'I'm getting around a lot easier now. And … I think we're both happy to have some time apart,' explains Scott, revealing little in the way of detail, but giving the impression of some unease at home.

Looking back out the windscreen I question whether what he's just said is even true, wondering if I can trust anything that comes out of his mouth. Another awkward silence hangs between us, our meeting so far not proving to be particularly fruitful.

We're only a few short minutes away from mine. With none of my questions answered and Scott offering up very little in the way of an explanation, I decide to be bold, forcing myself to speak up in my quest for some answers.

'Does she know? About me ... about us?' I ask, unsure I'm emotionally prepared to hear the answer.

'I don't think so,' says Scott, not exactly exuding confidence. He keeps his focus on the road ahead, giving me the distinct feeling he's happy to use our drive as a distraction from having to look directly at me.

'I feel awful,' says Scott, rubbing his hand over his face, a look of angst washing over him, his words sparking anger in me.

'*You* feel awful! Well, take that feeling and times it by fifty, and then you might just be able to comprehend how fucking awful *I* feel,' I snap, not in the mood to hear how hard done by Scott feels by this situation.

He doesn't react, instead we revert back to silence. Internally seething I stare back through the windscreen.

We arrive outside my flat; and I feel regretful that we've managed to resolve precisely nothing, our meeting leaving me feeling even worse, if that's even possible.

Scott pulls the car into a tight parking space. I release my seatbelt and just as I'm about to reach for the door handle ready to vacate the car and this dire situation, Scott speaks.

'I've known her for years. She's the sister of my mate Gaz.'

I presume 'she' is his wife. I pause my exit, allowing myself to relax slightly back in my seat, intrigued to hear what Scott has to say.

'A few years ago, we started seeing each other ... and about a month later she fell pregnant with Lola. It wasn't planned, but we were excited and I dunno, we'd already known each other for such a long time, we both figured maybe it was fate or something stupid,' says Scott, shaking his head in dismay.

'A few months before Lola was born we got married and very soon afterwards we realised we'd made a huge mistake. It was so rushed and the truth is we really didn't know each other as well as we thought we did. But by then we'd bought our place together and we had this little baby ... what were we meant to do?'

I watch Scott anxiously rub the back of his neck, frustration overcoming him as he explains a set of circumstances I had absolutely no idea about, the man before me as good as a stranger.

'We sleep in separate bedrooms, we have done for years. I think we unofficially broke up ages ago, but neither of us can afford to move out, so we just take care of Lola between us and do our best to avoid each other,' says Scott. He turns to look at me. His cheeks look red and flushed, his face displaying a look of sadness I've never seen from him before.

I stay silent, digesting everything Scott's just told me. The unplanned pregnancy, the loveless marriage. Everything so raw and convincing, but then I see it, once again, in my mind's eye, just like I've seen it a million times over and over again. That kiss. The kiss Lacey planted on Scott's lips from his hospital bed. The sight of which has been haunting me for weeks.

'That kiss. That wasn't the kiss of two people who hate each other,' I say, my voice quiet.

Scott shakes his head, as if to dismiss my witness account.

'It was the accident, the shock. She said she wanted us to start over ...'

'Have you slept together?' I ask, the question tripping out of my mouth, it nothing short of ridiculous. Why should it be any of my business if a husband and wife have slept together; but I have to know. I have to know if there was any part of him, of our relationship, that was sacred, that belonged to just us.

'No, I swear ... we can't fake what's not there. Things are already back to how they were.'

I breathe a sigh of relief, feeling to have won some kind of small victory. Feeling some kind of reassurance that not every piece of him has been shared with someone else.

'The way I feel when I'm with you, Lyd, it was never like that with her,' says Scott, looking into my eyes as he places his hand on mine resting on my leg. The sheer feel of him, even in such a minor way, sending a rush of feeling through my body, making me realise how much I've so desperately missed him.

'Why didn't you tell me you were married?' I ask, rubbing my forehead, this conversation nothing short of agonising.

'I'm not the only one that lied,' Scott says softly, as if the lies told between us cancel each other out.

'I never omitted the existence of anyone else. I never lied about *who I* was,' I say, unable to hide my upset, my voice raised slightly.

'Nor did I.'

I roll my eyes and scoff a laugh at Scott's comeback.

'You're someone's husband. That's who you are,' I say, as if to remind him of such.

'I'm still me, Lyd,' he says softly. 'I never meant to hurt you. And I know you're angry with me, but you have to believe me when I say I am so, so sorry.'

I look into his sorry eyes so full of remorse and guilt, and as hurt and angry as I am, I feel my defences begin to slide away.

'I miss you so much. I can't stop thinking about you,' he says as he reaches his hand to my face and strokes my cheek, and I can't deny how much I miss him, my body and soul pining to be near him.

'I miss you too,' I utter, unable to hide how I feel.

Scott moves in closer and places his lips on mine, kissing me softly. I move my body closer to his, placing one hand on his firm chest, the other on the stubble on his face.

Our kissing quickly becomes passionate, our tongues intertwining, our hands wandering, and in that moment it's as if nothing ever happened. As if we were back to where we were. In a state of passion and sheer happiness, wanting and needing nothing more than one another.

I feel Scott's hand drift up past my hip and waist, wandering its way underneath my breast, his open hand caressing my body through my clothes. Unable to resist the feelings he so easily ignites inside me I pull my lips away from his. I look at him and smile, and without saying a single word I reach for the door handle and climb out of the car.

In the pouring rain I trot along the pavement to my street door. Searching for my keys, I open the door as quickly as I can and head inside, leaving the street door wide open behind me, offering Scott a silent invitation to join me.

I sit on the edge of my bed and kick off my

shoes. I've only been in the flat a few seconds when I hear the street door close, followed by the clanking sound of Scott's crutches on the stairs.

As the sound gets ever closer, I look up, and to my relief I see Scott has followed me in. He closes the front door behind him, leaves the crutches by the door and with a slight limp in his step walks slowly over to me, taking a seat next to me on the edge of the bed. Our lips frantically meet each other's once again with our mouths opening and our tongues meeting. My hands instantly gravitate towards the bottom of Scott's sweatshirt, pulling it off over his head and discarding it on the floor.

I run my hands over his flat broad chest as he places one hand into my hair and the other on my waist. That hand soon drifts its way up to my boob, cupping it and massaging it through my top.

'I've missed you so much, baby,' he whispers, his voice soft and breathy.

'I've missed you too,' I respond, stroking his short hair as he begins to kiss along my neck.

I move my hands down Scott's chest, while his hands move towards the button on my jeans, and it's then a worrying thought enters my mind.

'Oh shit!' I say, a little louder than I'd intended.

Scott pulls away and looks into my face.

'What's wrong?' he asks, concerned.

'No, nothing,' I say, shaking my head. 'It's just ... I haven't shaved my legs in like four days,' I say, squirming at my confession.

'That's okay, neither have I,' chuckles Scott, banishing my feelings of discomfort, then kissing me on the lips while unbuttoning my jeans with ease.

I lift myself from the bed and stand myself between Scott's legs. Keeping my gaze firmly fixed on his I reach for the bottom of my top, pulling it over my head and dropping it to the floor, before slowly pulling down my jeans, taking my underwear with them, leaving everything on the floor by my feet. Standing before Scott in just a bra and no knickers, I notice the wide grin spread across his face. He reaches into the pocket of his shorts, pulling from it his wallet. Opening his wallet, he takes from it a red foil packet.

He places the wallet back in his pocket and makes to take off his shorts, lifting himself slightly and shuffling awkwardly, the hindrance of his damaged leg turning a simple seductive manoeuvre into something quite comical.

A small giggle falls from my mouth. I gently take the foil packet from him and still standing between Scott's legs, I place my hands on the waist of his shorts and along with his boxers manage to roll them down over his legs and giant boot, until they reach the floor.

With his cock already rock hard, I unwrap the condom and delicately roll it all the way down him. Scott runs his hands along my hips and my waist. I lower my face to his and we kiss passionately as Scott's hands wander over me. Reaching my vagina he places a finger inside me, my yearning for him obvious.

'How are we going to do this?' I say quietly, referring to Scott's damaged leg, and anxious not to damage him any further.

Scott slowly pulls his fingers from inside me and places a hand either side of my waist. Aligning my body with his I climb onto Scott's lap, straddling a leg either side of his waist. I place a hand around his cock, and guide it into me, burying it inside me as I lower myself down onto him.

We both groan out loud in the pleasure of each other as I begin to slowly rock myself on his lap, while Scott keeps a tight grip on either side of the lowest point of my hips, pushing me back slightly and guiding my rhythm.

To have him inside me feels amazing, as if a missing piece of me has finally been put back in its rightful place.

As my rhythm picks up pace, I wrap my hands around the back of Scott's head, pulling his face into mine, us kissing open-mouthed. I continue to bounce on his lap, my mind solely focused on the sheer pleasure of having him deep inside me. I feel Scott's hand wander up towards my bra. He pulls back the cup, freeing my breast, he cups it in his hand and places my nipple in his mouth, pleasuring me even further.

I soon feel myself building, the intense sensation of pleasure igniting my entire body. Knowing I'm about to climax, Scott moves his mouth to mine to kiss me. I move even faster as I pant and groan loudly, my body tensing. I grip Scott's arm tightly as I feel myself come, letting sheer pleasure release itself from my body.

I feel Scott's fingers gently trail a soft line from the very top of my neck, all the way down to the very base of my spine, the sensation making my skin tingle. I feel myself begin to relax, but before my body has a chance to slump down on top of his, Scott makes a grab for my hips and pushes me back slightly, using his hands to keep me rocking on him for a few moments longer. Moving his head, resting his cheek against mine, he calls out into my ear as he climaxes under me. 'Yes, Lyd! Yes, yes!' His hands stay on my hips while my rocking comes to a stop, allowing me to relax on top of him completely, burying my head into the area between his neck and shoulder.

Scott rests his head on my shoulder and I loosen my grip on his arm and wrap both my arms round his broad back, both of us waiting for our bodies to wind down before moving.

Scott kisses me softly on my neck.

'You okay?' he asks, his voice hoarse and breathy.

I lift my head and look into his eyes. I smile and nod, to which Scott responds with a smile of his own and kisses me on the lips. I gently lift myself from him as Scott swiftly removes his condom.

I decide to make myself comfortable and climb into the bed as Scott slowly limps his way into my bathroom.

He quickly returns and hobbles over to the bed, joining me under the covers. Scott lies next to me, and we cuddle into each other. I lay my head on his chest and gently brush my fingers through his chest hair. Scott wraps his arm around me and I feel him trail lines along the top of my arm with his fingertips.

Unsure as to what our encounter means, I feel an overpowering need to address what has just happened.

'So, what now?' I ask quietly.

Scott doesn't answer straight away, his failure to respond making me feel anxious.

'I already know what I want, Lyd,' Scott finally replies, his tone very matter-of-fact.

'I think you want to have your cake and eat it,' I reply, rolling my eyes at Scott's feeble answer.

'It won't be like this for ever.'

I sit up and look into Scott's face.

'But in the meantime you'll come here, fuck me, then return home to your family,' I say, my tone stroppy.

'No, it won't be like that ...I know it's not ideal,' Scott responds calmly.

I let out a deep breath, feeling frustrated with him, knowing that he has no actual concrete plan for any kind of real future together.

'You know what, Scott, I really don't want to get into this right now,' I rant, brushing my hand through my hair and climbing out of the bed, making it clear that I'm ready to wrap up this topic of conversation.

I turn to my chest of drawers next to my bed and pull the top drawer open heavy-handedly, unable to hide how pissed off I am. I pull out one of Steve's old T-shirts that I still sleep in and I pull it on over my head.

'Do you want me to leave?' asks Scott, his voice hesitant.

I stand and look at him in my bed. I'm so incredibly frustrated with him and not to mention angry with myself, knowing that he is my weakness. Knowing that I may well be on the cusp of agreeing to an arrangement that I'm not entirely happy with, for it's better than the alternative, a life without him.

I so desperately don't want him to leave and so I force myself to calm down.

'No. That's not what I said,' I say, then turn back to my drawers to dig out some clothes to pack for tomorrow's trip to Brighton.

I see Scott relax, snuggling himself down into my bed, making himself comfortable while I faff around the room preparing to pack for my night away.

CHAPTER 33

It's the morning after the night before.

Scott and I are standing at my street door. Scott's dressed in the same clothes from last night and I'm back in Steve's old T-shirt and not much else. Scott pulls me in closer to him by my waist as we say our goodbyes.

Scott's departure from mine has been delayed due to some morning 'entertainment', but I'm now eager for him to get going before Ruth arrives ahead of our trip to Brighton.

The thought of him returning to his wife and child leaves me feeling incredibly uncomfortable, not to mention guilty considering all the 'activity' that has taken place in my flat over the past few hours.

'Have a good time this weekend,' says Scott, before placing his lips down on mine.

My natural response would be to wish Scott a good weekend too, but I can't bring myself to do so.

'Thanks,' I say, keeping my response short, swallowing down my urge to fire off some bitter comment.

Finally we release our hands from one another. I give Scott a short wave as I watch him walk slowly over to his car, crutches in tow.

Just as Scott climbs into his car I hear the gravelly sound of a wheelie suitcase being pulled along the pavement. I look to my left to see Ruth walking towards my street door and shaking her head. Judging by the look on her face there's no point in hoping that she hasn't just witnessed Scott's departure from my flat.

I gently lean my head back, resting it on the doorframe, knowing I've been busted.

I see from the corner of my eye Scott's car pull out of its parking space, at which Ruth and I both turn our heads and watch the car drive past us. Ruth lifts her hand to give Scott an enthusiastic wave and I see Scott through the passenger window lift a hand from the steering wheel, acknowledging Ruth with a much less enthusiastic wave back.

Ruth and I stand and watch the car drive away until it's out of view completely.

'Dare I ask?' says Ruth, turning to me and arching her eyebrows.

I don't say a word, just stand there.

'Hmm, save it for the train!' says Ruth, walking past me and making her way up to my flat, clumsily dragging her suitcase behind her, whacking it heavily on each stair she climbs.

Ruth and I are currently three hours into

the longest possible commute from London to Brighton that two people have ever undertaken. From my flat we walked to Seven Kings Station and rode the train to Stratford, then travelled one stop back to Mile End. We then jumped aboard a District Line train and got off at Victoria. From Victoria we were hoping to catch the train all the way through to Brighton. However, Southern Rail being the menace that it is, rail works have interrupted our journey, throwing us and our luggage off at a little-known station called Three Bridges and forcing us to use the rail replacement bus service for the last leg of our journey to the coast.

Ruth and I have been sitting downstairs on a packed bus with our cases awkwardly placed in front of us for almost an hour whilst crawling along the dual carriageway; our entrapment on the slow-moving bus providing Ruth with the perfect opportunity to grill me on last night.

'So, he's *not* going to leave his wife?'

'He isn't in a position to leave her right now,' I say, looking out of the passenger window behind Ruth's head at the grey cloudy sky above us. 'But he says he's just going along with things at home for Lola's sake. He says that it's me he wants to be with.'

'And you believe that?' asks Ruth, and I'm unsure if that's a genuine question or if she's trying to point out what an utter idiot I am.

'Honestly? I don't know what to believe, Ruth.

I just missed him so much and it was so good to be with him. I am starting to wonder if I should stick by him—'

'What, and be the other woman? Is that really what you want?'

'No, it's not what I want! But nothing that's happened to me this year has been what I wanted! I didn't want Steve to kill himself, I didn't want to sell my house. But maybe life isn't about what I want. Maybe life is just about working with what I have,' I rant, leaning my head back and looking up at the low bus ceiling, exhausted by this conversation and my own confused feelings about the whole sorry situation.

There's a pause in the conversation and I look back at Ruth who's searching my face, trying to find appropriate words of comfort, she knowing all too well how truly horrendous this year has been for me.

'Certainly, I think there's an element of truth in that for all of us. But someone else's husband, Lyd? That's not you. It's just ... I remember a Lydia who refused to settle for anything less than what she deserved.'

There's a tight feeling in my throat as I cast my mind back to my past self. The Lydia who was more than willing to take on the world and bang down any door to get what she wanted. That Lydia would have stayed strong and told Scott to jog on and not to bother her again until he got his shit together. I miss her, and I'm worried that she may be gone for good, leaving behind nothing but a weak pushover who'll settle for less than she deserves.

It's only once we finish talking that we realise the bus has left the dual carriageway, finally bringing us into the residential streets of Brighton.

'Oh I stayed there!' exclaims Ruth, looking out of the window.

I turn my head and all I can see through the window is a small café with a glass bus shelter in front of it.

'Where? What am I looking at?' I ask, confused.

'There, look!' says Ruth, pointing enthusiastically.

'All I can see is a bus shelter,' I say, my eyes frantically searching for a possible place of accommodation.

'Yeah yeah, that's where I stayed!'

'The bus shelter?' I confirm.

'Ha yeah. I was nineteen. Me and my old boyfriend Seamus. We came to a music festival in Brighton and missed the last train back to London. We and a load of others spent the night under the stars in that very bus shelter.'

I look at Ruth, her nostalgia for her romantic night 'under the stars' filling me with concern.

'So just to confirm, you have booked us a hotel, right? That's not where we're staying, is it?' I laugh, pointing at the window.

Ruth rolls her eyes at me and laughs.

'I'm really looking forward to this weekend. It's been so long since we've all been out. You, me, Gav, Cher, Kylie, Madonna.'

'Yeah, me too,' I say sincerely, ready more than ever before to let my hair down, forget my troubles and dance the night away with my friends.

CHAPTER 34

On finally reaching our destination, Ruth and I went straight to the hotel to dump our cases. We'll be catching up with Gavin later on tonight after his show, so in the meantime we've decided to head out into the town to check out all that Brighton has to offer!

We're currently wandering through The Lanes, which are essentially a maze of narrow streets and alleyways all lined with unique independent shops and boutiques, selling everything from clothes and chocolates to rubber ducks and military memorabilia, but above all jewellery. Like a couple of magpies, Ruth and I can't resist pressing our heads up against every jeweller's window we pass.

Ruth has fallen in love with one piece of jewellery in particular. On our way back she can't resist a second look at the necklace displayed in the window of a jeweller's named Narnia. The necklace has six separate diamond-encrusted white-gold, or possibly platinum, thin chains. Each chain hangs lower than the one above it, bathing the cream-coloured bust it sits upon in undeniable sparkle and glamour.

Ruth and I both note there is no price shown, leaving us with no choice but to guess the necklace's value.

'I'd say five thousand,' I say, tilting my head to one side.

'Oh no, I'd say more!' says Ruth, dismissing my guess.

'It's thirty-two thousand pounds,' says a cheeky voice to our left.

Ruth and I look round completely stunned and see a young skinny man with curly mousy hair and dressed in a light blue shirt and smart grey trousers standing in the shop's doorway.

'Thirty-two grand!' exclaims Ruth.

'Ha, afraid so. We do sell cheaper pieces, I promise! Come in,' says the young man, waving his hand to beckon us inside.

Ruth turns her head back to me, shrugs her shoulders and walks into the shop.

Ruth is soon in her element playing dress-up with the shop's expensive master pieces. We're the only customers in here as we stand at the long glass cabinet at the back of the shop with the young man and an older lady with a short harsh black bob haircut and thin rectangular glasses perched on her puffy lined face.

'So how much is this one?' asks Ruth, holding her right hand up and admiring the ring on her finger, a ring with one large mauve-coloured diamond surrounded by a circle of clear diamonds.

'That's five thousand,' answers the young man. 'But we also design bespoke pieces. So we could make you this same ring using cubic zirconia for a much cheaper price.'

'Ah cubic zirconia, a girl's second best friend!' says Ruth, causing all four of us in the shop to laugh.

'That's a beautiful piece you have there,' says the older lady, lifting my left hand from where it's resting on the glass cabinet and staring intently at my diamond engagement ring. 'Whoever gave you that must worship the ground you walk on,' she says.

I look down at my hand with my lips pursed and I wonder, what with all this talk of jewels and their value, how much my own possessions are worth.

'How much would you say it's worth?' I ask.

'Lyd! No, what are you doing?' says Ruth.

'Calm down. I'm just curious. Say, I don't know, what if my lovely husband was to die and leave me to fend all for myself, how much would you say these two together are worth?'

The lady lifts my hand to her face, and pushes her glasses back further on the bridge of her nose to take a long hard look at my rings.

'Two platinum rings, this one with three clear-cut diamonds ... I'd need a proper look at them if you wanted to sell them, but you've certainly got a couple of grand sitting on that finger of yours.'

'Hmm, interesting,' I say, nodding my head.

'You're a lucky girl,' says the lady, letting go of my hand.

'Oh, so lucky,' I say, and I see Ruth roll her eyes at me.

'I can't take her anywhere!' says Ruth, while twisting the five-grand ring off her finger.

The sun is hiding behind a heavy grey sky, but the temperature is mild. Ruth and I have had a ball wandering around Brighton all afternoon. Ruth is eager to head back to the hotel for a quick power nap before tonight's events, but I've managed to persuade her to stay out for a bit longer.

We're currently sitting al fresco at a small round table outside the cutest little tea shop on the corner of a busy parade of shops, drinking tea and sharing a generous slice of chocolate fudge cake. A very elderly man and woman are walking slowly hand in hand past our table. They're holding on tightly to each other, guiding each other carefully along the wide cobbled walkway of the busy pedestrian-only street, both wearing thick winter jackets on a mild day. Then I see two men, possibly in their late twenties or early thirties, dressed as two of the four Beatles in Sergeant Pepper fancy-dress costumes, one in a red sergeant's suit, the other in a bright yellow one. They're both wearing thick stick-on moustaches and have dark floppy-haired wigs on their heads. They're walking past hastily with purpose, no doubt off to join their friends for some celebratory event, and I note that no one, not even the elderly couple, looks twice at their outlandish costumes.

'I love it here. It's just the right balance of kooky and traditional. I can't believe I've never been here before,' I say to Ruth, picking up my fork to take another bite of cake.

'I know, it's been for ever since I've been here. We should come again and stay a bit longer next time.'

'Yeah, defo. So shall we head to the pier after this?' I say, excited by the idea and wanting to continue exploring.

'What about my nap? Can't we go tomorrow?' whines Ruth.

'You know we're both gonna be hanging tomorrow! Come on. We'll go to the pier then I promise I'll let you nap!' I say, picking up my tiny pink-and-white teacup from its adorable matching saucer and drinking up.

CHAPTER 35

Ruth and I are clambering out of a minicab that's just pulled up outside a club named Her Ladyship in Brighton's Kemptown. There's no question as to whether we're in the right place. The small white building situated in a quiet street has stand-out rainbow-coloured lighting projected all across its front, as well as a large rainbow flag hanging high above the front entrance.

Ruth overslept a little once we got back to the hotel, so we were delayed getting out the door. We're conscious that we're going to be walking in a good ten minutes after Gavin's show has begun. Ruth links her arm through mine, hurrying me along the pavement into the venue.

We're both dressed to impress. Ruth in a fuchsia-pink vintage-style body-con dress that shows off her curvy figure while I've slipped myself back into the same LBD I wore the night Scott was run over.

Once at the front door of the club we're greeted by a short smiley skinny lady with large black-rimmed glasses and white-blonde cropped hair. She's holding a gold clipboard and is dressed for a night of standing outside in a thick black Puffa coat that reaches well past her knees.

'Hi, hi,' a flustered Ruth says to her. 'We're Ruth and Lydia, we should be on the list. We're guests of Gavin.'

The lady at the door looks down at her clipboard and crosses a line through at the top with her biro.

'Yep, okay, the show's already started so I'll take you to your seats,' says the lady,
walking ahead of us through the entrance and straight down a flight of dimly lit stairs.

We walk into the venue to the sound of the crowd clapping and cheering.

The venue is larger than the outside led me to expect, and it's very glamorous, designed to look like a regal French boudoir. The walls are painted a dark navy-blue, small crystal chandeliers fixed all along them. There must be over twenty round tables, all with clean white tablecloths. A heavy dark blue velvet curtain hangs behind the stage, which is decorated with small spotlights twinkling all the way along the edge as well as along a catwalk that spreads out into the audience.

Behind the tables at the back are comfortable high booths cushioned with navy-blue velvet seats and designed for smaller groups.

The nice lady hostess directs us to one of the booths at the back.

'Here you go, ladies. Someone will be over

shortly to take your drinks order. Have a great night,' says the hostess above the noise of the cheering crowd, before quickly scurrying off out of sight.

We clumsily climb into our seats just as the cheering begins to calm down and onto the stage walks Gavin's alter ego, Orgazma Sanchez!

Orgazma is dressed in a long-sleeved floor-length gown, saturated in small shiny gold discs that sparkle under the bright spotlight. The dress has a slit all the way up Gav's left leg, revealing a set of fabulous long legs, his feet tucked away nicely inside a pair of gold sky-scraper stiletto heels. I can see even from our seats at the back that Gavin's face is plastered in stage make-up and his eyes are decorated with bright pink eye shadow matched with the longest set of fake eyelashes I've ever seen on anyone. Gavin's wig is one I've seen him in before at previous shows. A large blonde beehive with a heavy fringe and large gold stars on one side.

'Wasn't he brilliant, ladies and gents!' announces Gavin from the stage, holding tightly on to a pink-crystal-encrusted microphone as the audience cheer once again in agreement. 'In trousers that tight; no wonder his voice is so high! Let's have the house lights up for a mo', I want to see who we have with us tonight!'

The crowd cheers as the house lights light up the whole floor and Gavin holds his hand up to his forehead, scanning the crowd in front of him.

'Oh goodness, we are a feral bunch, aren't we!' exclaims Gavin in disgust.

Ruth and I are still fidgeting to make ourselves comfortable after our late arrival when Gavin finally spots us.

'Oh, so nice of you to finally join us, darlings. Ladies and gents, I've got some friends in the audience tonight! My good friends from London, Ruth and Lydia. Did your watch break, darling!' says Gavin, lifting his arm and pointing towards our table, drawing the audience's attention to Ruth and me.

'I was having a nap!' Ruth shouts back over to Gavin.

'Having a nap! Are you sure you weren't in a coma, darling! Can I have two Red Bulls for table seven, please!' announces Gavin, much to the amusement of the audience.

'So who else have we got in tonight?' says Gavin, stepping off the low stage and out into the tables, ready to interact with his adoring crowd.

The club is empty, expect for the people that work here, Ruth and I the last remaining audience members in attendance.

After an hour and a half of burlesque dancers, contortionists, magic tricks and a roaring rendition of 'I Am What I Am' performed by Orgazma, the Her Ladyship cabaret show has finally come to a spectacular end.

Ruth and I are still sitting in our designated

booth, feeling very merry while finishing up the last of one of our many cocktails, waiting for Gavin to appear.

While Ruth enthusiastically sings her own drunken rendition of 'I Am What I Am', I reach for the straws in our glasses and use them as drumsticks on the table in front of us.

'I tell ya, the security here isn't what it used to be, who let these two lushes in!' sounds a very camp voice.

Ruth and I look up to see Gavin walking through the empty venue towards our table with a huge glowing smile and his arms lifted in the air to greet us. Ruth is the first to hurry herself out of our booth and charges towards Gavin to give him a big hug hello. It never fails to impress me how quickly Orgazma transforms back into regular old Gavin. His face clean-shaven and free of stage make-up.

'That was fantastic, Gav, we had so much fun!' says Ruth as she and Gavin hold on tightly to each other.

I make my own way out of the booth, feeling a little wobbly on my feet as a result of not having stood in over an hour as well as having a copious amount of alcohol running through my bloodstream.

Ruth and Gavin eventually let go of each other, at which I greet Gavin with a hug of my own. Gavin holds me tightly into him, then lets go, gripping my hands in his.

'Lydia darling. How are you?' he asks, staring with concern into my eyes.

'I'm good,' I reply, giving the most convincing smile I can muster.

'No really, how are you?'

'Really, I'm fine and all the better for seeing you,' I say, suppressing the urge to be too honest and crumple like an empty drinks can. I give Gavin's hands a squeeze, grateful for his genuine concern.

'Ha, yes, that's the spirit. Now I hope you ladies have brought your dancing shoes with you? Come on, let's get out of here!'

Gavin lets go of my hands and beams an excited smile. He turns on his heels and we follow, ready to be led on to the next exciting instalment of our evening.

Gavin has brought Ruth and me to a gay bar on Brighton's dark and windy seafront named The Pink Shrimp. The bar is situated under the promenade, overlooks the pebbled beach and is everything a gay bar should be with a pink and gold theme throughout. Gold sparkly wallpaper decorates the wall behind our pink PVC-lined booth, which just happens to be the closest to the dance floor where a gaggle of people are dancing along to Diana Ross's 'I'm Coming Out'.

Somewhere out on the floor should be Ruth and Gavin, who have been dancing away for most of the time that we've been here. I on the other hand have made myself comfortable at our pink booth with my new best friend and pal of Gavin's, thirty-five-year-old Latin and Ballroom dance instructor Franco.

Franco is practically pocket-size and far too handsome to have ever been straight. He has dark Mediterranean skin, thick floppy black hair and muscular arms under his tight black short-sleeved shirt.

Franco is listening to me pour out my story of the last few months as I finish my sixth, or possibly seventh, cocktail of the evening and lap up his unthreatening male attention.

'They never leave their wives. I'm telling you, I've been there. They fill you with hope and tell you you're the one, but no matter how much you laugh together, no matter how good the sex, he'll always go back home, trust me, I know,' says Franco in a thick Italian accent, his words so full of wisdom. He sips up the last of his own cocktail, then places the empty glass down on the table.

'But he said that I make him happy. In a way she never has,' I slur, trying to convince Franco that my situation is different from the thousands of other exact same situations that have come before.

'And that's probably true, but he won't leave her. He'll leave you high and dry, or in your case low and wet, while you sit and wait for him to come back from playing Mr Family Man.'

I drop my head to the table in despair, knowing that Franco is right. The table feels wet and suspiciously sticky on my forehead. I quickly regret placing my head down and lift it back up, at which Franco licks his thumb and presses it against my forehead, wiping away whatever residue it was.

'Same again, Franco?' I say, pointing at our tall empty glasses, ready to slide my way out of our booth and head to the bar.

'No! No more time for drinking! Now is time for dancing!' declares Franco, shoving me along until we're both out of the booth and up on our feet.

'No, no! I'm a terrible dancer!' I protest, waving my hand in front of me, more than happy to sit and bore Franco with my troubles a little longer.

Franco takes hold of my hand and drags me onto the dance floor just as the Pussycat Dolls mega mix kicks in with Nicole Scherzinger singing about how you wish your girlfriend were more like her!

Franco squeezes us through the many sweaty dancing men until we eventually pause at a spot somewhere in the middle where there's just enough room for the two of us under the coloured flashing disco lights. Franco keeps a firm hold of my right hand and twirls me around on the spot at least three times before pulling me back into him and placing his hands on my hips just as the music takes a slight change of pace, mixing into the song 'Buttons'.

'Oh yes, very sexy!' says Franco, approving of the song and my drunken dance moves, which I strongly suspect are playing out a lot better in my head than on the dance floor.

Suddenly, I feel a sharp slap on my backside. I turn round to see it's Ruth, who's dancing drunkenly away with Gavin by her side.

'Oh mind if I cut in!' interrupts Ruth, eager to have her own turn with the handsome Italian. Franco lets go of me and swaps me for Ruth just as the song quickly merges into yet another, this time 'Hush Hush, Hush Hush', the camp disco classic that samples Gloria Gaynor's 'I Will Survive'. The song starts off calmly, with Nicole telling us she never did need a man to make her strong, then suddenly bursting into the most camp up-tempo number in the world.

Gavin takes hold of my hand, throwing my arm into the air with his, and shakes his head from side to side. I copy his moves, then let go of his hand and sing loudly along to the song's lyrics.

I'm pretty sure it's the six or seven cocktails that have caused me to lose all my inhibitions, but as I hear the Pussycat Dolls sing about being 'broken but not defeated' I feel as if Nicole Scherzinger is my own personal masseur. Directly sending me her own empowering message, telling me how I too will survive my own broken love story.

As the string section of the 'I Will Survive' sample plays loudly throughout the bar, I throw my hands into the air and let my body get lost in the music. I dance along and shout out the lyrics, allowing myself to let loose and shake away all my troubles, feeling annoyed with myself that I've just wasted the last hour drunkenly talking through my woes, when I could've been dancing them away.

It's 3.30 a.m. I'm sitting with my sore feet inside an old weather-beaten rowing boat on the dark pebbled beach next to a small beach hut. Gavin and I are both sitting on the rim of the boat, each of us with a paper packet of chip-shop chips in our laps. The loose paper blows in the strong sea breeze along with my loose long hair that I can't be arsed to tie back, letting it flap over my face. The cold sea air and salty chunky chips seem to be helping me to sober up somewhat. While Gavin and I stuff our faces we watch Franco give Ruth a private dance lesson on the beach, the two of them dancing around in each other's hold about ten feet away from where Gavin and I are sitting.

'I hope you've had a good night, darling. I hope it's helped you to forget all about that wretched man,' says Gavin, great sympathy in his words.

I look out at the choppy sea, watching the waves rush up to the shoreline before crashing down on the thousands of small pebbles below. I take in the view of Brighton Pier in the distance, its sign shining brightly beneath the dark early morning sky. I let out a deep sigh as I reflect over the past few months, unable to remember the last time I had so much fun, and I'm honestly dreading the idea of the weekend coming to an end and having to return home tomorrow.

'You know, I thought, after Steve died, that that was it. That I was just going to disappear down this black hole that I'd never be able to climb out of. And then, I got my job at the pub and I met Scott and I thought, you know what, I can do this. I can move on with my life and support myself and be happy again, and now ... I just don't understand why life just keeps screwing me over,' I say, feeling defeated by all the hard knocks.

'Oh darling, life's not screwing you over, that's just life! Sometimes it's all smooth sailing, other times, the sea gets a little choppy, throws you overboard and all you can do is kick your arms and legs like your life depends on it,' says Gavin, throwing the chip that he's just picked up back into the white paper bag and wrapping his arm around me, pulling me in closer to him for a cuddle, his kindness causing my eyes to fill with tears.

'My darling, you are going to be fine. This storm, it will pass. You will be happy again. You will, I promise,' says Gavin reassuringly. He places a kiss on the top of my head as my loose hair flaps around his face then frees me from his embrace and throws another chip into his mouth.

'I know, you're right. I think I'm just gutted I have to go home tomorrow. I love it here. I've had so much fun this weekend,' I say, wiping my eyes with the back of my hand, blocking the route of any falling tears.

'Then why don't you stay?' suggests Gavin casually, as if recommending I try a new brand of coffee.

'What! No! I have a whole life in London to get back to!' I say with a small laugh at such a ludicrous suggestion, looking into my bag of chips and digging out another to throw into my mouth.

'And what life is that exactly? The one with your dead husband, or with your married boyfriend? And don't even get me started on your mother!' says Gavin with exaggerated hand gestures, waving his bag of chips around in front of him, trying to home in his point.

I slowly chew on the chip in my mouth, looking out at the choppy sea, knowing that Gavin makes a good point, and I try my hardest to think of a viable reason as to why it's imperative for me to return home.

'There's my flat and there's Ruth,' I say, pointing at her and Franco nearby. Both of them giggling loudly whilst moving their hips and holding each other in a ballroom pose.

'Oh please, she'll be fine! She has Ben and work. Anyway, it's Brighton, not Alcatraz, she'll be allowed to visit!'

'What would I even do here? I've got no job or place to stay.'

'Stay with me! I have a spare room that I keep meaning to advertise online. It's yours at a reasonable rate if you want it ...'

'Okay, but how would I even pay you rent with no job?'

'Hello! You're an experienced barmaid. You'll find a job in Brighton in no time, don't you worry about that!'

Gavin speaks with real enthusiasm, making the whole idea sound very appealing. However, I'm not sure I have the energy to start my life all over again for the second time this year.

'I dunno, Gav. I'm almost thirty. I should be thinking about marriage and kids. Not running off to the seaside,' I say, trying to talk myself out of Gavin's appealing proposal.

'Yes, you're right. Marriage, kids, mortgage, that's what you should be doing ... Sorry, now do remind me how that went the first time?'

I give Gavin a sideways glance, feeling no need to respond to his comment.

'Look, the room's yours if you want it. I'm going to message you my address. If you change your mind, even if you're already halfway home on the train, just turn round.' Gavin hands me his packet of chips as he reaches into the right pocket of his chinos and pulls out his mobile phone.

'Thank you. It's never going to happen, but

thank you,' I say, grateful for the kind offer.

'Never say never, darling!' says Gavin, looking down at his phone and tapping the screen to type out his address to send me.

I suddenly hear a load thump followed by the scratchy sound of pebbles. Gavin and I turn our heads sharply to our left to see Ruth has fallen on her arse and has consequently dragged Franco down with her, poor Franco straddled on top of her and struggling to get back onto his feet as the two of them laugh hysterically.

'Shall we go and rescue Franco?' I say, trying and failing to suppress a tired yawn.

'Ha, yes, that's probably wise!' laughs Gavin, placing his phone back in his pocket. He swings his long legs over the back of the boat, jumps down onto the pebbles below and reaches out his hand to help me off.

CHAPTER 36

The piercing high-pitched ringing of an old-school telephone sounds in my ears, waking me from my deep sleep, but I struggle to prise my eyes open. They feel stuck together, presumably by the residue of last night's make-up. I turn onto my side and lift the thin duvet from the bed over my tired head in a vain effort to escape the sound of the ringing phone. Irritated, I kick a leg backwards to wake Ruth who I assume is still next to me in the bed.

'Eurgh, I'm asleep!' moans Ruth as my foot hits against her warm bare legs and I feel her shuffling and rolling over onto her side in her own vain effort to escape from me.

'Eurgh,' I moan back, realising that Ruth isn't going to move, and haul myself out of bed.

I manage to open my eyes just wide enough to make out the fuzzy image of our small hotel room, the light grey-blue carpet coming into focus under my feet. Wearing nothing other than one of Steve's old T-shirts, I pad over to Ruth's side of the bed and pick up the receiver.

'Hello,' I say in a raspy voice.

'Hello, this is reception,' says a curt female voice.

'Hi,' I grunt, plonking myself down on the bed next to the back of Ruth's head.

'I'm calling to remind you that your checkout time was at 11 a.m. It is now 11.32. I will need you to leave the room as soon as possible, please.'

I feel a surge of shock and lift my wrist to take a look at my watch, which indeed states the time is 11.32 a.m.

'I'm so sorry! We'll be down straight away!' I say in a panic, slamming the receiver back down on its unit.

'Ruth! Ruth! Get up, it's half eleven,' I yell, standing up from the messy bed and throwing my hand down on Ruth's shoulder, giving her a shake to wake her.

'I'm asleep,' groans Ruth, refusing to move.

'Ruth, get up! We need to leave! We were meant to check out half an hour ago, our train leaves in less than half an hour!' I bark.

Ruth slowly sits herself up in the bed, rubbing her eyes and head. Ruth is also displaying a smudged face full of last night's make-up, her long blonde hair matted.

'But I wanted to have a ride on the carousel before we left,' yawns Ruth with a zero sense of urgency in her voice.

'Fuck the carousel! The twelve o'clock train is the only one today going straight through to Victoria!' I reply, my voice raised. I drop to my knees in front of my small suitcase, frantically pulling out a hoody and searching for a pair of socks.

'What you panicking for? We have half an hour, the station's only ten minutes up the road.'

'Because if we miss the twelve o'clock we have to jump on that replacement bus and I'm not doing that again, it took fucking forever!'

Ruth reluctantly throws the duvet off her legs and climbs out of the bed, still dressed in last night's pink dress, and meanders her way to the bathroom.

'Ruth, there isn't time for a shower. Get dressed!' I bark.

'Calm down! I'm doing a wee!' Ruth yells back from the bathroom, her words soon followed by the sound of gently trickling water.

'The station, please!' I instruct the back of the balding head of our cab driver as Ruth and I climb into the back of the white people carrier that's just pulled up outside our hotel. Ruth slumps herself down on the seat next to me, wrapping herself in her navy-blue parka, still displaying little sense of urgency when the only direct train to London is departing in less than ten minutes.

'So where is it you ladies are heading to?' asks the cab driver.

'Back to London, we just came for a weekend visit,' answers Ruth.

'My gran came from London to Brighton just for

a weekend visit. She ended up staying for forty-five years.'

'Wow! She must've had a really good weekend!' laughs Ruth.

While Ruth and the cabbie make small talk I pull my phone from my jeans pocket, checking it for the first time today. I have two unread messages. One from Gavin that simply reads: *2a York Place, Mead Road, Brighton, BN1 7SD.*

The other is from Scott; and I feel my tummy flutter as I tap the screen to open his message: *Hey, beautiful. Hope you had a good weekend x.* I take note of the time the message was sent, 9.21 a.m., and I wonder what Scott must have been doing at that exact moment. Sitting at the breakfast table waiting for Lacey and Lola to arrive home to the house they all share together? Or maybe they were already back, he sneakily texting me from the bathroom while his wife and child played downstairs? The possible scenarios in my head make me feel uneasy, as well as insanely jealous, knowing that for the foreseeable future I'll have to share my boyfriend with his wife, a situation I never imagined being faced with.

I stare down at Scott's message, my eyes glued to the screen as I wonder how or whether I should reply, when suddenly my uncomfortable thoughts are interrupted by the cab's sudden halt.

'The traffic's not moving up ahead, ladies. I'll

drop you here if that's okay? It's only a two-minute walk.'

I take a look at the time at the top of my phone: 11.56.

'Oh really?' says Ruth, finally springing into action.

Ruth and I look out of the cab window. The traffic is indeed at a standstill, meaning it may well be quicker for us to jump out of the cab now and run the rest of the way to the station.

I'm already sliding open the heavy cab door, trying to gather up my suitcase and handbag, still with my phone in my hand. I jump out of the cab onto the pavement, dragging my suitcase behind me, and I'm quickly joined on the side of the road by Ruth, dragging her own suitcase.

'That's okay, keep the change!' Ruth calls back to the cabbie, knowing we don't have time to wait for change if we want to catch our train.

Ruth hastily slides the car door shut behind her and we begin to run as fast as we can uphill along the busy parade of high street shops.

Hot, sweaty and out of breath, Ruth and I finally make it to the entrance of Brighton Station. I can feel sweat trickling its way down my back, making my thick hoody stick to my skin. We run towards the ticket barriers of the small Victorian station and stop in front of the small departures board, frantically searching it to find our designated train, and I notice the time at the top centre of the screen reads 11.59.

We have mere seconds to spare until our train leaves.

'Platform 4!' shouts Ruth.

Ruth is already running ahead of me and so I follow her, struggling to drag my suitcase behind me without losing hold of my phone, while frantically trying to find my travel ticket in the side pocket of my handbag. I feel the thin cardboard in my hand and pull out the ticket and try to pick up my pace. I see Ruth slot her ticket into the barrier, it opening and allowing her through. When I reach the barrier I waste no time in slipping my own card into the appropriate slot, ready to run through to our waiting train the second the barrier opens.

I can see Ruth running ahead of me, the wheels of her small case skidding behind her, then the barrier opens for me and I surge forward like a greyhound let out of a cage, desperate to catch up with Ruth, who's just this second jumped into the nearest carriage. My sweaty hand loses grip of my suitcase handle, the case crashing down to the ground. My legs are moving so fast that it takes me a second before I can stop and turn back to rescue it. I reach out for the long extended handle and grab hold of it, sweeping the case up from the ground and bolting forward. I hear the beeping sound signalling the closing of the train doors and knowing I only have seconds to spare I make it to Ruth's carriage, only for the doors to slide shut in my face.

'ARE YOU FUCKING JOKING!' I scream, throwing my suitcase and handbag down to the platform and waving my hands up towards the heavens in utter despair.

Ruth is standing on the other side of the train door, her face etched with panic.

A male station worker is standing next to me. He blows on the silver whistle in his
mouth and waves a white round placard over his head, signalling for the train to depart.

I hear a sound and turn to see Ruth tapping frantically on the window, trying to get the station worker's attention as the train starts to slowly move forward. She's making a telephone sign with her right hand and shouting some kind of instruction to me, but it's no use. I watch as the carriage moves further away from me; and I shake my head, knowing all hope is lost and I can do nothing but watch the train roll its way down the track, while I stand abandoned on the platform.

The station worker pulls the whistle from his mouth and lowers his placard. He turns to me, shaking his head.

'You can pick up the replacement bus service outside,' he tells me, pointing towards the station's exit.

I roll my eyes, letting out a loud defeated sigh, and watch as the train disappears. I bend down and reach for my handbag and then the handle of my suitcase. The station worker reaches out his arm in an effort to move me from the platform. Not wanting him to manhandle me, I quickly step away, turning my back on him and beginning the slow walk back up the platform, dragging my suitcase behind me.

At the end of the platform I see a sandwich board beside the barrier I just came through. A white sheet of paper pinned to the board reads: *Replacement Bus Service This Way* with a drawn-on arrow pointing to the left. I look left at the sullen face of a tarmacked car park. A dozen or so double-decker buses of all different colours sit under an overcast grey sky with queues of people waiting with their luggage ready to take the longest route home and I stop, thinking back to my own journey here and how long it took.

With my phone still in my hand, I look down to check the time: 12.02. I contemplate calling Ruth and so I swipe the screen, my phone unlocking itself and opening on my list of messages.

Scott's most recent message is at the very top with the first few words of the message visible. Directly underneath Scott's message is Gavin's message from last night, with the details of his address.

'You can't stay here, madam. I'm going to need you to move along!' instructs the same station worker, his words making me look up from my phone. He's walking towards me, his arm reached out, and I find myself moving forward, back towards the ticket barriers.

The last larger barrier at the end used for wheelchairs and buggies is wide open and I find myself drifting towards it in an effort to move myself out of the way. Once through the gate, I realise that I'm further away from the replacement buses and much closer to the station's exit and taxi rank.

Now out of the way of the stroppy station worker and the general public, I take a moment to look back down at my phone. My eyes are drawn to Scott's message and I feel at a complete loss as to how to reply to such a simple message.

I hold my thumb down over his name, until a tick box displays next to it, asking me if I'd like to delete his messages. Without any hesitation, I select delete all, then press the side button to lock the screen once again. I slip my phone into the back pocket of my jeans and start to walk forwards and out of the station.

I stroll to the station's taxi rank, where a dozen or so minicabs are waiting on a fare. There's no queue for the cabs, and so I dart straight towards the first one waiting in line.

'York Place on Mead Road, please,' I say through the window.

'No problem,' nods the cab driver. He quickly climbs out of his seat and walks around the front of the car over towards me.

'Jump in,' he says, as he lifts my suitcase and goes towards the boot of the car.

I open the back passenger door and, as

instructed, climb into the back of the cab. I place my handbag down on the spare seat next to me and I catch a glimpse of my wedding ring and my engagement ring on my left hand. I stare down at my rings. Two valuable pieces of stone and metal, once given to me as a sign of love and commitment, now nothing more than a reminder of a past life I struggle to relate to.

I loosely clench my fist, bring my rings up to my lips and give them a gentle silent kiss. I unclench my fingers, lifting my other hand to tug at my rings. They quickly begin to loosen and I manage to pull them off just as I hear the sound of the car boot slam shut and I place them into the palm of my hand. I fold my fingers over my palm, covering my rings, as the cab driver climbs back into the driver's seat.

I lift my head to see the reflection of the cabbie's dark brown eyes in the rear-view mirror.

'Ready?' he asks.

I look back down at my hand. I open it carefully and shift in my seat to bury my rings safely in my jeans pocket.

A small smile tugs at my mouth and I gently nod my head.

'Ready,' I reply, and the car pulls away, out of the station and back down the busy street.

I look up at the grey overcast sky above just as the cloud begins to break. A bright beam of sunshine shines down filling the cab with a glow and warmth and filling me with a sense of hope and excitement for all that's yet to come.

EPILOGUE

My body is drenched in warmth from the sun beating down on me. Keeping my eyes closed and with my body laid out flat, I effortlessly tune in to the background noise of the waves gently licking the sandy shoreline before they retreat again.

'Hey, bubs, look what I found.'

I feel a cold wet sensation, shocking enough to make me open my eyes and sit up. I look down at my bare stomach and see Steve has placed a gleaming white perfect heart-shaped stone about the size of a £2 coin on top of my belly button. Steve sits himself down next to me in the middle of my sun lounger. His wet slender body and dark brown hair glisten in the sunlight, his black swimming shorts exposing his wet legs.

'Wow, where'd you find that?' I ask, picking the stone up in my hand, staring at it, amazed by its perfect symmetry.

'I found it washed up on the beach. See that huge rock out there?' Steve points into the distance and over the crystal-clear blue sea in front of us.

On the horizon there's a huge black volcanic rock, the size of a small island.

'Someone told me there's loads of them washed up on that rock. I'm going to swim out to it now,' says Steve, enthusiastically leaping up from the sun lounger.

I hold my hand to my forehead to shade my eyes and look out past the white sandy shoreline and over the clear blue water towards the large rock.

'But it seems really far away,' I say, expressing my concern.

'It's not as far away as you think.'

'I'll come with you then,' I say, swinging my legs off my sun lounger and subtly readjusting my bikini.

'No, bubs, you need to stay here,' Steve says softly, wrapping his arms around my waist, pulling me into him so our bodies are pressed up against each other. I wrap my arms loosely round his shoulders joining my hands behind his neck.

'But what am I supposed to do while you're gone?' I pout, gazing into his gorgeous crystal-blue eyes.

'Whatever makes you happy, my love,' Steve responds. He lovingly pulls me in closer to him as he plants a soft gentle kiss on my lips.

Steve loosens his arms from my waist and gently pulls his body away from mine, and I watch as he turns away from me and jogs slowly into the sea.

'You don't need to wait for me!' Steve shouts

over to me, the calm water quickly washing up towards his knees as he wades further in. When the water's up to his waist he turns round and looks back at me with a warm loving gaze. 'Go and have some fun!' he yells as I watch him from my standing position on the sandy beach.

His body dips down into the water and he swims away out towards the black volcanic rock in the far distance.

I suddenly feel an ice-cold sensation on the very tip of my nose, the unfamiliar feeling making me open my eyes.

'Here you go, Sleeping Beauty.'

Directly in front of me, millimetres from my face, Gavin is holding a 99 ice cream out to me. The wafer cone in his hand is wrapped in a white paper napkin with the soft whipped ice cream sitting top-heavy, a chocolate flake sliced nicely through it. I take the cone from Gavin's hand and unwrap the napkin, using it to wipe the blob of ice cream off my nose.

Gavin sits himself down on the striped deckchair next to me holding his own ice cream, allowing himself to relax in the bright Brighton sunshine, and I hear his flip-flops crunch on the pebbles as he makes himself comfy.

'Not the worst way to spend your day off, eh?' says Gavin, wrapping his mouth around his ice cream to take a huge gulp from it.

'It certainly isn't,' I say, licking around the rim of my rapidly melting ice cream while looking out at the light blue sea in front of me. The warm sun is shining down on it, creating bouncing flickers of light on the ripples of the gentle waves in the distance.

I feel something digging into the skin at the top of my right thigh, just below the cut-off of my shorts, and I shift uncomfortably on my deckchair. I reach my hand between my legs, lifting my leg slightly, and I feel something hard, which I swiftly pull from under me.

'Jesus, darling! Have you laid an egg?' laughs Gavin.

Between my fingers I hold a shiny white perfect heart-shaped pebble, about the size of a £2 coin. I turn in utter bewilderment towards Gavin.

'Did you put that there?' I ask, completely dumbfounded by my discovery.

Gavin shakes his head, his mouth still wrapped around his ice cream.

I look down at the pebble, amazed by its simple beauty, and fold my hand tightly around it, feeling an overwhelming need to keep it close to me.

I lean back in my deckchair and take in the view of the sea as a peacefulness floods through me, happy to keep the memory of the love I was once given safe inside my heart.

The End.

Thank you for taking the time to read You're a Dream to Me. If you enjoyed this story, please leave a review on Amazon. Thank you.

Printed in Great Britain
by Amazon